M

Liars All

Liars All

Jo Bannister

Minotaur Books ◆ New York

LIARS ALL. Copyright © 2009 by Jo Bannister. All rights reserved. Printed in the United States of America. For information, address St. Martin's Press, 175 Fifth Avenue, New York, N.Y. 10010.

www.minotaurbooks.com

Library of Congress Cataloging-in-Publication Data

Bannister, Jo.
    Liars all / Jo Bannister. — 1st U.S. ed.
        p. cm.
    ISBN 978-0-312-61239-9
    1. Farrell, Brodie (Fictitious character)—Fiction.
2. Women private investigators—Fiction. 3. Mugging—Fiction.
4. Murder—Investigation—Fiction. 5. Mugging victims—
Fiction. 6. Jewelry theft—Fiction. 7. Guilt—Fiction.
8. Detective and mystery stories. I. Title.
    PR6052.A497L53 2010
    823'.914—dc22

                                                    2009041525

First published in Great Britain by Allison & Busby Limited

First U.S. Edition: April 2010

10 9 8 7 6 5 4 3 2 1

Liars All

Chapter One

They were young and in love, and like lovers everywhere they thought it would last for ever.

They thought they would, too.

They drove out to their favourite restaurant on the South Downs, the sleek, low car treading down drifts of fallen leaves in the narrow lanes. Tom had reserved a table as soon as he knew he was going to need it. Jane called him a control freak, but he wouldn't risk their evening for the sake of a phone call. He didn't want the occasion to be less than perfect.

Once he was sure this was the right thing for them he'd imagined proposing here: in a quiet corner of The Cavalier, with its long views over the patchwork fields and little spinneys of Chain Down. They'd come here the first time he wanted to impress her, again for their three month and six month anniversaries, and once in between to celebrate Jane's birthday. Of course he'd planned to take the next step here.

Events overtook them. After he'd done all his thinking, about what he wanted and also what was best for both of them, after he'd reached what he was sure was the right decision, even after he'd booked the table at The Cavalier, they were in her car – his was in the garage for a service – and somehow he couldn't wait a moment longer. He proposed to her in an elderly VW, with his feet among discarded crisp packets, in a queue of traffic waiting for the lights to change in the middle of damp and faded Dimmock. It may have been the least romantic spot for a proposal ever.

Jane did nothing to make it more memorable. She didn't come over all coy and indecisive. Coy and indecisive were not her style. She gave it less thought than the choice of her next gear, said, 'Yeah, OK,' and drove off without missing a beat when the lights turned green.

Tom was still trying to figure out what had happened when she spotted a parking space and pulled in. 'Er...you did say yes?'

She nodded. 'That's right.'

Puzzlement crinkled his brow. 'You didn't have to think about it?'

She breathed heavily at him. 'Tom, I've been thinking of little else for the last three months. All I was waiting for was for you to recognise the blindingly obvious and say something.'

He grinned; then a sudden fear wiped the grin from his face; then it too was gone and he managed a nervous, almost embarrassed little chuckle. 'So that's it? We're getting married?'

Jane nodded. 'We're getting married.'

Finally Tom looked around him. 'That's the jeweller's.'

'Yes.' It seemed she had a ring picked out.

The following evening they were on their way to The Cavalier, Tom's car humming between the high hedges, the autumn leaves a crisp russet carpet in the wash of the headlamps. The powerful engine was singing after its service, and his heart was too. Jane seemed to be taking engagement in her stride, much as she took everything else – calmly, clear-headed and purposeful. But when he sneaked a quick sidelong glance at her, Tom kept catching a smile of sheer happiness on her face. She masked it when she saw him looking, but if he looked again in a couple of minutes it was always back. He hadn't been fooling himself. She wanted this as much as he did.

It was dark by the time they ate. It hardly mattered. Today the soft views would have been wasted on them. They bathed in one another's gaze, and might as well have been eating rissoles from a lay-by chip van.

Over dessert Tom produced a box from an inside pocket. Jane arched a thin eyebrow, wiggled her finger at him. Diamonds glittered in the light of the candles. 'Got one,' she said smugly.

'Yes,' nodded Tom, 'and no. That's an engagement ring. It's a token of a contract. This is an engagement present. It's because I love you. And because, in a public place, this is the only way I can show you how much without being prosecuted.'

He put it on the table between them. After a moment she picked it up and opened it. Her face went still.

In mounting anxiety Tom looked from his gift to the

girl and back. 'You don't like it? It's all right, I'll find something else…'

Her hand slid across his wrist on the table. She had artistic hands: delicate, expressive, and strong enough to beat him at arm-wrestling. She pinned his hand to the tablecloth. 'Over,' she said quietly, 'my cold dead body.'

It was a necklace. Jane hadn't much experience of good jewellery – she'd always bought cheap, used extravagantly and given it away when she tired of it. This was something else. 'It's beautiful.'

'You like it?'

It wasn't a question she felt the need to answer. She peered closer. 'It's got a star in it!'

Tom laughed softly. 'My mother loved that star.'

'This belongs to your mother?'

'Not anymore.' She looked up at him, waiting for him to explain. 'She wants you to have it, Jane. My father bought it for her. She loved it for twenty years, but she hasn't worn it since he died. She won't wear it again. It'd give us both a great deal of pleasure to see you enjoy it.'

A jewel that carried that much family history alarmed her. But Tom was right. It *should* be worn. It was too beautiful to be kept for ever in a box. 'What is it?'

'A sapphire.'

'Sapphires are blue.'

'Not always.'

'But they are always valuable.' She made an effort to sit up straight, away from the grey-black gem with its golden many-rayed star. 'I can't take this. Tom, thank Imogen for me, but it's too precious.'

He'd anticipated this. 'It's a gift,' he said simply. 'The value doesn't come into it. Tell you what,' he reached for the box, 'put it on while you're thinking about it.'

She knew what he was doing. He thought that, once she'd worn it, she wouldn't want to give it back. But she lacked the resolve to stop him lacing the gold chain about her throat. 'Well…maybe for tonight,' she murmured.

It was late before they left The Cavalier. They were the last to go; less scrupulous waiters would have been clearing their throats and tapping their watches. But eventually they realised what the time was, made their apologies and headed across the road to the car park.

People talk about a car coming out of nowhere, but they never do. They're always there, they're just not always very noticeable. Particularly if it's late at night, and you're talking and laughing and you have other things on your mind. And the car in question has no lights on, and the engine is idling barely audibly, and you step out into what you think is a clear road.

The engine roared. By then the car was so close the sound seemed to be all around. The startled couple spun, Tom one way, Jane the other, looking for it; they bumped into one another and clung together like frightened children. The one thing they didn't do was the one thing that might have saved them – pick a direction, any direction, and hurl themselves as far as they could from the centre of the road. So the car hit them. It hit them both, threw them into the air and hit them again as they came down.

Disasters – real disasters – have a strange effect on the human mind. Time slows right down. There seems to be plenty of it, for making and filing observations, for rational thought. Jane, lying in the dark road with Tom's arm across her throat and one of her own legs twisted under her body, thought: *He must have been drinking. He must have left The Cavalier just ahead of us, and because he'd been drinking he forgot to put his headlights on. The police will throw the book at him.* And only after that did she think: *I hope we're all right.*

After the second impact the car stopped. Jane's sideways view of the lit windows of The Cavalier was momentarily occulted by a pair of legs. The man stooped over her.

She said quite clearly, 'Get help. At the restaurant. Call an ambulance.'

She thought he was shocked too, that he couldn't take in what she was saying. She tried again. 'Call an ambulance. Don't touch us. Get help.'

Her handbag was still over her shoulder. She felt the strap tug and pull free. She saw the stooped figure take the watch from Tom's outflung arm and then rifle his pockets for his wallet. Then he turned back to her.

'And that.'

They were the only words he ever spoke to her. But he lifted her head by the hair and fumbled for the catch at the nape of her neck. Not shocked at all – he knew better than to break the necklace with a snatch. He freed it carefully, and used her hair to wipe her blood off it, and then he let go of her. The sick crack as her head hit the tarmac yet again was the last thing she knew.

Chapter Two

Brodie Farrell was the perfect person to meet off a plane. There was no missing her. She was tall and striking, with a plume of dark, curly hair tossing about her shoulders. And usually she was the centre of a knot of people. Sometimes she had to ask for assistance. But usually it was volunteered, as even busy people made their days harder in order to make hers easier. It was absurd. She was a woman in her mid-thirties, as strong and capable of looking after herself as she would ever be, yet people she'd never met danced attendance on her, as if she was something special. A natural-born VIP. It was laughable. But as it was also convenient she did nothing to break the spell.

Today, though, the magic had failed. There was no little press of people wanting to serve her. Which was a pity, because today she could have used some help. She had a tired, fractious baby and a month's worth of luggage, and she was exhausted by the long flight and the hard weeks that had preceded it. This, of course, was why she was left to fend for herself. Exhausted, she looked pretty much like everyone else.

Except to Daniel Hood. However tired and grey she was,

for Daniel she would always stand out in any crowd. He saw her the moment she came through the door. If he'd had his back turned – if he'd been blindfolded – he'd have sensed her presence. She lived on his nerves. Though he worried about her a lot, he was never worried that something might have happened to her. If something bad happened to her, even on the far side of the world, he would know.

He hurried to help with her burdens. She didn't see him until he reached to take Jonathan. She was dead on her feet. He hadn't seen her for almost a month. She looked years older.

He knew what her first words would be. And she didn't disappoint; or only in a way.

'Where's Jack?'

'He couldn't make it. He's in court.'

She fixed him with a predatory eye. She was taller than him, so it felt a bit like a rabbit's-eye view of a stooping hawk. 'Couldn't *make* it?' she echoed imperiously. 'He's in *court?*'

'Brodie, he had no choice,' said Daniel patiently. 'It's a murder trial, he was called this morning. He sent me.'

Her look said, *Oh great.* 'Where's the car?'

Daniel gave her back the baby, took the luggage. 'In Haywards Heath. It'll be easier to take the train from here. I've got the tickets…'

'What you mean is,' she said nastily, 'you still don't like driving in heavy traffic.'

He didn't deny it. But it was also true that the railway platform was closer than the car park, and if she hadn't been so tired Brodie would have thought it was a good idea too. Instead she said sourly, 'Go on then – let's join the wage slaves.'

When they were settled, with Jonathan asleep on his lap, Daniel said quietly, 'Do you want to talk about it? Or shall we wait till we get home?'

In fact, all he didn't already know were details. He knew where she'd travelled in the States, the hospitals she'd visited, the neurosurgeons she'd talked to. He knew what they'd told her. The reputable ones told her the odds were too long.

A month earlier she'd left, full of hope and enthusiasm, sure she'd find someone able and willing to perform the surgery that would save her child's life. Money would be an issue but not an obstacle. She and Jonathan's father were both prepared to sell their homes to finance anything with a realistic chance of success. In fact, Daniel was too. A brain tumour might kill Jonathan Farrell but lack of funds wouldn't. It was the one bit of good fortune he'd had in his short life.

Now they were back, failure written in every line of Brodie's face. She'd had setbacks before. She'd been told, by people she respected, that they'd run out of viable options. But she'd always clung on to some hope. With all the baggage that she'd lugged back from America, it seemed she'd left that hope behind.

'There's nothing to talk about,' she said wearily. 'The tumour is inoperable. Everyone who knew a scalpel from a screwdriver told me the same thing.'

She didn't say it as if it was her baby's death sentence. But Daniel wasn't shocked. Firstly, because he'd known her too well for too long to be surprised by much that she did. And secondly, because he knew she'd have done all her raging, all her grieving, in private.

Halfway through her trip the outcome was already clear – that the best advice a continent had to offer was the last advice she wanted to hear. She'd had time for it to sink in. Not to come to terms with it – no one ever comes to terms with such a thing – but to build walls in her mind to section off the horror so it wouldn't rampage through every corner of her life. It was immense, unbearable and inescapable. The walls were to protect her. They weren't bombproof. Some days they seemed to have been fashioned from paper, so that a cautious finger put out to test their strength would have gone straight through. But whatever protection they could offer, she needed.

'I'm sorry,' said Daniel softly. His pale-grey eyes, sheltered by thick glasses, brimmed with compassion.

Someone else might have argued. Might have thought she needed cheering up, that even false hope was better than none at all. But there was no room between them for lies. If Brodie had found the courage to face the truth it would be an insult to tell her anything different. If the best paediatric neurosurgeons on two continents could do nothing to help it was certain that Daniel Hood, sometime maths teacher, couldn't do any better. Except that he could be there for her. That was the story of his life: not doing but being. Finally, the one thing he could offer might be the thing she needed most.

As the train picked up speed Brodie seemed to nod off, and Daniel turned his attention to the baby he was cradling. Slumbering, his tired restlessness was stilled, his thin cries silenced. Now the funny white eyes were gone there was nothing about him – no hideous growths or disfigurements – to mark him as different, as doomed. But Daniel had seen him grow less substantial with every week that passed. He was pale and listless, his cheerful complacency giving way to a sad dullness, as if now he lacked the energy to complain. Sixteen months old, he seemed like a tiny pensioner, beginning to find life more trouble than it was worth.

Daniel had been wrong. Brodie wasn't asleep, she was watching them. She said quietly, 'Do you see much change in him?'

'A little,' admitted Daniel. 'Brodie—'

She anticipated his question. 'They said to bring him home and make him comfortable. They said I wasn't going to have him much longer, and to make the most of it.'

Her honesty rocked him. He tried not to let it show. 'What did you tell them?'

This was the human being who knew her better than any on Earth – better than her ex-husband, better than Jonathan's father. He hadn't been with her when the world's experts on retinoblastoma demolished her hopes with a few carefully chosen sentences, but he might as well have been.

'I made a bit of a scene,' she remembered. 'It really wasn't what I was expecting. Not the first time, not even the second. The whole world of medical science, it's like a cavalry charge – full speed ahead, unstoppable. You read constantly of the things they can do this week that they couldn't do last week, of the things they'll be able to do by the end of the month, and you think that nothing is impossible. They've mapped the human genome. They can produce cells in a Petri dish that can be turned into heart cells, or liver cells, or brain cells, and set about curing life-threatening diseases from the inside. They can perform surgery with beams of light instead of knives.

'And you think the answer you need has to be out there somewhere. It's only a little cancer. The whole baby isn't very big. How can all these experts be beaten? But they were.' There was a kind of wonder in her voice.

Instinctively Daniel held the sick child closer, as if he could protect the tiny body with his own. But he couldn't. Not from this.

'I haven't given up, you know,' Brodie said sharply.

'Of course not.'

'I mean it. So surgery isn't the answer. There are other things. One day chemotherapy will replace surgery entirely. Everyone says so. The precise combination of drugs that will save Jonathan's life may be sitting on someone's lab bench right now. I'll find them.'

Daniel felt his heart sink. 'Maybe you will.' She'd spent the last six months alternately trawling the internet and touring the world, taking the weakening child to appointments in San Francisco and Geneva and Johannesburg, only to receive one gentle rebuff after another. He'd hoped she would give up now, make the most of whatever time was left to them.

Brodie heard the note of censure he'd tried to keep out of his voice and her pointed chin came up in a kind of tired belligerence. 'This is what I do, Daniel, remember? I find things. Things that other people think are gone for good. But I find them. If they're out there at all, I can find them. I can do this. For Jonathan? Damn right I can.'

'I'm not doubting you,' said Daniel softly. 'But I don't want you blaming yourself if you can't find something that actually isn't there yet – that might exist in another year or five years, but doesn't exist yet.'

'It *does* exist,' she insisted with the stubborn sophistry of the very desperate. 'Somewhere. It has to.'

He said no more. He hoped that when the jet lag subsided she'd be more open to reason.

He'd felt the same way when she got back from Geneva, and from Johannesburg.

In the end the defendant changed his plea. Detective Superintendent Jack Deacon supposed it was the sight of the girl in the wheelchair waiting to give her evidence that did it. Perhaps the defence team had thought she'd bottle out, or be too frail to take the stand. But Deacon had got to know her over the last nine months, knew she'd be up there telling what happened if she had to drag herself into the witness box on her hands and knees.

Robert Carson's counsel must have come to the same conclusion, and realised how it would look; that this was a man sufficiently depraved not only to mow down a young couple in his car, not only to rob them while they lay broken-bodied in the gutter, but to make a crippled girl relive the worst moments of her life rather than admit to doing what the dogs in the street knew he'd done. They'd had a serious word with him after opening submissions. As soon as the court reconvened they asked for the charges to be put again, and this time Carson pleaded guilty.

The first thing Deacon did was look at his watch. But it was too late to head for Gatwick. They'd be on their way home by now. If Daniel hadn't got lost.

Deacon returned to his office in Battle Alley, meaning to immerse himself in work. In fact, though he had plenty to do, all he did was stare at the papers spread across his desk until the print blurred and ran. It might have been cuneiform, reporting crimes in ancient Ur.

Finally a hand closed the file he was peering at. Deacon blinked and checked where his own had got to; but they were still where he'd left them, one each side of the anachronistic blotter, half circling the reading matter in a protective embrace like harbour walls. So someone else had recognised the pointlessness of what he was doing and rescued him from it.

Detective Sergeant Voss said quietly, 'Why don't you go to her house and put the kettle on? They'll be back soon, and she'll be desperate for a cup of tea.'

Deacon gave a bear-like shrug. He growled, 'There are things that need doing.'

'Yes, there are,' agreed Voss with a solemn nod of his ginger head. 'And I'd be able to get on with them if you'd stop cluttering the place up. Go and meet Brodie. See if there's any news.'

'There isn't,' said Deacon. He made no effort to move. 'I talked to her last night. Nobody's holding out much hope at all.'

'All the more reason you should be there when she gets home.' Charlie Voss was more than twenty years younger than his boss. All they had in common was the job. In spite of which, a relationship had developed between them that was as close to friendship as Deacon was probably capable of. Voss talked to his superintendent in ways that would have prompted Deacon to throw anyone else out of his office, then follow him along the landing in order to kick him downstairs.

This was less to do with Deacon having a soft spot for his sergeant – general consensus at Battle Alley was that The Grizzly didn't *have* any soft spots: not for his officers, his partner or even his sick baby – than with Voss's management skills. Like the best butlers he knew when to listen, when to speak and when to speak frankly; and even Deacon had eventually realised that it was no coincidence that his professional life had suddenly got both easier and more productive. A good sergeant is indispensable to a superintendent. It wasn't just that Voss's legs were younger than his own. Sometimes his brain was quicker. And he was better with people. Deacon thought of people as a necessary evil. Voss understood that they were what made the job worth doing.

'Maybe you're right,' grunted Deacon. He pushed his big body back from the desk and stood up. 'If anyone's looking for me…'

'I'll let you know,' nodded Voss. It wasn't the first time he'd lied to his boss, and was unlikely to be the last.

Chapter Three

Halfway across town, with sudden uncharacteristic sentimentality, Deacon thought he should take them something – flowers for Brodie, a toy for Jonathan – to welcome them home, and bring a brief smile to their weary faces.

The flowers were easy. He went into the flower shop and pointed. But Mothercare frightened the life out of him. He grabbed a rubber ball with tentacle-like protrusions and a prettily chiming bell inside, slapped down the money and ran.

He ran into – almost literally – a man he'd known most of his life, and spent the last ten years trying to arrest.

The curious thing about Jack Deacon and Terry Walsh was not that they had made good careers for themselves on opposite sides of the law. It was that they had more in common now, and even in an odd way liked one another better, than when they were growing up in neighbouring streets in London. Each recognised the professionalism of the other even though it made his own job harder. It was a kind of respect. But it wouldn't stop Walsh selling Battle Alley Police Station to a gullible developer if he could, or prevent Deacon putting Walsh in Parkhurst if the opportunity arose.

Walsh was a shorter man than Deacon, his sturdy frame giving him a squarish appearance. The black crinkly hair was salted now with grey, the humorous brown eyes almost lost in a network of laughter lines. A tan that might have meant too many hours on a sunbed in fact testified to his love of sailing – he kept a sleek Camper & Nicholsons sloop called *Salamander* at the marina on the River Barley. Ostensibly he was in the bulk paper trade. Anyone who didn't know him well would have thought him a prime example of a self-made man and a credit to the capitalist system. And in a way they'd have been right.

He wasn't alone. A young woman, taller than him, dressed in jeans and a rugby shirt, long fair hair pulled back in a rough ponytail, had her arm linked through his and they were laughing together. Deacon's immediate reaction was absolute astonishment. Nothing he knew about Walsh – and he knew a lot more than he could prove – suggested he was other than a devoted family man.

His second thought, hard on the heels of the first, was: *Caroline will have your goolies...*

Walsh saw Deacon a second after Deacon saw Walsh. He gave him a friendly grin devoid of concern and hugged the girl's arm closer. 'Don't look at her, Jack. She's not fit to be seen in public. I tell people, She's not my daughter. My daughter has a respectable job in an art gallery in Eastbourne. She washes and wears clean clothes.'

'Sophie?' Deacon wasn't sure he'd managed to keep the surprise out of his voice. He should have known. She wasn't going to stay a fourteen-year-old girl on a pony for ever. She'd be...what...in her twenties now.

'Hello, Mr Deacon,' the girl said cheerfully. 'Ignore my dad. He's still in denial about my new career. He'll feel differently when I win Badminton.'

Deacon frowned. 'You play badminton?'

Happily, Sophie looked more like her mother than her father, but the grin was pure Walsh – mischievous without malice. Even people who knew what Walsh was capable of had to fight not to like the man. 'Three-day eventing. I'm a working pupil at an eventing yard. My dad thinks it's not a proper job.'

'It's a proper job,' admitted Walsh. 'It's just not a very *clean* job.'

It was a mud-spattered hatchback that Sophie Walsh got into. Walsh waved her off and, after a moment, somewhat embarrassed, Deacon did too.

'I'd buy her a better car,' said Walsh, 'but she wants to pay her own way. Which you have to admire, particularly since she earns a lot less than she did in Eastbourne. I keep the horses for her, and every so often her mother despairs of how she looks and buys her a new outfit. Apart from that she's self-sufficient. Actually,' he admitted, 'I'm rather proud of her. This was her dream and she was willing to make sacrifices for it. Which is more than you can say for a lot of kids.'

The smile of fatherly contentment froze on his face and he looked at Deacon with concern. 'Sorry, Jack, I wasn't thinking. Isn't Mrs Farrell due back about now? Is there any news?'

People who worked for him – people *he* worked *for* – were nervous about encroaching on Deacon's private life.

Everyone at Battle Alley knew about him and Brodie, knew that her baby was his, knew that the child was sick and getting sicker. But only Voss and Chief Superintendent Fuller would have dared ask after him. Except that Mrs Merton the tea lady knitted bootees for him. Even she never broached the subject with Deacon directly, but every couple of weeks he'd find another pair of tiny knitted socks left on his blotter.

Terry Walsh had nothing to fear from Deacon's moods. If he'd been capable of damaging Walsh he'd have done it years ago. He was still trying, couldn't try any harder however much the man annoyed him. It left them free to be themselves with one another.

Deacon shrugged wearily. 'Nothing good. Yes, they're on their way home about now. I don't know, Terry, but I think maybe we've exhausted the possibilities.'

Walsh *believed* in possibilities. He was a walking testament to what could be achieved by sheer determination. He shook his head crisply. 'You don't know that. You don't know what the future holds – what's just around the corner. It might be just what you need.'

'That's what Brodie says.' The two men had fallen into step, the crime boss and the senior detective, pacing slowly down High Street like old friends. 'She won't give up. Every time she gets knocked back, she goes on the internet and finds another imminent breakthrough. Then she calls the airline. She only comes home to do laundry.'

Walsh was eying him sidelong. 'You don't approve?'

Deacon picked his words carefully, not because he worried what Walsh might think but because the words were important. They didn't just describe how he felt, they helped define how he felt. 'I think that time is past. It was the right thing to do six months ago. There might have been something out there that would have helped. Six months ago I backed her to the hilt. Now I think it's just stubbornness. Refusing to accept the inevitable.

'Even that wouldn't matter if she had only herself to consider,' he growled, head down, talking like thinking aloud. The other man's quiet companionship let him say things he desperately needed to say and had no one to say them to. Brodie talked like this to Daniel. Deacon hadn't realised there was anyone he could unburden himself to. 'She can make up for lost time later. But Jonathan is spending the last months of his life living out of a suitcase, and there's no longer an excuse for it. He should be at home, as comfortable as we can make him, getting a bit of pleasure out of his life. Giving us all some worthwhile memories. What Brodie's doing can only be justified if she succeeds. If she doesn't, she's depriving me of my son and Paddy of her brother. And herself, too, of good times to remember when he's gone.'

Terry Walsh was what, at heart, Deacon was not: a family man. The joys and, now, the pain of fatherhood that had come as such a surprise to Deacon were second nature to him. He may have understood more of what Deacon was going through than Deacon did. 'I'm so sorry, Jack. If you can think of anything I can do… I mean, if money would make a difference…'

Deacon was more touched than he would have admitted. He stopped dead and turned his searchlight glare on the shorter man. 'You seem to forget, Terry, I know where your money comes from.'

Walsh laughed lightly. 'Of course you do. Scandinavian paper forests. As my daughter never tires of telling me, my money really does grow on trees.' The easy smile died. 'All the same…'

Deacon sighed. 'I know. Thanks, Terry, I appreciate the offer. But perhaps it's as well I shan't need to take you up on it.'

Walsh leant closer, as if someone might be listening. He said fiercely, 'Whatever else I have, I have a good, fully documented income from the bulk paper business. If your son can use any of it, I want to know.'

Deacon dredged up a craggy smile. 'I know. And I will remember, and some day I'll do you a favour in return. Extra snout on visiting day, something like that.'

Walsh chuckled, and they parted at the corner of the street where Deacon had left his car.

Brodie appreciated the flowers. Even more, she appreciated the tea that was brewing in the pot.

Jonathan liked his jingly ball too, and fell asleep clutching it to his wan cheek. Deacon stood looking into the cot. To a baby – at least, to one that could see – it would have felt like being observed by a mountain. 'He looks tired.'

Brodie nodded. 'It's partly the drugs. He hasn't had a fit all the time we've been away, but I guess there's no such thing as a free lunch. This is the price he pays.'

'Or else he's getting worse,' Deacon said, his voice low.

If he thought that hadn't occurred to her, he was mistaken. 'Of course he's getting worse,' Brodie said shortly. 'It's a progressive condition. He's going to go on getting worse until we find the answer to it.'

'If there is an answer.'

'There *is* an answer.' She took a bite out of her tea, savage as if it had challenged her. 'There has to be.'

'Actually, no,' growled Deacon. 'There doesn't.'

She stared at him, her gaze hard and tired and angry. 'And this is why God gave children two parents. Because if they only had fathers they'd be written off the first time they put anyone to any trouble. After all, it's so much more fun to make another one.'

'And if they only had mothers,' retorted Deacon... but intellectually he was better at the marathon than the sprint; he was still hunting for an apposite retort when Daniel rescued him by standing up.

'If you two are going to fight, I'm going back to the office. Do let me know which of you manages to hurt the other most.'

They looked at him. Brodie's glance could have cut silk; Deacon's would have concussed an armadillo. But Brodie spoke for them both. 'Oh, sit down, Daniel. You know perfectly well it's only having you here that stops us ripping one another's throats out. You're a calming influence.'

Daniel hesitated. He'd been called a lot worse – in fact, he'd been called worse by the two people in this room. All the same, a man might wish for a different kind of compliment from the woman he loved. She loved him too – he knew she did – just not the same way. Which was why he found himself acting as referee between Brodie and the father of her baby.

He sighed. He was accustomed to it now, this endlessly repeating pattern in which he martyred his needs to hers. He'd long ago accepted that he couldn't make her happy but he could make it possible for her to be happy. Though it wasn't what he'd have chosen, Brodie's happiness mattered more to him than his own. He did as she said and sat down. 'But you'll have to play nicely,' he instructed them.

They were all getting older, mellowing. When they first knew one another, Deacon wasn't a man to trifle with. Even carefully; even if you were much bigger than Daniel. He was still intimidated by Deacon but he'd learnt to appreciate his finer points as well. He was utterly honest. He was utterly reliable, even if some of the things he could be relied on to do were not desirable. And what you saw was what you got. He said what he thought to your face, even if he had to hold you up by the lapels to do it.

So now, instead of snapping Daniel's head off, he cleared his throat and started again. 'So, do we know anything now that we didn't a month ago? Had anyone any useful suggestions?'

Brodie's lips tightened and she shook her head. 'They said we should enjoy the time we have left. Enjoy! Enjoy watching a child grow weaker, knowing he's going to die. Anything has to be better than that. Any hope, however tenuous – however stupid. *Anything.*'

Daniel said nothing. But Deacon had the right to contradict. 'What you have to ask yourself is whether you want Jonathan to die in an airport lounge. Because if you don't, at some point you have to say he's done enough. Maybe that point is now. Maybe he's travelled far enough, seen enough experts. Maybe you've tried hard enough. Maybe now we move on to plan B.'

'I'm not ready to give up on him!' Her voice was thick with the tears she refused to shed.

'It's not giving up,' said Deacon, stubbornly hanging on to his temper. 'It's choosing what's best for our son in a situation where the options are narrowing.'

Brodie stared angrily at him. She'd been ready for an argument. It said all you needed to know about their relationship that she found it easier to deal with him when they were both shouting than when he was calm and rational. It was like arguing with Daniel: you had to think your case through because otherwise he'd deconstruct it. She ground the heels of both hands into her eyes, tried to explain how she felt.

'We're only going to get one chance at this. When it's over, we want to feel we gave it everything. I know the odds are long, and getting longer by the day. I know it would be easier, on all of us, to stop now. But if we do that we're never going to be sure that one more effort wouldn't have saved him. That the very next doctor wouldn't have something to offer that'd make all the difference. If we keep going, for as long as Jonathan can take it, at least we'll know there wasn't a treatment waiting for him behind a door that I turned back from.'

She breathed quietly for a moment, marshalling her thoughts. 'You're Jonathan's father, you get a say in this too. I've been taking all the decisions, and maybe that's not good enough. If you can honestly say to me that what I'm doing is wrong, that a slim chance of finding a cure isn't worth dragging a sick child halfway across the world, I'll stop. But before you say that to me, Jack, you've got to be absolutely sure. This is a live show. No rehearsals, no second takes.'

Deacon bit his lip. She was right: it was easier to criticise someone else's life-and-death decisions than take your own. He *thought* it had gone on long enough. He didn't think there was anything to gain by going on any longer, and he didn't think Jonathan should be living his last few weeks like this. But sure? How could anyone be *sure*? You just had to take your best guess.

Which was what Brodie was doing. And perhaps he'd have played it differently; and perhaps, when his son died, he'd have thought he'd got it wrong. There were no certainties. All you could do was play the game as hard as you could for as long as you could.

He shook his head. 'I don't know. I honestly don't know. If you think this is what we should be doing, I'm not going to argue. I want what's best for Jonathan. I also want what's best for you. If we lose him' – it was in his voice that *if* was just a kinder way of saying *when* – 'I don't want you wishing you'd done something different. If that means you have to keep looking, keep looking.'

She drank his words as if she'd walked a hot desert in search of them. Her voice wasn't entirely steady. 'Thank you. Daniel?'

Daniel's pale eyes flared behind the thick glasses. 'I don't get a vote.'

'You're our friend,' she said, 'and you talk more sense than anyone I've ever known. I want to know what you think.'

He considered for a moment. Long enough that, if Deacon resented his involvement, he'd have said so. When he didn't, Daniel said, 'I think you should set some kind of limit. Agree now the point at which you stop.'

Deacon frowned. 'Such as?'

'He's on painkillers, isn't he? How about, when you need to up the dosage again, you come home?'

Chapter Four

When Daniel returned to the office Brodie went into the bedroom to check on Jonathan. There was space in the flat for a pint-sized nursery but she'd never wanted to move his cot out of her room, feeling instinctively that she should keep him near her. Even before he fell ill, she was conscious that his inability to amuse himself by looking at the objects around him would make time alone seem both long and empty.

But he was tired after the flight, sleeping so deeply that the chiming ball he was still clutching was entirely silent. Brodie went back into the living room. She cast the comfy chair a glance, then went and sat on the sofa beside Deacon. After a minute one weighty arm went round her shoulders. They sat a while longer in silence.

Finally she said, 'It's not that I'm expecting a miracle.'

'I know,' said Deacon gruffly.

'I just want to feel that, if there is a miracle out there, we didn't miss it.'

'I know.'

She let out a slow sigh. There were a lot of things these two didn't agree on – in truth, most things, and probably this too. It was at least a minor miracle that they hadn't let it come between them. So far. But all her instincts, as well as her doctors, were telling Brodie that the end was coming. If they'd got this far without tearing one another apart, they'd get to the end.

She said, 'What about your case? Adjourned?'

Deacon shook his head. 'He changed his plea. Didn't even hold out for manslaughter. Not that it was a runner. He hit two people with a ton of car in order to rob them – there was nothing casual or careless about it. Maybe he didn't need anyone dead, but what he did that resulted in the boy's death was entirely deliberate and the word for that is murder.'

'Why do people do that?' asked Brodie, puzzled. 'Change their pleas. A case takes months coming to court – they must have thought about what they were going to say. But as soon as the jury files in, all at once they go from *Goodness me, certainly not, it wasn't me, and if it was then that isn't what I did* to *Er, well, actually, hands up, yes it was.* Proving to all concerned that they're not only guilty as charged but they're liars too.'

'I suppose, when you're facing life for murder, you're not too bothered if people think you tell porkies as well.' Deacon gave a disparaging sniff. 'And the reason they wait till the last minute is that something can always go wrong. This time, everything hinged on the girl. If she hadn't been able to testify, or if she had fallen apart in court, we'd have struggled to prove intent. He'd offloaded everything he stole before we caught up with him and none of it's turned up. Without the girl, there's no proof that Carson took anything. The thief could have been a bystander, a paramedic, someone at the hospital – anyone. Without Jane Moss, all I could actually *prove* was dangerous driving causing death. That's why he waited. In case she couldn't go through with it.'

Brodie's eyes widened. 'You think he tried to nobble her?'

Deacon shook his head. 'He's not that class of villain. Bobby Carson is just a mugger with a really big cosh. All his defence had to work with was the hope that someone who'd suffered life-threatening injuries might be too traumatised to take the witness box. Or that, if she got there, she'd buckle under cross-examination – agree that she couldn't be sure who took her necklace.'

'Was there any danger of that?'

'Oh no,' said Deacon, with some satisfaction. 'Physically, of course, she's frail; but she looked…well, she looked the way *you* look when somebody says you can't do something. Determined doesn't come close. There was no way the defence were going to shake her, and trying would just have made things worse. They did the only thing they could – took Carson into a quiet room and told him to 'fess up and get the very few Brownie points still available.'

'So he's going down.'

'All the way.' Deacon looked at her. 'I'm sorry I wasn't at the airport.'

Brodie managed a smile. 'Couldn't be helped.' She added, deadpan, 'Daniel parked the car in Haywards Heath.'

Deacon rolled his eyes.

* * *

Daniel walked back into town. For years he'd walked everywhere because he didn't have a car, indeed had hardly driven since passing his test at eighteen. When they stopped being just friends and he started working for Brodie, after she found she was carrying Jonathan, she scorned his belief that you can get most places on foot or by public transport and said she wasn't paying for time spent waiting at bus stops. She gave him a refresher course in driving skills and put his name on her business insurance. But he still didn't have a car, and only got Brodie's when (a) it was essential for work and (b) she didn't have a more pressing need for it, like shopping or picking Paddy up from school. Daniel still went most places on foot or by public transport.

He genuinely didn't mind. His grandfather taught him to drive, but too many years had passed when he wasn't using the skill and he didn't think he'd ever be entirely at ease behind the wheel. Not like Deacon, who drove on autopilot while doing the mental gymnastics that were part of his job. Daniel thought better while walking.

And because he was thinking, he didn't pick up on the fact that he was being followed.

Brodie bought her office when Shack Lane was a run-down little side street between Fisher Hill and the Promenade. The building had been empty for two years and the roof was letting in. Even in its prime it was only a little two-up two-down mid-terrace house at the unfashionable end of a second division seaside town, and the top floor was someone's flat. But it was perfect for her needs, for two reasons: her divorce settlement was enough to buy both it and her flat in Chiffney Road; and an unfashionable side street was the ideal location for her kind of business. She didn't want passing trade. And the trade she did want often wanted to pass unnoticed.

She called it Looking for Something? She specialised in finding things – lost things, wanted things, personal things, occasionally quite big things like houses and, once, a sailing barge. When people had exhausted their own ideas, if they still wanted something enough to pay her commission, they came to Brodie Farrell.

It wasn't quite true that she could find anything. But research is a catacomb, full of dark passages and intersecting avenues, and the secret to doing it well is doing it long enough to acquire the techniques. It only seemed like magic when Brodie produced a painting of someone's house or a photograph of their great-grandfather. In fact it was just a professional being very good at her job.

Daniel wasn't particularly good at the job. Partly because it wasn't his field – he trained as a teacher, his passion was for mathematics – and partly because much of Brodie's success was based on having skin like a rhinoceros when it came to asking impertinent questions. Brodie was bold and striking and memorable, and often people were oddly flattered to have her poking her nose into their affairs. Daniel was small, plain and self-effacing, and he hated asking personal questions of people he didn't know, or even those he did. He did it for one reason only: because Brodie needed him to.

He took it on when she found herself pregnant – a situation that couldn't have taken her more by surprise if it had been a virgin birth. And he kept it on when it became clear that Jonathan's problems would keep his mother fully occupied for the foreseeable future. Sometimes in the early months they'd swapped roles, because while Brodie was much better at running the business Daniel was pretty good at looking after the children. More recently, though, with Brodie chasing the fireflies of medical advancement, Daniel was left alone with the business and Brodie's daughter Paddy was living with her ex-husband. It wasn't ideal, just the best that could be managed.

Daniel's route across town took him through the park, under the shadow of the monument. Which was where it all started for him and Brodie, four years ago now. They'd covered a lot of ground together in that time. And if the journey hadn't left him exactly where he'd have chosen to be, it had been a hell of a ride. Taken all in all, he never wished they hadn't met.

Two hundred metres down the Promenade, then left into Fisher Hill and left again into Shack Lane. And there, three doors short of the smart burgundy one with the discreet slate nameplate, he stopped and turned round. 'If you're looking for Looking for Something? it's here. If you're looking for something else, perhaps I can help.'

Daniel hadn't entirely wasted those four years in which he'd swapped the challenges of a maths class for the even more exciting realm in which Brodie Farrell moved. He'd thought there was someone following him when he entered the park. By the time he'd wandered round the monument, apparently studying the architecture, and she was still with him, he was sure.

She didn't look like a stalker. She was a woman in her mid-fifties wearing a linen jacket and a hat – a sure sign of respectability, unless it's a baseball cap worn backwards. She wore beige leather court shoes and carried a matching handbag. And from the way her eyes flew wide, she was astonished that her subterfuge had been discovered.

Her obvious embarrassment, and the way she swallowed it rather than making an excuse and leaving, told Daniel she was at least a potential client. She wasn't here to waste his time, because the girls in the office dared her, or because Brodie had stepped on her toes in the course of some earlier commission and she wanted to give him a piece of her mind.

'Mr Hood,' she stammered. 'I'm sorry, I just…I needed to… I wanted to be sure I was doing the right thing.'

Daniel nodded amiably and took out his key. 'This is our office. Why don't you come in and tell me about it? It's a very small office – if you change your mind you can be outside in three strides. If I don't think I can help I'll say so.'

She followed him inside, holding her handbag close as if unsure what lay behind the burgundy front door.

He saw her seated, then went through to the adjoining kitchen. She heard the rattle of cups. 'Milk? Sugar?' He wasn't at all what she'd been expecting, neither Humphrey Bogart nor Sean Connery so much as a Renaissance cherub who, in growing up, had lost the wings and gained a serious pair of spectacles. With his diminutive stature, bright yellow hair and grave politeness, he might have been a thirty-year-old choirboy.

He returned with the tray and a reassuring smile. 'Do you want to tell me your name? Or would you rather hear something about what we do first?'

He might have had no great talent for the work but Daniel was good at putting people at their ease. The woman relaxed visibly. 'Margaret,' she said. 'My name is Margaret.'

'I'm Daniel.'

'I know.' She returned his smile uncertainly. 'I made enquiries before I came here. I'm sorry if that seems rude, but I needed to know you were the sort of person I could deal with. I hadn't planned to come here today. But then I saw you in town and...'

'And am I?' prompted Daniel. 'The kind of person you can deal with?'

'I think so.' She cast him a nervous glance over the top of her cup. A little like Dimmock itself, there was a certain faded gentility about her. As if once she'd enjoyed a better life. 'I'm not sure *I'm* the sort of person you can.'

Daniel had a simple test for this. 'Have you done anything wicked?'

'No!' Then she gave it a little more thought before repeating, with an odd mixture of insistence and despair, 'No. But something wicked was done.'

'Is it a police matter?'

'The police *were* involved. I think they're finished now.'

'Then I don't see any reason we shouldn't talk about it. If you want to.'

'There's one,' said the woman. Another of the anxious, troubled little glances. 'Shame.'

Daniel neither recoiled nor leant forward like an overeager social worker. He sipped his tea pensively. 'The funny thing about shame is, the people who feel it most are usually those with the least reason. Those who acknowledge their responsibilities. To feel shame you need a conscience.

'You say you've done nothing wicked and I believe you. You say the police were involved, but whoever they've locked up it wasn't you. Are you sure you've anything to be ashamed of?'

'Oh yes,' said Margaret with a terrible certainty. 'People were...hurt. Worse than hurt. And it wasn't an accident, and it wasn't carelessness or stupidity – it was deliberate. I didn't know anything about it. I didn't expect it to happen, I didn't want it to happen, perhaps I couldn't have prevented it. But it couldn't have happened without me.'

Daniel was thinking. 'Can I tell you something about me and my boss? Mrs Farrell – this is her business really, I'm only helping out while...well... The point is, she's the expert. She probably *could* find a needle in a haystack. She found me.

'That's how we met. Four years ago. Somebody came in here one day, said I'd stolen money from her and asked Mrs Farrell to find me. And she did. But she was being lied to. I hadn't stolen anything. Someone thought I'd done something I hadn't, and knew something I didn't, and wanted Brodie to find me so he could ask me about it. And I don't mean just *ask*. I was hurt too – quite badly. Brodie blamed herself. She'd no way of guessing how the information she provided would be used, but she felt responsible. Without her help they'd never have found me. They'd never have…'

His voice faltered. Even four years on, even knowing that the worst time of his life had led to some of the best times, he found it hard to get the words out. As if he could deal with what had been done to him in the privacy of his own head but was afraid what might happen if he let it out.

He flicked his visitor a shy little grin. 'Sorry. The reason I'm telling you this is not to play for sympathy. It's to make the point that bad things happen to good people. Sometimes, bad things happen *through* good people. What matters is the intent. Brodie never meant to hurt me. I never blamed her, and I think even Brodie's forgiven herself now. If what's troubling you is at all similar, you're probably being harder on yourself than anyone else is.'

'Perhaps.'

He thought she wanted to say something more, but Daniel waited and still it didn't come. He wasn't sure what to do for the best. 'You haven't committed yourself to anything by coming here. You can finish your tea, go home and never come back, and if we meet in Tesco's we needn't so much as exchange a glance. The trouble with that is, nothing will have been resolved. The problem that made you want to see me will still be there.

'So I'm going to say something that might make it

easier. If it's indiscreet, I'm sorry. You call the shots; I really am only trying to help. And it might help if I say I think I know who you are.'

She looked as shocked as if he'd slapped her. For a moment words evaded her. Then: 'How?' she stammered. 'You can't. I wasn't... I didn't... How can you know that?'

'Don't be upset,' Daniel said quickly. 'Please...that's the last thing I want. But you gave me your first name as if you were afraid your second name might mean something to me. And even in Dimmock a murder trial is unusual enough to attract attention. I put two and two together, and I thought – maybe I was wrong – that you might be Robert Carson's mother.'

Chapter Five

Margaret Carson vented a breath so long she might have been holding it for most of the last nine months. Since her son was arrested she hadn't had a full night's sleep. She hadn't spoken to anyone, even friends and family, without wondering how much they knew and what they thought about it, about her. She hadn't walked down a street without the fear of being recognised. Once, when a man in a shop raised a hand to scratch his nose, she actually flinched.

Now this young man with his pale, weak eyes and his mild, engaging personality was telling her it might have been for nothing. That her responsibility for her child's behaviour ended when his childhood ended, and the man in the shop and the people who glanced at her in the street probably didn't know who she was, and might not care if they did. The thought brought a lump to her throat.

What it didn't do was undermine the resolve which brought her here.

'Are you all right?' asked Daniel quietly.

'Yes.' She dabbed her eyes with a tissue. 'I'm sorry. I

suppose I'm feeling a bit emotional.'

'It must have been an emotional day for you,' said Daniel. 'Were you in court?'

Mrs Carson shook her head. 'I couldn't face it. I couldn't face people looking at me, thinking I was there to support him. And then, the last I heard he was pleading not guilty. I didn't want to listen to his lies.'

'Did you know they were lies?'

'Oh yes,' she said. 'I mean, he never laid his head on his old mum's shoulder and confessed what he'd done. I didn't *know* in that sense. But I knew he was capable of it. From the moment the police came to my door I never doubted that Bobby had done what they thought he'd done.'

Daniel didn't know where all this was going. When he guessed who she was, he'd supposed she wanted him to seek out evidence for an appeal. He thought he was going to have to explain that she needed a private investigator for that, and her son's solicitors would organise it. Now it seemed that wasn't what she had in mind.

Conscious that time was money, Brodie would have asked her outright. Daniel took a rather gentler approach. He did this job because Brodie needed him to, but he genuinely liked helping people. If all someone needed was a cut-glass decanter to complete the set her Aunt Dotty left her and *somebody* didn't pack properly when they moved house, he took pleasure in her delight when he found a replacement. If he could help extricate a client from a sea of troubles emanating from the fact that something had been lost, or sold, or thrown or given away when he'd no idea how his future would be blighted by his failure to keep it safe, that was even better. They were rarely life-and-death matters. But the people who came through the burgundy front door usually left a great deal happier, which gave Daniel considerable satisfaction. He was in many ways a simple soul.

He said, 'Tell me how I can help you.'

Margaret Carson swallowed. 'How much do you know about the case?'

'What was in the papers, that's all.'

'He ran them down. In his car. He knocked them down so he could rob them.' Her voice was a measured monotone. If she'd allowed any feeling to surface it would have run away with her.

'Yes,' said Daniel softly.

'They'd just got engaged. That's what they were doing in the restaurant – celebrating their engagement. She was wearing her ring, and a necklace he'd given her. Good jewellery – expensive. You can say that about my Bobby.' She barked a bitter laugh. 'He has an eye for quality. The police never found the stolen items. It took them five days to catch up with Bobby, and by then he'd disposed of them.'

Listening to her told Daniel something about Margaret Carson. She was well educated, and there was no history of crime in her background. She lacked the vocabulary. Anyone to whom armed robbery was a familiar field would have used different words, and used them less awkwardly. The way she spoke went with the linen jacket and the summer hat. She wasn't a wealthy woman, but nor was she living in poverty. She was accustomed to a modest degree of comfort. She was someone who paid her taxes, observed speed limits, didn't park on yellow lines. The hat didn't lie: she was in every sense a respectable woman. Except that she'd raised a son who killed people for money.

'Detective Superintendent Deacon – do you know him?' Daniel nodded. 'He said they interviewed an antiques dealer who bought the necklace – apparently in good faith – the day after the robbery and sold it again within twenty-four hours. The police never managed to trace either it or whoever bought it.'

Most people's experience of crime is limited to what they learn from TV drama. Daniel didn't watch much television: most of his experience of crime was personal. But between them Jack Deacon and Brodie Farrell had an encyclopaedic knowledge of crime, and a lot of the time they were talking, Daniel was listening. He knew that jewellery was an attractive proposition for thieves because it could be broken up. Good stones retained their value even after the ring, the necklace, the brooch had been rendered unidentifiable.

He guessed that this was not what his visitor wanted to hear. 'Mrs Carson, I still don't know what it is you want me to do.'

She seemed to change the subject. Her gaze strayed off round the room. It was only a little office, there wasn't much to occupy it there – before long she had to look at him again. Her voice fell soft. 'You think, maybe he'll be a scientist. Maybe he'll find a cure for cancer. You know it isn't very likely, but one day some mother's son is going to and you think, Maybe it'll be mine. You look at him in his cowboy hat and his scuffed trainers, and he grins up at you, and you think he's the most perfect thing in the world. Five or six years old, a bundle of pure potential wearing a silly grin.'

Even knowing what followed, she couldn't keep from smiling at the memory. 'And you tell yourself, Don't be ridiculous. For every Nobel Prize winner there are a million GPs. And that would be great – a good profession, helping people. Who wouldn't want a doctor in the family? Then you notice he's got the trainers on the wrong feet and you think, Maybe he's not going to be that academic. Maybe he'll have more of a practical bent. And that's fine too. People will always need car mechanics, electricians, plumbers. If a man works hard enough at anything to raise a family, he's been a success by any yardstick that matters.'

Her gaze fell. She had to make herself keep going. 'What you never, ever think is that he'll grow up to be a murderer. A criminal, a thug and finally a murderer. Where did that little boy go? What happened to all that potential? What *happened* to turn a six-year-old in a cowboy hat and a silly grin into a young man who'd run people down in order to rob them? And if you're his mother' – she dared a quick, agonised glance at Daniel's face – 'you think, What did I do wrong?'

Daniel didn't go in for platitudes. They were too close to easy lies, a way to avoid hard truths. But the truth never went away. It just hung around like a rightful heir, waiting to be acknowledged. Daniel believed passionately in truth. He thought that the one thing that was harder to deal with than a hard truth was an easy lie. So instead of demurring kindly he said, 'Do you think you did something wrong?'

She didn't have to think. She'd thought of nothing else for nine months. 'I raised him the same way I raised his brother and sister. He had everything they had. I didn't treat him any different, I didn't love him any less. A part of me still loves him. I hate everything he's become, everything he's done, and yet still somewhere in the heart of me he's that six-year-old in the cowboy hat with all his life ahead of him. Only now, as well as that, he's a self-confessed murderer.'

Daniel was nodding slowly. 'I suppose they're the unacknowledged victims of crime – the criminal's family. Everyone feels for the injured parties and the people who love them. And of course that's right. They're the ones like us – the ones who woke up that morning with no idea their life was about to be derailed, who had no say in what happened, who suffered because of someone else's greed or anger or stupidity. Of course we sympathise.'

Behind the thick glasses the mild grey eyes saw things that Margaret Carson could not have put into words. 'But all that applies to you too, doesn't it? You didn't want this to happen. No one *wants* their son to turn to crime. And it's easy to think you should have seen it coming and stopped it, but how? Realistically, how do you prevent someone becoming a criminal? But your family were as much affected by his career choice as the families of Bobby's victims. You *are* his victims. The first time he hurt anyone, he hurt you too.

'Tom Sanger's family, and his fiancée, weren't the only ones to suffer a bereavement. You lost your son too – the one you loved and had hopes for. I suppose you feel that the man in court today murdered him.'

She looked at him as if he'd given her absolution. He hadn't – Daniel didn't do religion – but his understanding went most of the way. Her eyes glittered with unshed tears. She mumbled, 'I agonised about coming here. Whether I should come at all, and if so, when. I put it off as long as I could. I told myself that if I came before the trial it could prejudice the case. But I knew that if I didn't come as soon as the trial was over I wouldn't come at all. I thought it was going to be a lot harder. Thank you for that.'

'I haven't done anything yet,' said Daniel.

'Yes, you have.'

He considered a moment. 'But that wasn't why you came. If talking about it has helped, I'm glad. But you must have had something else in mind. There are grief counsellors out there. There are priests, if you feel that way inclined. Nobody comes to a finding agency because they need someone to talk to – they come because they want something finding. Mrs Carson, what is it you want me to find?'

Brodie left Jonathan with his father – both of them sleeping, the baby in his cot, the detective sitting bolt upright on the squishy sofa as if he might be under observation – and went to pick Paddy up from school. She was tired and didn't want to go out again, and the second Mrs Farrell was happy to collect the child as she'd been doing for a month. But Brodie had the sense that this was something she owed to herself and Paddy both. It was the last day of the school year. Next year she'd make her own way home from school. It was another milestone – the last walk home together. She didn't want to miss this one as well.

Everything in a household plays second fiddle to a sick child. At eight going on thirty, Paddy understood that as well as anyone. She didn't complain about the amount of her mother's time and energy the baby needed. Perhaps she was aware it wouldn't be for ever, and she and Brodie would have time to make up for lost opportunities in a way that Brodie and Jonathan never would.

But now she was home, while Jonathan didn't need her Paddy took priority. Over tiredness; over being jet-lagged; over everything else. She drove as far as the park and walked the rest of the way to the school, hoping the fresh air would blow some colour back into her face and soul.

Paddy was expecting her stepmother. She liked Julia, enjoyed staying with John and his wife, but when she saw Brodie waiting at the school gates her face blossomed like a rose. Brown pigtails bouncing ecstatically, schoolbag swinging, she ran the rest of the way. Brodie caught her in a hug and swung her round and round. Her heart was so full it ached. The child looked so healthy! She'd almost forgotten what that looked like.

And the other thing that struck her, after not seeing her daughter for a month, was how little she resembled either of her parents. She had something of Brodie's colouring, but without the drama – rosy cheeks and glossy brown hair would never turn heads the way her mother's classic features and cloud of dark curls did. And she'd inherited something of her father's asceticism – a thoughtful, considerate, conscientious child who might one day follow in John Farrell's footsteps as a solicitor. Unless she stuck with her first love which was tractors. But of all of them, thought Brodie, the one she favoured most was Daniel, with whom she shared no genes.

Of course, there's more to family than DNA. Paddy had known Daniel for half her life. They were interested in the same things: not the tractors so much but the world and the stars and the way things work. By the time she was five she knew there were a lot of questions that Daniel could answer better than her mother. She didn't think of him as a father: she had one of those and found him quite satisfactory. And she knew he wasn't her mother's boyfriend, because that was Uncle Jack. Perhaps that was why she was so fond of Daniel. If he didn't come with a label, he was free to be her friend. Paddy had learnt early what it had taken Brodie thirty years to discover: the strength, the support, the sheer contentment to be found in friendship.

The child mumbled something into Brodie's midriff. Brodie ducked down to her level. 'What was that?'

'How long are you home for?'

That stabbed her in the heart. She could brush aside Daniel's reservations, deflect Deacon's concerns, but when Paddy's first words to her after a month apart were to ask when she was leaving again, that pulled her up short. Was it possible, after all, that she was doing this wrong? That she was risking too much on a gamble she had little chance of winning? She held her daughter close. 'For a while, anyway.'

'It's all right,' said Paddy, gazing up at her. 'I know it's important. I don't mind.' She thought for a moment. 'Auntie Julia does proper cooking.'

Brodie didn't know whether to laugh or cry. 'Well, take notes, then you can teach me.'

They walked back across the park. 'I called Julia, she knows you're coming home with me. If you want to. If you don't mind eating out of the freezer,' she added ironically.

Paddy grinned and nodded. After a moment the grin faded. 'How's Jonfon?' It wasn't a lisp, she just thought Jonathan was too big a name for a baby.

'Not great,' admitted Brodie. 'But there are things we haven't tried yet...'

The words dried in her mouth as she became aware that Paddy was giving her Daniel's look. She hadn't told Paddy how serious Jonathan's condition was, not wanting to share her burden with a child. But it was like an elephant in the drawing room: Paddy didn't need it pointing out to know it was there. The atmosphere at home, and the way her mother and Uncle Jack stopped talking sometimes when she came into the room, had kept her abreast of developments.

Now she asked, quietly, matter-of-factly, 'Is Jonfon going to die?'

It was a nexus moment. Maybe Brodie hadn't been entirely candid with the little girl – she was, after all, only eight – but she hadn't lied to her and she didn't want to start doing so now. Which meant being honest with herself. However much she might wish otherwise, however hard she was prepared to fight for him, the only honest answer was Probably.

She sighed. They were nearly at the car but this wouldn't wait. She stepped aside from the path to a handy bench and Paddy sat down beside her.

'I think so,' she said, and her womb bled to say it. 'We're doing all we can. All of us – me, Uncle Jack, Daddy and Auntie Julia, Daniel… And you – being so helpful, so undemanding. We could none of us have got this far without your contribution. And we're not finished yet. Anything we can think of, we'll try. But a point comes where you have to face up to what's probably coming. We're probably going to lose him.'

They sat in silence, side by side, for a couple of minutes. Then Paddy slipped her small hand into Brodie's and her small voice mumbled, 'I'm sorry.'

Brodie squeezed her fingers. 'Me too.'

Looking back, Brodie was aware that Paddy never again called her brother Jonfon. As if the fact that he was unlikely to grow into his proper name made it important to use it now, while there was still time.

Chapter Six

As soon as she decently could, Brodie dropped in on Daniel at work. She wanted to monitor his success as her locum. She picked up a bit of shopping first and tried to look as if she was passing. It was barely ten o'clock the next morning, which was a Friday. 'Just wondering how you were.'

He gave her that cool, calculating, sceptical look that Paddy had learnt from him. 'You saw me yesterday.'

Brodie gave a negligent shrug. 'Jet lag. So, how's things?'

'You mean, have I ruined your business yet?'

She demurred, unconvincingly. 'I trust you, Daniel, you know that.' But her eye was touring the tiny office, looking for the desk diary. Even Brodie would be embarrassed to ask for the accounts, but she could get a good idea of how much work he was getting from a casual glance at the diary.

She'd always kept it on top of the desk. He'd moved it. She thought he'd done it to annoy her. He took it calmly out of the top left-hand drawer and opened it without a word.

The only cool thing for Brodie to have done at that point was laugh lightly and turn away, leaving the pages unread. But for Brodie, cool always took second place to profit. She was a businesswoman to the tips of her well-manicured fingernails. Looking for Something? wasn't just a way to pay the bills: it had provided her with a life worth having after John left. It had made her who she was. And she liked who she was, even if the cricket on her shoulder was embarrassed sometimes.

She was grateful to Daniel for babysitting it. And it was true that she trusted him. But they both knew it wasn't a business he had much talent for, and she trusted his instincts much less than she trusted her own. So she inspected the diary carefully, ignoring his unwavering gaze.

'Who's Margaret Carson?'

'Someone who's trying to buy back the past.' Daniel told her about the murderous thief and the guilt of the woman who spawned him.

Brodie frowned. 'What does she want us to find?'

Daniel noted that *us* without commenting. 'The jewellery. The engagement ring, and a necklace belonging to the boy's mother. They were the last things Tom Sanger gave to Jane Moss, and Mrs Carson wants to give them back.'

'Were they valuable?'

Daniel regarded her levelly. 'Yes. They cost a life.'

Brodie had learnt not to rise when he took the moral high ground. 'Financially. What were they worth in hard cash? What do we base our percentage on?'

Daniel shrugged. 'I've no idea. The necklace was in the family for a generation. I suppose there's a receipt somewhere for the engagement ring, but Mrs Carson wouldn't know where to find it. Anyway, is that what we base our fees on? When Carson fenced the things, he'd get a fraction of their actual value.'

With world travel and still the hope of expensive medical procedures to fund, Brodie couldn't afford to be sentimental. 'We base our cut on what the jewels are worth, not what a fence would give for them. Apart from anything else, it'll be a costly business tracking them down. If Mrs Carson wants to return the jewels, how's she planning on paying us? Or their new owner?'

'She says she'll sell her house if she has to. And maybe, if someone bought them in good faith, he won't want paying.'

'Yeah, right,' said Brodie, heavily ironic. 'I keep telling you, Daniel, most people don't share your delicate scruples. Nobody is going to return valuable jewellery for nothing but the satisfaction of doing a good thing. They're going to want at least what they paid.' She shook her head. 'I don't think this is one for us. If the police couldn't find the jewellery, I don't see how we can.'

'But that's always the case,' Daniel pointed out. 'People only ever come to us after the usual paths have petered out. What we can do, that Jack or an insurance investigator can't, is spend time looking. With a big organisation behind them, they have to cost their time at hundreds of pounds an hour. Even good jewellery wouldn't be worth a week's searching. We can do it for a lot less than that. You know that's so. If it wasn't, this business couldn't exist.'

Brodie was watching him with her head tilted to one side like a bird's. 'You want to do this, don't you?'

'I felt sorry for her,' he nodded. 'She feels terrible about what her son did. She wants to try to make amends. She can't bring the boy back, or undo the damage to the girl. This is all she can think of – to restore the jewellery to its owner. It's the only kind of peace she's going to find. I'd like to help her, if I can.'

'They're not lost property, though, are they?' Brodie reminded him. 'They were stolen in the course of a pretty horrendous crime. Whoever has them now probably knows that. Even if he doesn't, the people who laundered them certainly do. These are bad people, Daniel. Some of them aren't much better than Bobby Carson. Asking them what they did with Jane Moss's necklace could get you hurt.'

'I thought of that.' Daniel flicked her a slightly nervous smile. 'Then I thought, I'm not the police. Nobody needs to talk to me. If I get too close for someone's comfort, they'll just shut the door on me. They don't need to hurt me, they just need to clam up. What can I do about it? They're safe. If Jack could have nailed them he'd have done it by now.'

Brodie was puzzled. 'Then what do you expect to achieve? These aren't, on the whole, people with a conscience. They won't give the things back because you tell them a sob story.'

'I don't expect them to. I'm hoping they'll find a way

to sell Mrs Carson the jewellery. As stolen goods, it'll have been changing hands at a fraction of market value – she may be the only person around who's willing to pay more. If I can put the word out, maybe someone will want to do business with her.'

'Or rip her off,' warned Brodie.

'Or rip her off,' agreed Daniel. 'That's part of my job, isn't it? To stop anyone ripping her off. To make sure that, if she parts with her money, at least she gets what she wants in return.'

Brodie's whole demeanour was doubtful. 'There are more ways this can go wrong than right. The chances are you'll put in weeks of work and have nothing to show for it.'

'She knows that. She's willing to pay for time and expenses if I can't finish the job.'

That satisfied at least some of Brodie's concerns. But there was a part of her that wasn't just businesswoman. 'There has to be some prospect of success before we take someone's money. Even if they're up for a gamble, we shouldn't let them throw their money away. I just can't see how you're going to find some stolen jewellery nine months on. It'll have been turned into something completely different by now. I doubt if even an expert could say that the diamonds in one ring originated in another.'

Daniel nodded. 'The stones from the engagement ring may be in a dozen different pieces by now. But the necklace is something else.'

'Why? Because it's older? These are not sentimental

people. They won't give a second thought to destroying a period piece if they can make themselves richer, or safer, by making it unrecognisable.'

'I don't think they *can* make this unrecognisable.' He put a photograph on the desk in front of her.

It had been taken for insurance purposes. The lighting was carefully angled, the background a plain white card, the focus close. A small ruler had been included in the picture. There was nothing glamorous, nothing alluring, about it. But it did show very clearly a necklace comprising a gold chain, a gold filigree setting, some seed pearls, and an oval stone the like of which Brodie had never seen before. 'What *is* that?'

'It's a star sapphire.'

'Sapphires are blue.'

'Not always. That's a black sapphire.' It wasn't, however, black but an indeterminate shade of translucent grey, as if someone had dipped a pen in water and the ink had run.

'And that...' She pointed. 'That isn't a trick of the camera?'

Daniel shook his head. 'That's what makes it a star sapphire. It's called asterism – it's caused by light refracting off inclusions of tiny rutile needles.' He'd done his homework. 'That's a twelve-ray star, which is pretty rare. It's the one thing about that stone that will always be recognisable. You couldn't alter it without making it worthless. So the stone at least still looks today the way it looked when that picture was taken. It can be found.'

Brodie didn't know how to put this politely so she just came out and said it. 'By you?'

He smiled at her lack of confidence. His smile lit up his whole rather ordinary face, and Brodie's heart as well. 'We won't know that till I've tried.'

Chapter Seven

Brodie suggested he talk to Deacon first; then she told Deacon to talk to Daniel. Deacon had a regrettable habit of dividing the world into those who could help him and those who weren't worth his time.

'Of course we tried to recover the stolen goods,' growled Deacon. It was lunchtime on Monday and they were in The Belted Galloway, the nearest hostelry to Battle Alley and Deacon's second office. It wasn't that he was much of a drinker – he was too conscious of the danger of being outsmarted even when sober, not just by old lags but also by young policemen. But he liked the atmosphere here. It was dark going on gloomy, which both suited his demeanour and encouraged the trading of confidences in a way that the well-lit interview rooms around the corner did not. And the publican didn't believe in canned music. Deacon hated canned music with a passion.

He took a moody bite out of his weak shandy. 'We were too slow. By the time we caught up with Carson he'd fenced them. They probably went through three or four different handlers in the first seventy-two hours. The only one I found was Paul Sinclair at Top of the Hill Antiques'

– his sour-lemon expression attested to his dislike of clever names – 'and he said he bought the necklace in good faith from someone who claimed to be clearing out his late mother's house. He sold it on the same day. Cash, both times.

'Which is enough to make you wonder,' he added dourly, 'but not proof of anything. It's a cash trade. People dealing in antiques really do wander round with a few thousand pounds in their back pockets in case they spot something that's worth a little bit more. I might have my suspicions about Sinclair's honesty, but I can't prove he did anything wrong.'

'Did the insurers conduct their own investigation?'

'Of a kind. That necklace was a valuable piece. The ring was worth a bit too, so was the boy's watch – but they were modern, there'll be others like them around, they were always going to be easier to disappear. But the star sapphire was distinctive, much harder to cash in. The insurers offered a reward for information leading to its return but no one took the bait. Of course, Sanger was dead – it was a murder inquiry, and no one wants to be associated with that. The insurers paid out when it started to look like the cheaper option.'

Already Daniel was starting to feel he was boxing above his weight. He frowned earnestly into his glass. It contained even less alcohol than Deacon's shandy. 'So how do I go about finding them?'

Deacon barked an incredulous laugh at him. Even after four years Daniel Hood retained the ability to surprise him. 'Daniel, you don't. They're gone. *I* couldn't find them, and I'm paid to. The insurers paid out because *they* couldn't find them. No one's talking. No one's *going* to talk – it's not in their interests to. All the people who had a hand in the deal took their cut and kept their mouths shut. When Carson went down without involving anyone else, they heaved a sigh of relief. They're not going to put their hands up now just because you ask nicely.'

Daniel looked disconsolate. 'They wouldn't get greedy? My client's willing to pay…'

'There's greedy,' said Deacon deliberately, 'and there's downright bloody stupid. Most of the downright bloody stupid ones are behind bars already. The rest put their liberty first. Crime's like any other business: sometimes you walk away. And sometimes you run.'

'What am I supposed to tell Mrs Carson?'

Deacon had no sympathy at all. 'Tell her you can't do it. Tell her you underestimated the size of the task and overestimated your own ability. Tell her that when it comes to finding stolen goods the police are the experts – if we luck out she's probably better keeping her money in her purse.'

Daniel wasn't quite ready to concede. 'Some of the things Brodie's found, everyone else had given up on. Including the police.'

Deacon gave him a slow sideways glance laced with dislike. People sitting each side of them instinctively shuffled up in case spilt pints and swinging fists should follow. But Daniel knew better than to take it personally. Dislike was Deacon's default position. In fact, it had taken Daniel a couple of years to graduate to mere generalised dislike from a position of very specific disfavour.

'That's Brodie,' growled the detective. 'She's good at what she does. But right now she's doing something else, so this is going to be you. You asked my opinion and this is it. You can't do what this woman wants. Don't waste your time and her money trying.'

Daniel bit his lip. Another time he might coax a slightly more helpful response from Deacon, but right now he too was preoccupied. He said softly, 'Jack, I'm sorry Brodie didn't bring back better news. You must be going through hell.'

Deacon looked again at him, almost furtively. He *was* going through a kind of hell, but only Daniel, Terry Walsh and maybe Charlie Voss had noticed. Everyone else was sorry his son was ill, but sorry in the same way as if his car was on its last legs or his house needed underpinning. Bad news – really bad news – people were genuinely sympathetic, and yet there was no acknowledgement of the scale of the loss he faced. He thought it was because he and Brodie weren't married. That people considered a love child somehow less precious. As if their reactions were unconsciously mitigated by a sense of *easy come, easy go*.

He said slowly, as if to the shandy, 'I never wanted a child. I never expected to have one. You know he was a mistake?' Daniel nodded silently. 'If Brodie had said she didn't want to proceed with the pregnancy, I wouldn't have argued. I think I'd have been relieved.

'But that was *a* baby. And this is *this* baby. My son Jonathan. I had no idea what a difference it made. In here.' He thumped his chest hard enough that the glasses on the bar slopped. 'Daniel, I'd rip my own arm off if I thought it would save him. But it wouldn't. And I feel cheated. It's like… It's like, you buy a lottery ticket. You don't expect to win the jackpot. You expect to throw the ticket away on Monday. But against all the odds your numbers come up. You've won five million quid. You didn't need it, you never expected it. But you won it and now it's yours.

'And *now* someone steals the ticket. That's how it feels. Like this was something I'd been needing all my life, and I never even knew it. And now I understand that, I'm going to lose it.'

Jack Deacon was a famously inarticulate man, even among policemen. If a situation couldn't be resolved by a mixture of threats and clichés he floundered. It wasn't thinking that gave him trouble. He was a good thinker: clear, accurate, occasionally imaginative. His difficulty was translating those thoughts into words that resonated in other people's minds. It stemmed mainly from a lack of practice. Deacon's authority, even before he had the authority of rank, had always derived from substance. People tend not to argue with big men. Daniel was good with words because they were usually the only defence he had. Deacon was bad with them because nothing he said made as much impression as the shadow he cast.

So it was a rare privilege to hear him speak from the heart. Daniel knew how desperately Deacon must need to talk to use him as a listener. He tried to be worthy of the policeman's trust.

'Are you aware,' he murmured, 'that's one of the reasons Brodie's so determined to find an answer? She thinks she let you down. She gave you something, and it wasn't as perfect as it should have been. She blames herself. However much she wants Jonathan to get well – and of course she does, desperately – she wants it even more for you than for herself.'

Deacon's look came from the place where wonder meets disbelief. If he'd been talking to anyone else, disbelief would have won. But Daniel would walk through fire rather than lie. If he said it, he believed it to be true. 'How…?' Emotion cracked his voice.

'How do I know?' Daniel smiled gently. 'Jack, you *know* how I know. It's driven you mad for the last four years. I know how she thinks, how she feels. I know what matters to her, and how much. Sometimes I know what matters to her before she does. But we haven't talked about this, if that's what you're wondering. We haven't been discussing you behind your back. I've hardly seen her since she first took Jonathan abroad.'

'Then *how*?'

Daniel's mild grey eyes glinted with the tears that still formed a little too easily but seldom fell anymore. 'You want me to say it? Again? I love her, Jack. That's how.'

'And you think I don't?' said Jack Deacon fiercely. The fierceness was essential to getting it out. The words didn't come easily. 'But I don't know her the way you know her.

I don't understand her the way you understand her. And she doesn't talk to me the way she talks to you. I would lay down my life for them both. For Brodie, and for Jonathan. You know me well enough to know that isn't just words – I would literally die for them. And it isn't enough. It isn't enough to keep them safe. We're going to lose him. And when we lose Jonathan, I'll lose Brodie too.

'And the reason is – the bottom line, the can't-get-round-it reason is – he's all we have in common. A baby neither of us wanted, who's been nothing but a worry since we found out he was on his way, who in spite of that has managed to do what two healthy adults couldn't: cobble together some semblance of a family. But semblance is the word. We aren't a proper family. We don't behave like family. Because of Jonathan we've both made an effort – me to support her, Brodie to let me. But it shouldn't be this hard. If there was something there worth having, it wouldn't be. When Jonathan's gone there'll be nothing left between us.'

He looked up then, and in his craggy face Daniel read an odd mixture of humour and despair. 'It isn't me she'll turn to for comfort then, Daniel, it's you. Hang on in there, stud. Your chance is coming.'

But Daniel shook his head. 'My chance came a while back. I had the choice of settling for a friendship I could keep or spoiling everything by asking for more. I took what she was happy to give. Maybe it was a coward's choice – risk nothing, gain nothing. But realistically, it was the only part of her that was ever available to me. And it's so much more than I ever had before. It's almost enough.'

'Almost?'

Daniel shrugged. 'Nothing's ever quite enough, Jack. The secret of happiness is knowing what's almost enough.'

Deacon gave a little snort and turned back to his drink. Then he changed the subject; or rather, reverted to the one they'd been discussing earlier. 'You could talk to Sinclair, I suppose, though I don't think it'll do any good. When I interviewed him, he stuck like glue to his story because he knew I had nothing on him. Why would he talk to you now?'

'Because I'm not the police? Because I'm no threat to him?' hazarded Daniel.

Deacon didn't think that way. 'I don't think Sinclair bought the necklace directly from Bobby Carson. I think it had already been through other hands first. All the same, Sinclair knew it wasn't kosher. He knew he was one stop in the wash cycle.'

Daniel was looking confused, so he explained. 'The goods go in dirty at one end. They change hands quickly, earning a little more legitimacy each time, until they come out at the other end clean enough for Joe Public. The system depends on people not asking questions. I think Paul Sinclair knew better than to question the man who was clearing out his mother's house, and the guy who spotted the necklace under Sinclair's counter later that day knew better than to question Sinclair. When he sold it on, at an antiques fair or to someone in a pub, it was a bit cleaner again. Today it's probably with someone who genuinely did buy it in good faith.

'I don't think you'll get anything useful out of Sinclair,' he decided thoughtfully. 'But I don't think he'll follow you into a dark alley for asking.'

Mention of dark alleys made Daniel nervous. 'I don't expect I'll get anywhere with this,' he agreed hurriedly. 'But at least I can go back to Mrs Carson and say I tried.'

Chapter Eight

Paul Sinclair looked down his nose at Daniel. This took more determination than you might think because he wasn't much taller. He was a man in his mid-thirties with thinning fair hair, a cut-glass accent, a fondness for cashmere sweaters in shades of peach and mint, and – according to Brodie, who was never wrong in these matters – a nineteen-year-old toy boy who worked at the marina. He looked at Daniel as if he'd come in on somebody's shoe.

'You want what?'

Patiently, Daniel said it all again. That he was acting for a client. That he was trying to trace the star sapphire necklace that Sinclair had bought and then sold. That any information he might have that would assist in finding the purchaser would be helpful.

'The police asked me the same thing. I wasn't able to help them. What makes you think I'll be able to help you?' The tone was barely the right side of objectionable.

'Because nobody's going to jail, or getting leant on, or having their books looked at because of anything I hear. So people don't have to be quite so careful what they say to me. The police are only interested in facts. I'll be grateful for anything that might put me on the right track. Any impression you gained about the man who bought it – where he was from, if he was living in the Dimmock area, what sort of business he was in, who the necklace was for. Anything. Probably it won't get me very far. But it might.'

'And what are my other customers to make of the notion that I'd discuss private business with a third party?' demanded the antiques dealer.

'Unless they've got something to hide,' murmured Daniel, 'I don't see why they should be concerned. I'm trying to buy the thing, not repossess it. Wherever that necklace is now, it might be for sale again. You and I are just helping someone who's anxious to buy it make contact with someone who might want to sell.'

Sinclair had been leaning slightly back, to facilitate his sneer. Now he leant slightly forward. 'No questions asked?'

It was a trick. But Daniel wasn't as green as he'd been a year ago. He pursed his lips. 'It's not actually lawful to make that kind of offer. But I wasn't hired to find out who did what, only to locate the necklace and buy it back.'

Sinclair's eyes slipped out of focus as he considered his options, and how big a gulf stood between the safest, which was to say nothing, and the most profitable, which was to help put a deal together in return for a percentage. He said distantly, 'Let me think about it. If anything occurs to me, I know where to find you.'

* * *

I know where to find you… If Daniel had watched fewer science documentaries and more soap operas on the television, the words might have resonated with him in a way that in fact they did not. After all, Looking for Something? was a business – Daniel needed people to be able to find him.

But he doubted he'd hear from Paul Sinclair again. Too much time had passed. Even if the dealer knew more than he said about who bought the necklace, in the intervening months the thing could have travelled halfway round the world. The stone could have been reset in a ring, or a brooch, or the staff of office of an Eastern potentate. Deacon was right. If he'd been unable to pick up its trail a week after the crime, Daniel's chances nine months later hovered somewhere between microscopic and none.

He said as much to Brodie after he'd pondered the problem for twenty-four hours. 'I think you were right. I'll have to call Mrs Carson and tell her I've drawn a blank.'

Brodie nodded absently. It said everything about her state of mind that she could hear talk of lost commission and not automatically rush to salvage it.

She didn't think of herself as mercenary. She'd refused numerous commissions in the last four years, and even returned a few as being less achievable than she'd first thought. But she didn't do it lightly. The clients for her curious little business were her only source of income, and thinking their odd requests weren't worth the trouble of following up would be a short cut to bankruptcy. Eighteen months ago she'd have thought Margaret Carson's quest was a runner. She'd have found out how much the star sapphire was worth, and thus how much her commission should be, and after she'd picked herself off the floor she'd have locked the door, put the phone on voicemail and concentrated all her efforts on locating the missing stone. And she'd have expected to succeed. Even nine months after the event.

Now she had even more important matters to think of. And it wasn't Brodie looking for Jane Moss's sapphire but Daniel, which meant the hunt would be less fun and the prospect of success smaller. She would always be grateful to Daniel for keeping her business afloat when she'd thought she'd have to close it, but gratitude didn't blind her to the fact that he would never be her professional equal. The chances of him completing the commission were so slight that losing the fee cost her little grief. She'd never really expected to see it. 'Maybe that would be best.'

'Sorry,' said Daniel.

Brodie smiled at his disheartened expression. 'Don't be. You do pretty well. Not everything *can* be found – not by you, not even by me. That sapphire is long gone. It's in a numbered bank vault somewhere, waiting for someone to put together a fake provenance before it can be sold again. Someone paid peanuts for it, and they don't care if they have to sit on it for twenty years. It's an investment. They were never going to sell it to Margaret Carson.'

'I shouldn't have taken the brief, should I? I should have known that.'

Brodie topped up their glasses from the bottle on the table. They were eating in her kitchen though Daniel did the cooking. He'd had everything on by the time she'd got the children to bed. 'It was worth making some enquiries. If the necklace had never reached an end-user it might still have been in Dimmock – stashed under a squeaky floorboard by a small-time local dealer who was now terrified he was never going to get rid of it, who'd have been glad of a chance to get back his stake. Sometimes you have to try. You just have to recognise when you've tried hard enough.'

Daniel was thinking outside the box. He said slowly, 'I keep wondering if there isn't another different way to approach this. If I can't help Mrs Carson without finding the necklace.'

Brodie was puzzled. 'I don't see how. I mean, she could have the thing copied, but it would never be the one Tom Sanger gave to Jane Moss. It was a gift from the man who was going to be her husband, its value to her is personal. Even a perfect copy would be just eye candy. If Bobby Carson's mother bought *me* a replica and thought that made things OK between us, I'd slap her face.'

Daniel winced. The last thing he wanted to do was hurt anyone's feelings. He wanted to help Margaret Carson, but not by turning a knife in Jane Moss's side. 'You're right, of course. It would seem like blood money. She'd be deeply offended.'

The prospect of offending people didn't much trouble Brodie. And Jane Moss wasn't the one footing the bill. 'Jane wouldn't be offended if she thought it was the real thing.'

Daniel looked up with a start like a shying horse, eyes flaring behind the thick glasses. 'You're saying we should *lie* about it? Pass it off as something it isn't?'

Brodie rocked a non-committal hand. 'I'm not saying to lie. I'm not saying we should make any claims for it. But Jane Moss only had that stone in her possession for a couple of hours, and most of that time she was looking at Tom Sanger. And she's not a jeweller. Would she recognise it if she saw it again? If it was taken out of the setting and put on a table in front of her, with two or three others of generally similar appearance, would she be able to pick it out? Because if she couldn't, she might get as much comfort from a stone that we couldn't vouch for but which just might have come from her necklace as she would from the real thing.'

'You are,' said Daniel flatly, accusingly. 'You're suggesting we lie to her. And that would mean lying to Margaret Carson too – telling her we've found the stone when all we've actually done is find one that looks a bit like it.'

'Everything's black and white with you, isn't it?' Brodie grumbled into her wine. 'Either it's the stone Jane was given, though she wouldn't know it from a bauble on a Christmas tree, or it's one just like it and she's being cheated. But what if it's not actually about the stone? What if it's about her feelings? She lost the man she was going to marry, and also the last thing he gave her. If she got it back, she wouldn't cherish it because of what it was worth, she'd cherish it as a memento of Tom.'

Daniel was unable to follow her reasoning. 'But if it wasn't the stone from his mother's necklace, there would be no connection to Tom.'

'But if she *thought* it was the same stone she'd get the

same comfort from the lookalike as she would from the original. Nobody's cheating anybody. Jane gets a stone identical to her fiancé's last gift to her, and she puts it away among her treasures, and maybe she takes it out sometimes to look at it and maybe she doesn't, but she knows it's there and while it's there she feels he's not entirely gone.

'And maybe, years down the line, when she's fallen in love with someone else and had five kids, and she's wondering how to get them through university, she takes the stone out and thinks this is something Tom would have liked to do for her. And she sells the stone. Well, as long as it's worth as much as the original, she still hasn't been cheated.'

'And what do we tell Margaret Carson?' Daniel's eyes were appalled.

'The same as we tell Jane Moss. That we've found a stone that matches the description of the stolen sapphire. That we can't establish a provenance for it, but that could mean it came onto the market via the back door. That it's up to her whether to proceed or not. She'd know there was a chance the stone wasn't right, but she wouldn't be paying any more than it was worth. If she decided to go ahead, she too would get what she needs – the feeling of having done all she could to make amends. If Jane Moss flung the thing back in her face, it could be sold again and all the exercise would have cost her would be our fee.'

They regarded one another over the kitchen table. Sometimes Brodie worried Daniel quite a lot. Even after all they'd been through, sometimes he couldn't be sure if she was being absolutely serious or enjoying a joke at his expense. She made a good case. Daniel could only see one thing wrong with it. '*We'd* know it was a lie!'

Brodie shook her head. 'It's not a lie unless we claim the stone is the original.'

'It's a lie if we know it isn't and don't say so!'

'No, that's just a tactical omission. As long as Mrs Carson knows there's a chance it's not the same sapphire, it's her call. She has to decide whether the stone we've found can do what she needs it to do, for her and for Jane.'

Daniel's pale brows lowered in a censorious frown. 'Plus, we get paid.'

Brodie grinned. 'Well, yes. That's kind of the point, Daniel. That's what keeps us in business. Not the warm fuzzy glow of helping people.'

'The warm fuzzy glow is important too.'

'Of course it is. And you would be helping them – both of them. If the real thing can't be recovered, this is probably the only help we or anyone else can offer.'

He was horribly afraid she was serious. Outrage bubbled in his chest. 'Brodie, you're not making a liar of me!'

She gave a negligent shrug. 'Suit yourself. Let them go away disappointed.'

They continued their meal almost in silence. But a couple of times when Daniel glanced up he caught Brodie secretly smiling.

Chapter Nine

Four years ago Daniel had come home, to this same odd little shack in the shadow of Dimmock's ruined pier, and found men waiting who almost killed him. It had been months before he could climb the iron steps to the front door, let himself in and check the four small rooms for intruders without feeling physically sick. It was a year before he stopped checking for intruders.

Tonight as he went through the door, before he even got the key out of the lock, someone grabbed him, swung him round and slammed him into the wall hard enough to break the glasses on the bridge of his nose and set off a volley of fireworks in his head.

He didn't pass out, not quite. He slumped in a boneless heap, and though he saw the living room light come on, all it did was brighten the red mist in front of his eyes. He felt the silken touch of blood on his face and heard a plaintive mewling protest that he supposed was his.

He had no idea what had happened, who had ambushed him or why. He didn't know how many of them there were, and whether that made much difference to a man still struggling with the concept of *up*. The only thing he knew for sure was that he was in a lot of trouble.

He heard the rings rattle as someone drew the curtains so that the netting shed would look the way it looked every evening when he was home. Anyone who had seen him walk down the beach wouldn't be puzzled that, minutes later, he still hadn't switched the lights on. None of the casual acquaintances he'd made along the seafront, in the shops and cafés and B&Bs, who wouldn't have called him a friend but still took an amiable interest in his activities, would come to check that he was all right.

Strong hands fastened on him. Instinctively, he cringed. But they only straightened him out, and carefully picked the remains of his glasses out of the bloody flesh of his cheek, then lifted him bodily and put him down in his own armchair. 'Better?'

He didn't recognise the voice. It was a man, but he'd known that from the force with which he'd hit the wall.

The scattered starlings of his wits were beginning to settle back on the telegraph wires. He mumbled, 'Better than just now. Not so good as ten minutes ago.'

The man chuckled, genuinely amused. 'OK. Well, that's fair enough. I needed a quick chat with you. I wanted to get your attention. Have I got it?'

Daniel said nothing. But as the big figure loomed closer the urge for self-preservation grabbed the wheel and he nodded quickly.

'Good. You seem a reasonable sort. We're not going to fall out over this, are we?'

Again the interrogative pause. Again, Daniel's desire not to get beaten up shook its head and hoped the rest of him would join in. Round a thick lip he mumbled, 'I was afraid we already had.'

'No.' The man sounded surprised and concerned that he'd been misunderstood. 'Not at all. If we'd fallen out you'd be picking your teeth out of the carpet. No, this is just friendly advice. I know you were just doing your job, and I know you didn't mean any harm, but you've managed to wander in where angels fear to tread and you need to back out again before anyone gets hurt.'

'I don't know what you're talking about,' whined Daniel. 'What are you *talking* about?'

The man gave a disappointed little sigh. 'Come on, sonny, don't piss me around. The sapphire. Bobby Carson's retirement fund. You've been asking questions about it and you're making people uneasy. They asked me to pop over and tell you what you need to know. That the stone is gone. You'll never find it. No one will ever find it. Forget about it.'

The frantic, terrified part of Daniel's brain was semaphoring wildly: *He's right. There's nothing more you can do. You'd already decided that. Tell him. For pity's sake, tell him!* But the other bit, the bit that didn't like being pushed around, the bit that long ago recognised that being pushed around is a habit which is hard to break, said, 'What people?'

The man gave an incredulous laugh that reminded Daniel of Jack Deacon. 'Oh come on, Danny! I know you're not very good at this, but nobody's *that* bad! If I told you that I'd have to kill you. And that's not the worst of it. *They'd* have to kill me, then they'd have to kill one another just to be sure. You don't need to know who they are. You don't need to know who *I* am. You just need to know that it's time to move on and find some lost dogs or something, because you can't find that stone but you could get hurt trying. Do you understand me?'

Daniel nodded slowly, his head bowed, blood from his nose dripping on his shirt. It was no lie; he understood perfectly. Someone was putting the frighteners on him. And it was working. Whoever sent this man would be gratified to know how scared he was. The thing about facing death is, it gives you a taste for life. Every day seems infinitely desirable after you've looked into the void.

The thing about human beings is, they're made of more than raw instinct. They can be very frightened and still not allow the fear to rule them. Despite the shock, despite the jackhammer pounding in his head and the squibs exploding behind his eyes, Daniel knew that his life was in no immediate danger. If someone had wanted him dead it would have been easier, quicker and safer to do it as he came through the door. Everything that had happened since had been unnecessary unless the object was that he live and learn. Unless he was stupid enough to tell this man that nothing he could say or do would deflect Daniel from his task, this was as bad as it was going to get. Any moment now he was going to leave.

Daniel could have made him stay. He could have explained carefully that, when he indicated that he understood, this wasn't to be taken as consent or compliance. He could probably ensure that he got himself beaten senseless, and there was always the possibility that his visitor's instructions ran to shutting him up if he couldn't be scared off, and even Daniel didn't put that high a price on the truth. It could be argued by a purist that letting the man leave in the belief that his job was done was a kind of lie. But Daniel hadn't created the situation in which absolute honesty could get him killed. *Necessity,* he observed wryly to himself in that quiet no-man's-land where the mind can stand aside and observe calmly the most alarming events, *makes liars of us all.* Anyone who insisted that, even in such circumstances, his probity was worth more than his life was probably going to lose his life, and probably deserved to.

And then, he'd learnt things from the encounter that he'd like time to think about. This man knew a lot about him. He hadn't just been given a name by someone who'd heard it from Paul Sinclair. He hadn't gone to the office in Shack Lane: he'd come here, to the shore. Lots of people knew where Daniel lived, but they were people who knew Daniel. There wasn't a sign up. And his assailant hadn't followed him – he'd got here first, he'd been waiting.

He'd known Daniel would be alone. He'd known that he wouldn't be armed – well, this was England, he might have guessed that – and that he wouldn't fight back, at least not very effectively. And he'd known that, to protect his own identity, he didn't need a stocking over his face or a silly plastic mask, he just needed to remove Daniel's glasses. Lots of people wear glasses, but most of them have some useful sight. To know that Daniel was sufficiently blind without his to render any disguise superfluous, you had to know him reasonably well.

His search for Jane Moss's necklace hadn't just alarmed someone. It hadn't just alarmed someone who was prepared to use violence to stop him. It had alarmed someone he knew.

'Do you understand me?' the man said again.

Daniel spat out blood and the sharp chip of a tooth. 'Of course I understand you.' It took no effort at all to let his voice quaver timorously. *Leave it at that,* urged the little internal Daniel who cared more for his skin than his image. *That covers it. Don't say another word.*

'Good.' The man leant forward again, and seemed satisfied when Daniel flinched. He patted the smaller man's shoulder much as you might pat a good dog. Then he reached out and tweaked his nose. 'It's all right, that's not broken. Stick a tissue up it and try not to blow for a day. You'll be as good as new tomorrow.' Then he was gone.

Deacon peered judiciously at the damage. 'I'm not sure he was right about the nose.'

'The nose is fine,' whined Daniel adenoidally. 'Forget about the nose.'

'Suddenly you're an expert on noses?'

'I'm an expert on *my* nose,' insisted Daniel. 'It's fine. Now, can we talk about what's going on here?'

Deacon considered. Daniel had called him at work, and he'd dropped in on his way home. He hadn't thought it warranted blues and twos. 'What do you think's going on?'

'I think I've managed to rattle some cages. I didn't mean to. All I set out to do was find a missing necklace and buy it back, but all at once I'm in the middle of a Hitchcock film. That wasn't Bobby Carson, reaching out from whichever of Her Majesty's secure establishments he's currently occupying. It *was* someone who heard I'd been talking to Paul Sinclair. Someone we know, Jack.'

Deacon looked singularly unsurprised. 'Probably. Daniel – what were you expecting when you started asking questions about a robbery that put one person in the ground and another in a wheelchair? That all the big-hearted old lags would gather round and try to help you? Got news for you, Danny. Old lags don't have big hearts. If they had they wouldn't mug people for a living.'

'But we know who the thief was,' objected Daniel. 'Bobby Carson. And he's in prison. Why would anyone else want to get involved?'

'They're not *getting* involved,' Deacon explained carefully, as if to a child, 'they *are* involved. Carson's the one who ran those kids down and stole their valuables, he's the one we caught, but everyone needs contacts. Either he was taking orders from someone, or someone bankrolled him, or someone offered to move the gear on in return for a cut. Someone we never found. Someone who was relieved when Carson went down without talking, and doesn't want you raking over the coals again.'

'He used an old car – why would he need bankrolling?' asked Daniel. 'And you know who moved the necklace on – Paul Sinclair. Innocently, or more likely not, he had it through his shop and he sold it on where you couldn't trace it. He's also the only one I've talked to. It must have been him who sent Godzilla round.'

Deacon shook his head. 'Not his style. He wouldn't mind being one step along the way towards legitimising stolen goods but he'd want credible deniability. He wouldn't have taken the necklace directly from the thief. He wouldn't know if Carson had a partner, or a boss. All he'd know was who offered him the jewellery.'

Daniel took that on board. 'So it's someone further up the chain who's worried. Maybe the one who took the stuff directly from Carson's hands. Sinclair must have warned his contact, who warned *his* contact, who warned him.'

'Probably,' agreed Deacon. 'But Carson knew better than to implicate him. It wouldn't have saved him much time and it would have put him in a lot of danger. The guy who sent your visitor round would have no trouble getting at Carson, even inside. Instead of which, when he finally gets out, whoever he's protecting will remember that he's owed a favour.'

'This is a local man,' said Daniel, trying to put it together. 'He was in the area nine months ago when this was going down, and he's still here now. On top of that, he knows me. So I know him.' He rolled his eyes in frustration. 'I just don't *know* that I know.'

'Welcome to my world,' growled Deacon. Then, seeing Daniel wasn't going to let it lie, he sighed. 'OK, let's go through it again. Your visitor – did *he* seem familiar?'

'No,' said Daniel. 'I'd have recognised the voice if it was someone I know.'

'But he didn't want you seeing his face. And he knows you're as blind as a bat without your glasses.' Political correctness had largely passed Deacon by. 'So he thinks he's in the family album.' He meant the library of photographs CID maintained against this eventuality.

'He called me Danny.'

'*I* call you Danny.'

'Only when you're annoyed with me. Everyone else calls me Daniel. So he doesn't so much know me as know *of* me. Someone who knows me better – well enough to know I wouldn't recognise the queen of England without my glasses – gave him my name and address and sent him round with instructions to scare me off.'

'Did it work?'

Daniel thought for a moment. He sounded a little surprised. 'No.'

'Well, it should have done. You're getting in deep here. The sensible thing now would be to give it up.'

'Yes, I can see that.'

Deacon waited a bit longer. Daniel said nothing more. Deacon knew why. 'So,' he said heavily, '*are* you going to give it up?'

'No,' Daniel said again.

'May I ask why not?' In the less well-lit parts of Dimmock the sound of Deacon being polite made strong men turn pale.

'Because…' After he'd started the sentence Daniel found that the answer wasn't as obvious as he'd thought. 'Because I said I'd help Margaret Carson. She needs help, and no one else has much sympathy for the mother of a killer. It isn't her fault, she doesn't even think it's her fault, but she *feels* as if it is. She needs some kind of redemption. I want to help her.'

'Enough to send out the message that this' – he flicked the end of Daniel's nose for quite unnecessary emphasis – 'wasn't enough? That whoever did it should come back for another go?'

'This is just a thought,' said Daniel, blinking back tears. 'But you don't suppose that, now I've reported a violent assault to my local detective superintendent, he might take steps to prevent that?'

Deacon shrugged carelessly. He almost seemed to be enjoying himself. 'I can't protect you when I don't know who you need protecting from. Let's face it, Daniel, most of the people you know have felt the urge to break your nose at one time or another.'

Daniel clung onto his patience. 'So what do you suggest?'

'My best advice? Drop it. It isn't worth getting hurt over. But since you never take my best advice, my second best advice would be to change your locks. Maybe buy yourself a Rottweiler.'

'Thanks, Jack,' said Daniel coldly.

Chapter Ten

He hadn't expected to get much sympathy from Deacon. He didn't expect to get much from Brodie either, and he thought her advice would be the same – and harder to ignore since she was, at least technically, his employer. He waited for her to notice his thick lip and demand an explanation.

But he saw nothing of her the next day, and on the Thursday she phoned to say she was taking Jonathan to Switzerland that afternoon.

'How long will you be gone?'

'How long's a piece of string? I don't know what they'll tell me yet. But there's a new chemo treatment this particular clinic's pioneering and I want them to look at Jonathan.'

At least it wasn't the other side of the world. 'Shall I drive you to the airport?'

'Or at least, as close to the airport as you can park without having to go in backwards?' He heard the hint of humour in her voice and didn't take offence. 'Thanks, Daniel, but no. Jack's taking us. I'm just letting you know. Is there anything you want to ask before I disappear again?'

He wondered if Deacon had told her about his close encounter. He hoped not, because if she didn't know she couldn't tell him what to do about it and he wouldn't have to refuse. 'No,' he said carefully, 'I don't think so.'

'OK. I'll call you in a day or two.' Still she didn't ring off. It was as if she was waiting to be prompted – as if she wanted to say something but didn't know how to get started.

Sometimes he could read her mind. But not this time. 'OK then. Well… good luck.'

Her patience snapped. She was no good at tiptoeing round things. For all her faults, and they were many, she was a forthright woman. 'Oh Daniel, I wish you'd just say what you think!'

Behind his second-best glasses he blinked. 'About what?'

'About chasing wild geese, that's what! That's what you think, isn't it? That I'm wasting time – mine, but more importantly Jonathan's – chasing moon-shadows.'

'I never said that.' Daniel kept his voice low.

'I know you didn't. Your silences speak volumes!'

He understood where this was coming from. Sometimes Brodie used him as a sounding board, when part of her questioned the wisdom of something the rest of her was intent on. He sighed. 'Brodie, you're mistaken. I don't think what you're doing is wrong. I don't know. I don't know what I'd do in your place. I *do* know this has to be your decision – something you can live with. I wish I could help. If sounding off at me makes you feel better, fine. But don't think I'm criticising you when I'm not. Not out loud; not even silently.'

Perhaps no one else would have heard, over the phone, the catch in her voice. But Daniel did. 'I'm sorry. I'm just… I'm tired. And worried. And missing you.'

'I'm here,' he said softly. 'I'm right here. I'm going to be right here when you get back. I'll always be here.'

It never occurred to him that he was making a promise he might not be able to keep.

He only had one lead, so his choice was between following it and giving up. He went back to see Paul Sinclair.

He got a certain amount of satisfaction from the way Sinclair jolted when he saw Daniel's face. It might have been that he was surprised to see him again so soon. Or it might have been that Daniel looked like he'd come second in a headbutting contest with a goat, and Sinclair knew more about that than he'd have been happy admitting.

Daniel smiled pleasantly at him. 'I'm looking for more cranberry glass for Mrs Campbell-Wheeler.' It wasn't a lie. He was always looking for cranberry glass for Mrs Campbell-Wheeler.

'Er…right. I'll, um…'

'Have a look in the back?' suggested Daniel encouragingly. 'In case there's something you haven't got round to cleaning up yet?'

'Er…yes.' The dealer made no move. He couldn't seem to take his eyes off Daniel's face.

'Mr Sinclair? Oh,' he said then, as if suddenly remembering, 'the shiner. Yes. Somebody mugged me last night. Funniest thing. Didn't take anything, just wanted to talk. About that necklace. You know – the one I asked you about.' He let the pause stretch until its sinews creaked. He was waiting to see if Sinclair would take another breath. Only when the man started turning blue did Daniel take pity on him. 'In fact, the *really* funny thing is, you were the only one I *had* asked about it.'

'I-I didn't...I'd no idea...' stammered Sinclair. 'It was nothing to do with me!'

'No? Who was it to do with?'

The man was so flustered that the entry-level trick almost worked. But at the last moment he realised that the words about to come out of his mouth could earn him a call from Daniel's visitor. His eyes widened and his mouth shut tight as if he'd swallowed a goldfish.

After a moment Daniel went on, in the same calm, amiable tone. 'And I'm not sure what to do about it. Somebody's plainly got the impression that I'm some kind of a threat, and I'm not. As far as I know, the courts dealt with the guy who was responsible for what happened. All I want to do is buy the necklace back. That's my only interest in this, Mr Sinclair. I thought I'd made that clear.'

'I-I didn't... It wasn't...'

'You?' finished Daniel helpfully. 'Oh, I know that. This guy was bigger than you and me put together. But you see, the only way he'd have known I was looking for that necklace was if he'd been talking to someone who'd been talking to you. When I left here, who did you call?'

'No one.' Clearly a lie, it struggled out of his throat as if someone was strangling him.

'So when you told me you'd give it some thought, you'd actually no intention of doing so?'

'No. Yes! I mean, I thought about it. I just couldn't think of anything that would help.'

'So who did you tell?'

'No one.'

'You must have.' Daniel being adamant was like a small glacier grinding its way through a mountain pass. 'No one mugged me on the off chance. I'm not suggesting you sent him. I'm suggesting that you did what I asked and put out a few feelers, and one of them made someone uneasy. So, who did you speak to?'

But Sinclair just shook his head. Daniel's visitor could have got the information out of him. Perhaps Deacon could. But nothing Daniel was prepared to do would persuade Paul Sinclair that he had more to fear from a maths teacher than from the kind of man who considers locked doors a minor inconvenience. He'd hit a brick wall. Another one.

Deacon wasn't lying when he told Daniel the trail had gone cold. From a purely pragmatic point of view – which, in view of the CID budget, was sometimes all he could afford – he'd done what was required: found the killer, brought him to court, made the charges stick. Recovering the loot would have been the gilt on the gingerbread, but for a pie-and-chips man the main course is what counts.

Deacon always described himself as a pie-and-chips man. In fact he had a taste for French provincial cooking. There were many things about Jack Deacon that contradicted what his enemies thought they knew about him, and what he allowed his friends to think.

So, driving north towards Gatwick with Brodie beside him and his son strapped safely in the back, he allowed his mind to toy with this new development in what he'd considered a closed case. Someone was scared. Of Daniel? It didn't seem terribly likely. At least, to know there was something to be scared of you had to know him reasonably well. Most casual acquaintances saw a diminutive thirty-year-old ex-teacher reduced by post-traumatic stress to doing odd jobs for an old flame. Not a terribly scary prospect, even to the sort of person who jumped when cars backfired and rolled balls under the bed at night.

You had to look quite a lot closer to see that, while the facts were correct, they represented the truth hardly at all. Daniel's mental health hadn't always been fragile – it had been ripped apart by an act of extraordinary violence. Even so, he was not so much a victim as a survivor. And Deacon knew what Brodie did not: that he'd have been back teaching for eighteen months, that he was well capable of returning to a job he loved, except that he'd placed Brodie's needs above his own. As he always had, almost from the moment they met. She wasn't an old flame. She was the other half of his soul.

All of which, had it been common knowledge, would have made a lot of people review their opinion of Daniel Hood. He was smarter than he looked. He could be stubborn for England. And he was a zealot – he did what he thought was right even when it wasn't going to be easy.

And somebody knew this well enough to be nervous about his interest in the Carson robbery. Deacon didn't know who. Right now he didn't know how to find out who. But he was pretty sure that, if he put his mind to it, he could work it out.

He'd have liked to bounce a few ideas off Brodie. He didn't, for two reasons. She was preoccupied with her trip to Switzerland – expecting it to be another wasted effort yet unable to ignore the remote possibility that this time would be different. Like a busted gambler buying one more hand, because you only have to win once to pay for all your losses.

And the other reason was, Deacon knew Daniel had said nothing to her about his visitor. That he'd avoided seeing her because his bruises would have prompted questions he wouldn't lie to answer. Knowing that running her business had put him in danger would have given her a terrible dilemma. She'd still have gone to Switzerland, but the knowledge would have added vastly to her burdens. So Daniel stayed where she couldn't see him, and Deacon said nothing.

As the traffic began to build approaching Gatwick, Brodie said with a trace of a grin, 'Maybe we should have taken the train from Haywards Heath.'

Deacon gave a deep chuckle. The last few months had taken a lot out of her. But they hadn't taken the resilience – the inbuilt knowledge that, when things are as tough as they can get, they aren't going to be made worse by a bit of black humour. When this was all over – however it ended – she'd still be there: battered, sad, but capable at some point of starting to pick up the pieces.

She loosened her seat belt and turned to smile at Jonathan, secured on the back seat. 'Jack…'

* * *

They were directed to the Urgent Treatment Centre at Crawley Hospital. By the time they got there the baby was breathing normally again. But neither of them believed it was anything other than a significant deterioration in his condition, and by the time he'd been examined and his history considered, the consultant confirmed it.

'I don't think you can continue your journey, Mrs Deacon. I think we should admit Jonathan for twenty-four hours, just to monitor what's going on. Then, if he's stable, you should go home.'

'Farrell,' said Brodie absently – unaware that, by correcting the error, she was driving a fresh scalpel under Deacon's ribs. 'My name is Farrell. So's Jonathan's. Can I stay with him?'

'Of course.' The doctor was checking his notes, wondering how he'd got the name wrong. 'Try not to worry too much. I don't think this is a quantum change in the situation. You say he's had seizures before?' Brodie nodded. 'I think he's just very tired and rather poorly, and by tomorrow he'll seem a good deal better. But home's the place for him now. I understand why you've been doing so much travelling, but I think now it's time to stop.'

Brodie felt as if he'd quietly, politely but very firmly shut a door in her face.

Deacon said gruffly, 'Are we down to the last week? The last month?'

The consultant shook his head. 'There's no reason to think so. See your own specialist in the next few days, she'll be able to tell you better, but I don't see this as the beginning of the end. Just a warning that it's time to rethink your plans. He's not getting any stronger and you need to reduce the stress. On everybody. Your wife as well as your baby.'

Deacon said nothing until he saw that Brodie was about to. 'She's not my wife. I'll call the airline, cancel the tickets.'

'Tell them…' For a moment Brodie was going to ask him to have them hold the ticket rather than cancel it. As if a few days might make all the difference. As if next week they'd be able to go to Switzerland after all. As if nothing the doctor had said had registered with her.

Then cold, hard reality laid its hand on her. Held her against the wall and spoke directly into her face. This was the end of the line. She'd done everything she could do. All that was left was to wait for events to take their course. It had been an uneven contest from the start. Now it was time to submit.

Deacon saw them settled into a mother-and-baby room before heading back to Dimmock. He'd have stayed longer except that Brodie made it clear she'd rather be alone. 'I'll call you tonight.'

'It's not necessary…'

'It is to me,' he said firmly. 'And tomorrow, if Jonathan's OK, I'll come and pick you up.'

'Yes.' She managed another wan smile. 'Thanks, Jack.'

And his heart raged, because she'd got it wrong again and he hadn't the words to tell her. That she didn't need to thank him. That this was his son, and he was dying, and Deacon too was just doing the best he could.

Chapter Eleven

Brodie spent the rest of the day beating herself up. Everyone had told her it was time to stop, that she was sacrificing the last good times for a faint hope of something better. Now Jonathan himself had told her. She'd exhausted and sickened him until he'd struck back with the only weapon he had – his frailty. He was in hospital tonight because of his mother's obstinacy.

No one at the hospital said that to her, although she believed they were thinking it. They were kind and considerate, and told her she'd have him home tomorrow and no harm done. But it was an end, just the same. The end of her hopes. The end of her efforts to turn the dice by sheer force of will. She was beaten. And she didn't get enough practice to know what to do next.

'He's settled now,' said one of the nurses. 'Why don't you go for a walk? Get some fresh air before you go to bed.'

'Where?'

'There's a garden…' She glanced at the window, slick with rain. 'Or how about the chapel? Even if you're not religious, it's a nice peaceful spot to sit for a bit.'

Brodie listened to her directions mostly to be polite. She was never a churchgoer. But as she wandered aimlessly through the long corridors, trying not to think about what she was doing here, somehow she found herself looking at a carved sign on a wooden door. After a moment she put her hand out, half expecting the door to be locked; but it was open, so she went in.

The chapel was quiet, the lighting subdued. In fact it was empty. Someone had left a card saying how the chaplain could be contacted, but Brodie didn't need ministering to and didn't want company. She sat down near the front and after a minute she closed her eyes. She didn't cry. But, shorn at last of the stubborn conviction that there would be an answer and she would find it, she felt grief wash over her like a tide.

She could not have said how long she'd been sitting there when she heard the door behind her open and the grate of a chair leg as someone sat down. Suddenly Brodie felt a fraud. If someone wanted to use this place as it was designed to be used, she had no business here. She stood up and, head bowed, walked out.

While she was trying to remember the way back to the paediatric wing the chapel door opened again and there was a woman standing beside her. 'I hope I didn't chase you away.' Her voice held the soft slur of an American accent.

Brodie put on her brightest smile. 'Of course not. It's time I was getting back, that's all.'

'Then I mustn't keep you. Only...' Brodie looked at her in surprise. The woman was embarrassed. 'I wanted to ask if you need anything. If I can help.'

'No. Thank you.' Brodie turned away and headed briskly towards the stairs.

But she travelled only a few paces before slowing, and stopping, and turning back. 'I'm sorry, I didn't mean to be rude. I don't need to rush back, my baby's asleep. Do you fancy a coffee?'

They found a machine, and sat by a window looking down on the lights of Crawley. They introduced themselves. The woman's name was Hester Dale. Brodie said, 'Are you with a patient here as well?'

'My mother. I like to stop in on the chapel when I've been to see her. Only a couple of minutes, sometimes. It reminds me there's someone looking after both of us.' Again, the embarrassed little smile. So she'd been in England long enough to know that here, while it was all right to worship anything, or nothing, it was considered faintly impolite to talk about it.

'Is she getting better?'

Hester shook her head. She was rather older than Brodie: mid-forties, perhaps. 'She isn't going to. Her heart's very weak now. You try not to give up, but...' She sighed. 'She is nearly eighty. The time comes you have to accept it gracefully.'

'Yes,' said Brodie softly. 'Yes, I think it does.'

Hester was watching her with compassion through the steam off the coffee cups. 'You said, your baby?'

'Jonathan. He has a brain tumour. I was taking him to a clinic in Switzerland. He had a seizure on the way to the airport, that's how we ended up here. Tomorrow I'll take him home. And start working on the graceful acceptance.'

'It must be so much harder when it's a child.'

'Everyone assumes that,' said Brodie. 'And maybe it is so. But why? I haven't had him a fraction of the time you've had your mother. There's no one depending on him, the way they would if he was the father of a young family. There's really not that much invested in him. And yet...'

'He's your baby,' Hester said simply. 'Every cell in your body is programmed to believe he's the most important thing in the universe. If it wasn't, no one would ever raise a child. They're a lot of trouble, a lot of heartache, and sometimes not much reward. We have to believe at a genetic level that they're worth it.'

Brodie found herself thinking about Margaret Carson. About the baby that had been the centre of her world. About how her hormones had insisted he was worth any effort, any sacrifice, to protect and nurture. And how history had proved she should have drowned him in the bath.

'I just feel so *angry*, all the time,' she whispered.

'Of course you do,' murmured Hester Dale. 'It isn't fair. It isn't reasonable.'

Brodie had been wrong about one thing: she was glad of some company. And Hester was easy to be with – a quiet, gentle, unassuming woman who had mastered the knack of being there without invading other people's space.

Brodie said, 'Back there, at the chapel. How did you know I needed someone to talk to?'

Hester's smile reminded her of Daniel's. 'Most people who go into a hospital chapel are having a hard time. They don't all want to talk. But it doesn't do any harm to ask.'

Brodie was taken aback. 'You've done this before?'

'Yes. Quite often.' That trace of wryness again. 'It's something we do. In a prayer group I belong to. We keep an eye open for people who might need a friendly word. And we really don't mind if they don't.'

Automatically, Brodie gave a disparaging sniff. 'I haven't a lot of time for religion.'

'That's all right. There are people who don't believe in gravity. That doesn't mean their apples fly upwards when they drop them.'

Brodie laughed out loud. 'Just then, you sounded *exactly* like a friend of mine!'

'Is she a God-botherer too?'

'No. Exactly the opposite. And it's a he. And he has this way of…surprising you with the things he says. The way he thinks.'

Hester appeared to give that some thought. Then she said, 'Can I risk surprising you again?'

Deacon did what he always did when he was upset. He went to work.

There's nothing like a police station for rumours: everyone knew what had happened before he got there. Almost everyone avoided him. It wasn't meant unkindly. They were trying not to add to his woes. All the same, he appreciated it when Chief Superintendent Fuller came upstairs to ask if there was any news, and when ten minutes later Detective Sergeant Voss brought him coffee and a sandwich.

'I thought you mightn't have got a chance to eat.'

Deacon had neither eaten nor realised he was hungry. He ate the sandwich mainly to please Voss, but he felt better for it. 'Have I missed anything?'

Voss shook his ginger head. 'Nothing much. But I think I know who Daniel's visitor was.'

That perked Deacon appreciably. Voss couldn't be sure if it was the prospect of solving a crime that had cheered him or being reminded of Daniel's misfortune. 'Who?'

'Littlejohn.'

'Who?' But immediately Deacon's frown cleared. 'Can't have been. He retired. Went to live with a daughter up north.'

'I believe,' said Voss, deadpan, 'there is a thing known as the transport infrastructure. That, with sufficient planning, it is possible to travel north of the Watford Gap. And even back again.'

Deacon scowled mainly to keep from grinning. He liked young Voss. He thought that by scowling a lot he could keep the sergeant from knowing this. 'Less of the cheek, Charlie Voss. I am aware that the world doesn't end at the M25. I once took a holiday in the Lake District. My point is, Lionel Littlejohn has not been an active blagger for five years. I'm surprised you remember him. What makes you think it was him?'

'I did a trawl of the CCTV. There's nothing covering the shore, of course. But I got someone walking on the Promenade just a few minutes after it happened. Disappeared up one of the entries – must have parked his car up there.'

'And you think it was Lionel because…?'

'It looked like him. Walked like him. You know, he's a big guy – lumbers a bit but still manages to look pretty fit. Anyone who calls him Fatty had better be able to hit the four-minute mile from a standing start.'

'That sounds pretty much like Lionel,' admitted Deacon. 'But what would bring him back here after five years? As far as I know, he is genuinely out of the game.'

'That's a valuable piece of jewellery Daniel's looking for.'

'Lionel was no jewel thief! If he found the Koh-i-noor in his Christmas cracker he wouldn't know what to do with it. He stole cars to order, did a bit of cut and shut, boosted industrial quantities of spirits and cigarettes, and provided muscle on an ad hoc basis for people who'd more sense than to employ psychopaths. Made a steady living at it. A few short prison sentences and a couple of longer ones, but on the whole he was pretty successful. Then he got into his mid-fifties and thought he'd done it long enough.' He sniffed lugubriously. 'I know how he felt.'

'Have a look at the footage.' Voss put it on the monitor.

Deacon was almost persuaded. 'It could be him. But why would he lean on Daniel?'

'Like you said,' hazarded Voss, 'he provided muscle when it was needed. Maybe one of his old employers wanted a bit of muscle that wouldn't be traced back to him.'

'Carson stole the necklace,' objected Deacon. 'We know that. We don't know who fenced it for him, but it's a bit of a detail this long after. Is that worth bringing Lionel Littlejohn all the way down from Carlisle?'

Voss didn't have an answer. 'Do you want me to go and see him?'

Deacon indicated the monitor. 'This is all we've got?' Voss nodded. 'Well, you couldn't call it evidence. We can't prove it's him; and even if we could, we couldn't prove he was doing anything he shouldn't have been. Daniel never got a proper look at him, and the courts don't like speech identification unless it's been recorded and can be analysed. In a nutshell, Charlie Voss, the only one who could incriminate Lionel is Lionel, and he's too much of an old campaigner to make that mistake. I don't want to spend good money proving it.'

Reluctantly, Voss accepted his judgement. The unpalatable truth was, the budget was important too. If you exhausted it investigating minor offences on the basis of speculative evidence it wouldn't be there when extra manpower would make the difference between finding a dangerous man and leaving him to wreak havoc. No one in government will tell you that you can only have the level of safety you're prepared to pay for, but everyone in the police service recognises the fact. 'Anything I can do that wouldn't cost much?'

Deacon gave it some thought. 'You could talk to some of the people Lionel used to work for. Chances are, if he was brought down specially, it's one of them. They won't know how little we've actually got. Someone might just be rattled enough at hearing his name to let it show.'

Daniel got no sleep. Partly because his face still ached, mainly because he kept running recent events through his

mind and every time he hit the same wall. The problem
was not the man who said he shouldn't pursue his inquiries.
The problem was that he'd asked all the questions he knew
to ask of all the people he knew to question, and nothing
he'd been told suggested a way forward. He thought there
might be nothing more he could do to restore the star
sapphire to its rightful owner.

It wasn't a conclusion that sat easily with him. Not
just because he'd been threatened but because it meant
disappointing someone he wanted to help. He wasn't quite
sure why Margaret Carson's situation had touched him,
but it had. He felt sorry for her. He wanted to make things
better, if only a little.

And, thinking like that, in the blackness of the night
with the high tide sucking and tinkling the pebbles under
his window, he found himself revisiting the possibility of
helping Bobby Carson's mother to some kind of redemption
without actually achieving the task she'd set him.

Deacon got no sleep. When he finally went home there
was nothing to stop him thinking about his son and the
increasingly obvious fact that he wasn't going to have him
much longer. At least Brodie was going to bring him home
now. But the fact that Brodie was giving up underlined, as
nothing else would have done, how hopeless the situation
had become. Deacon had never known her to give up on
anything before.

Brodie got no sleep. The bed the hospital provided for
her was comfortable enough but she tossed and turned all

night, what she'd been told blazing through her head. It made no sense. At the same time, it was something else to try and it couldn't possibly do any harm.

It would be tomorrow, Hester Dale had said, before she could contact the members of her group and organise something. She'd warned Brodie against expecting instant results, or possibly any results at all. But it was a hope. A last, faint, forlorn hope perhaps, but a hope when she'd thought all hope was gone, and Brodie had snatched at it as it drifted past and was gripping like a hawk with all the strength of her blood-red nails.

Oblivious of all this, Jonathan slept like a baby.

Chapter Twelve

Deacon was on his way back to Crawley before the doctors had done their morning rounds. When Brodie called him he was only five miles away.

He wanted the details as soon as he saw her. But she wanted to get on the road, and talk in the car.

'But he's OK to come home?'

'Yes. They say he's no worse than he was this time yesterday.'

Deacon carried the baby. After he'd installed him safely on the back seat he looked curiously at Brodie. 'You look rather better.'

'Something's happened,' she said. 'I don't know if it's of any significance or not. I think it might be worth following up.'

Deacon frowned, the corners of his mouth dragged down by dismay. 'The doctors said we shouldn't travel him anymore...'

'We don't need to,' said Brodie. 'Oh Jack, I don't want to get your hopes up for no reason. But we're down to last resorts now, and it's one of those. And I don't know why but I feel it's worth pursuing. Get in the car and I'll tell you about it.'

For a man whose career consisted of asking questions, Deacon wasn't a terribly good listener. He interrupted as soon as he spotted a flaw or inconsistency. His default position was disbelief, his whole approach adversarial. After thirty years in which his job was the most important part of his life – he might almost have said the only important part of his life – he struggled to recalibrate, to find the different tone needed to conduct personal affairs.

Before they were even out of the hospital car park Brodie said sharply, 'Jack...just shut up and listen. I'll take questions later, all right?'

In the event, though, she'd already answered most of them by then. 'You want to know if I believe in this? I don't know. I know it can't do any harm. I know it doesn't involve dragging him halfway round the world again, so even if it doesn't help it doesn't waste whatever time he has left.

'You want to know if Hester Dale believed in it. I think so. She didn't make many claims for it. She said that, statistically, it seemed to help in more cases than you could explain as spontaneous recovery or misdiagnosis. She didn't try to convert me, or get money, or anything like that. There's nothing in it for her except satisfaction if it pays off.

'And you're wondering how much it matters if we *don't* believe. I don't know. Hester didn't know. What she said to me was, "You want him to get well. Believe in that." Look, Jack, I don't know how this could possibly help. And yet – unless she's lying to me, which I don't believe – it seems to. When it's used, people have a better chance of recovering. Why? I don't know. How? I don't know that either. I don't know how homeopathy can possibly work, when all the preparations really consist of is water, yet loads of responsible people testify that it does. Maybe not all the time; maybe not for everyone. Nor does conventional medicine. We know that. We've tried everything else. Now I'm going to try this.

'And I want your help. Not just yours – everyone I can rope in. Numbers seem to be significant too. Hester's group will be working on it, but she thinks it might help if I can get family and friends involved as well. So I will. This may be the last thing I can do for him. I'm not going to baulk at it because it seems silly.'

Finally she ran out of words. She sat back, drained, waiting for the avalanche of scepticism she was sure he was about to dump on her.

But all Deacon could find to say was: 'You think people praying for him is going to save Jonathan's life?'

It was a long time since Daniel had felt so nervous. Worried, and occasionally afraid, but not nervous. Nervousness suggested you were doing something that you didn't have to do, where you were uncertain of both the outcome and the wisdom of starting. Daniel did a lot of things he didn't strictly have to do, where uncertainty was the best that could be said of the probable outcome, but he was blessed – or possibly cursed – by such sureness of purpose that he seldom questioned the wisdom of starting anything. He didn't do things on the spur of the moment. He gave serious thought to every dilemma he encountered, and passed them through various moral and ethical filters before reaching a decision. But once he was sure the decision was right, practical considerations such as effort entailed, risk versus reward, even the chance that a desired object might be unobtainable didn't trouble him. He'd been beaten before now. He'd hardly ever given up.

But this was different. Not because he was being paid for his services but because his actions had the potential to hurt someone. Someone who'd been hurt already; who hadn't deserved that, and certainly didn't deserve to be hurt anymore. Yet he believed that what he was doing was right. That was why Daniel was standing on this doorstep with a dew of sweat on his upper lip, clasping and unclasping his hands, putting them in his pockets and then behind his back, like a teenage boy calling for his first date.

The doorstep was in River Drive, as good an address as you'd find in Dimmock without going up onto the Firestone Cliffs. This had rather puzzled Daniel at first. His understanding was that Jane Moss had been a couple of footmen below her fiancé in the social system – that the Sangers were the ones with money. Charlie Voss had explained. Jane's flat was high in a tower block, far from ideal for someone in a wheelchair. Imogen Sanger's house, echoingly empty when she found herself living there alone, was large and expansive, with wide doorways and enough rooms to make a separate living space on the ground floor. When Jane was discharged from hospital, this was where she came.

And this was the step on which Daniel now stood, nervous and unsure what to do with his hands, wishing someone would answer his ring and at the same time hoping no one was at home. He hadn't phoned ahead. He doubted she'd have agreed to see him if he had.

A change in the light falling on the glass panel above his head suggested movement inside. At the last moment he clasped his hands behind his back, on the basis that they could get into less trouble there, and prepared a friendly (but not too friendly) and courteous (but not smarmy) smile.

When the door opened, Daniel found himself smiling inanely at mid-air.

A voice said pointedly, 'Down here.'

Daniel winced. She was in a wheelchair. He *knew* she was in a wheelchair. She'd have had to be standing on a stool to be where he was looking.

'Sorry,' he mumbled. 'I'm used to looking up at people.'

Eyes as sharp as hazel diamonds ran him up and down – took in the lack of stature, the lack of substance, the thick glasses, the expression of a slightly simple choirboy, the bruises. Then she gave a grim, gusty little chuckle. 'Trundle a mile on these wheels.'

He thought it might be best to start again. 'Miss Moss, I'm Daniel Hood. I work for a firm that specialises in finding things for people.' He offered her one of Brodie's cards. It seemed to do nothing to ease her puzzlement, and when he looked closer he saw it was in fact his membership card from the Astronomical Society. 'Er...'

'Mr Hood,' said Jane Moss briskly, 'what do you want?'

The ground to swallow me up, he thought. 'I'd like to talk to you. And, if you think it appropriate, to Mrs Sanger.'

'What about?'

If he told her she wouldn't let him over the threshold. She'd sit there screaming and throwing things at him until he was out of range. He needed a harmless little subterfuge to get him in and get the conversation started, so he could edge up on his actual purpose. But Daniel didn't do subterfuge, even harmless little ones. Even when he should have done. 'Robert Carson.'

Whatever she was expecting, it wasn't that. Half a dozen different emotions flitted across her face, so quickly it was impossible to name any of them. But he wasn't stupid: he knew he'd done the equivalent of kicking her in the ribs. She would be shocked, hurt, upset and probably very angry to be confronted with that name on her own doorstep.

But she didn't burst into tears. She gave him a penetrating look, then an odd little half smile. 'Daniel Hood, you said?'

He risked a little smile in reply. 'Yes.'

'Daniel…would you help me stand up?'

Surprise widened his eyes. 'Of course. I didn't know… Of course. Tell me how.'

She used her hands to lift her legs, one by one, and put her feet on the floor. She folded the footrests of the wheelchair out of the way. Then she extended both arms. 'Hold on and brace yourself. I can do the rest.'

There wasn't a lot to her. There hadn't been before the attack, and months in a wheelchair had robbed her of much of the muscle mass of her lower body. But her arms and shoulders were strong. When she hauled, Daniel had to resist being dragged down. But then she was standing in front of him.

'Not the most elegant procedure in the world,' said Jane Moss, 'but I'm getting better.'

'That's great,' said Daniel, and meant it. 'Can you – I don't know – can you walk at all?'

'No,' she admitted, 'not yet. I can't even stand for very long. Just long enough for this.' And she slapped his face so hard that he reeled against the doorpost.

With nothing to hold on to she too keeled over. She grabbed for the wheelchair but missed, and ended up spilt across the hall floor. Daniel was stunned. Not for himself, though he never saw the blow coming; not even for his nose, though it was throbbing again like a toothache. He saw the helpless girl sprawled across the black and white tiles, and was appalled at what he'd done.

But the indignity of her position was the last thing on Jane Moss's mind. She was too furious to care. And she'd hit the floor a lot of times already in her struggle with the wheelchair. 'I want to know what gutter rag you're from,' she demanded fiercely. 'I want to tell your editor, in person, what I think of his crappy reporters.'

Gingerly, Daniel pushed his glasses back in place. 'Miss Moss, I'm not a reporter. And I do understand how bitter you must feel. If you tell me to go, I'll go. But I wish you'd give me the chance to explain. Not because there's something in it for you – I don't think there is. But the bombshell that tore your life apart caused collateral damage to another woman, and while no one would blame you for not giving a damn about Robert Carson's mother, it would be an act of real generosity to at least listen to her regrets. Will you give me five minutes?'

She went on staring angrily at him, but without the same certainty. She was not exactly a pretty girl, and probably never had been. Nine months ago, before the scars on her face faded to mere silver lines, she must have been quite disfigured. Now what you mostly saw – after you'd registered and forgotten about the wheelchair – was determination. There was a strength in her that was separate from the physical strength needed to cope with her disability. Her face was strong. Her eyes were straight and challenging, the set of her jaw firm, and her straight brown hair was cut short and flicked out of her face as if she'd more interesting things to think about. Daniel knew, having done his research, that she was twenty-four and an archaeology graduate.

'Get me up,' she said tersely.

'Er...' It wasn't reluctance, he just wasn't sure how.

'Oh, for pity's sake!' She arranged herself like Copenhagen's Little Mermaid, dragging the chair behind her. 'Bend down.' She put her arms round his neck, and when he straightened up – which was an effort but less than it should have been – she slid back into the chair.

She looked up at Daniel then, her eyes hard. 'Five minutes. Unless something important comes up.'

Chapter Thirteen

'Faith healing,' Deacon said flatly.

'They prefer to call it distance healing,' said Brodie. She was watching him out of the corner of her eye as he drove, still expecting some kind of explosion. 'Success seems to depend less on the faith of the subject than the conviction of the intercessors. And they can be anywhere.'

'Intercessors?' said Deacon, still in that same flat monotone that suggested he was keeping something on a tight rein.

'That's what they call them. Prayer groups. People meeting in their churches, or their temples, or their houses – many are Christians but not all – praying for someone who's sick because they think it'll help.'

'Is that what you think?'

'I don't know,' Brodie admitted. 'But I'm pretty sure being prayed for isn't going to do Jonathan any harm. It's not as if we're giving up on anything to do this. We've done everything his doctors wanted to do. I've done things they didn't see any point in doing. None of it got us anywhere. Maybe this won't either, but there's nothing left to lose. I'm going to give it a try.'

Deacon drove another mile in silence. Then: 'Does it mean taking him somewhere?'

Brodie shook her head. 'All they want is a photograph and a few details. I told Hester a bit about him, and she took a picture on her phone. She'll email it to the groups asked to pray for him.'

He gave a muffled snort.

'What?'

'It seems weird. People so mediaeval in their thinking as to reckon you can pray people better, but they're connected to the internet.'

'*That's* the bit that seems weird?' said Brodie, her voice climbing.

It was a long drive, which was a good thing. They kept coming back to the subject. 'Are there any statistics on this?' asked Deacon, whose instinct was always to look for evidence.

'There have been studies,' said Brodie. 'How authoritative they are depends on who you ask. Hester says some of them produced significant and occasionally remarkable results – but she admits that such results are hard to replicate. Which is what the scientific community expects to be able to do. Repeat a procedure and get the same outcome every time.

'But that's kind of the point. It *is* a matter of faith. The people praying over those photographs are doing it because they believe it will do some good, not because they think the statistics will be significant. If it works once and never again, that would be dismissed by science as a fluke – but for that patient it would be a miracle. I suppose it depends on where you're standing.'

Deacon thought some more. Haywards Heath came and went. 'What do we have to do?'

Brodie didn't comment on it, but she appreciated that *we*. 'We don't *have* to do anything. But there's a general feeling that it helps if those closest to the patient join in the prayers. I said we'd do that.'

He gave her a sidelong glance. 'I didn't know you were religious.'

She swept a distracted hand through her thick curls. 'I'm not. What I am is desperate. I'd crawl over broken glass for him – I'll sure as hell get down on my knees and pray for him.'

'All right,' said Deacon.

'You'll do it too?'

'Like you say, there's nothing to lose. I might feel silly. It's not much of a price to pay for even a tiny chance of saving my son's life.'

'Thank you,' said Brodie, genuinely touched. 'And I know Paddy will, and Marta' – from the flat above hers – 'will. And John and Julia will. Which just leaves…'

'Oh,' said Deacon, casting her a startled glance. 'Yes. Will he do it?'

'Yes,' said Brodie firmly.

Deacon wasn't so sure. 'You know how he feels about religion. *All* religions. All trappings of religion.'

'For me,' said Brodie, 'he'll do it.'

'Well…lots of luck,' muttered Deacon.

* * *

Voss had been going through the files. Many of them were on computer now, though some were still on paper and the best of them were in Detective Superintendent Deacon's head. Still he'd managed to amass some interesting facts.

Lionel Littlejohn lived and worked in Dimmock for eighteen years, if you included the five and a half when his putative address was the Woodgreen estate but his actual whereabouts were whichever of Her Majesty's prisons had vacancies. He'd worked for himself and for other people. Among the other people he was on record as having worked for were most of the middle-sized players in organised crime on the south coast. Voss presumed that meant he'd also worked for the big players, only they'd arranged things better and he hadn't got caught.

Five years ago he'd decided he didn't get as much fun out of blagging as he used to and retired, moving close to where his married daughter lived in Carlisle. Voss looked for any indication that he'd returned to his old ways and found none. This in itself was unusual. In the same way that most old lags leave prison with the intention of going straight, most really old lags need at least two attempts at retiring. More fail than succeed because making an honest living requires more commitment than petty crime.

But Voss found no suggestion that Lionel Littlejohn had been involved in anything illegal, in Carlisle or Dimmock, during those five years. And five years is a long time. Most people who've given something up for five years will manage to stay off it.

So what had happened to tempt him out of a

comfortable retirement? Not the sudden need for cash. Carlisle may be well north of Watford but they don't do things *so* differently there: a man of Lionel's experience could always pick up casual work if he wanted it. No, thought Voss, this smacked more of a favour for someone he considered a friend.

Two names came instantly to mind. One he felt safe dismissing. Wherever Joe Loomis went after bleeding his life out on Brodie's carpet, Voss doubted there were telecommunications with Carlisle.

And then there was one. That didn't automatically make him guilty, but all his instincts told Voss he'd be wasting his time doing anything before he'd eliminated Terry Walsh from his inquiries.

Chapter Fourteen

It wasn't that Jane Moss didn't have any furniture. In her living room were a comfortable sofa and an armchair by the fire. But she didn't invite Daniel to sit, so – having been brought up by his grandparents with manners that were considered polite in the 1950s – he continued to stand.

It should have been easier for her to bring her visitor down to her level. But she'd learnt to use her otherness as a power play. Daniel felt like a small boy again, summoned before the headmaster, kept standing while the one in charge commanded the room from behind his desk.

'You're wasting your time here. You do know that?' There was an edge like steel on her voice.

He wasn't her guest. She hadn't invited him here – it was a minor miracle that she let him over the threshold when she learnt why he'd come. She was entitled to her opinion of him. At least she was listening. He took a deep breath.

'Margaret Carson didn't raise her son to be a thief and a killer. She saw it happening, she tried to stop it, she failed. She wanted him to be a doctor. She'd have been satisfied if he'd grown up to be a decent brickie's labourer, and proud if he'd also managed to be a good husband and father. But by the time he was sixteen it was obvious that wasn't going to happen. She tried loving him despite who he was turning into. She tried to *not* love him, in case that might help. But nothing did. If you believe in the concept of bad eggs – that some children don't have it in them to grow into decent individuals who make mistakes but make amends and leave the world a little better than they found it – then Bobby Carson's one of those.'

'You reckon?' gritted the girl. There was a world of venom in the words.

Daniel swallowed. 'Mrs Carson can't do anything about what her son did to you. If she could she would. She feels terribly guilty and desperately sorry. And she's the sort of person who thinks you should try to make up for your mistakes. That's what she hired me to do. To find a way of restoring a little of what was stolen from you.'

For a second, sheer astonishment booted the anger out of Jane's eyes. Her mouth rounded. The fading scars on one cheek kept her lips from forming a perfect circle. 'How…?' Her voice cracked. She cranked it down and tried again. 'How can she *possibly* think she can do that?' But mixed in with the astonishment, and the furious indignation, was just a gnat's whisker of curiosity. It wasn't a rhetorical question: she wanted an answer.

And that, thought Daniel, was the nearest thing to a way in he was going to get. If he couldn't use it the commission was finished. He'd have to tell Mrs Carson that he'd failed.

'She wants me to get your necklace back,' he said simply. 'She doesn't care what it's going to cost her. She's prepared to mortgage her house if she has to. It's not that she thinks it'll make everything all right. It's more, that's the one thing you lost that money could buy back. She hopes that, in time, having it might be a source of comfort to you. It was the last thing Mr Sanger gave you. It was a family piece, it meant a lot to him. It would have meant a lot to you too. Mrs Carson hopes that, one day, it will again.'

At least Jane no longer thought he was a reporter. She went on staring at him as if she no longer knew what to think. As if the cogs of her brain had stopped whirring, there was nothing behind the shock-stretched eyes. Daniel was beginning to think they might remain there, frozen in this moment, until one of them died. He murmured, 'Shall I help you stand up again?'

She blinked, and a flicker of appreciation passed through her eyes. 'No. I'll throw you out in a minute. In the meantime, sit down while I try to get my head round this.'

He took the sofa. Now he didn't know what to do with his eyes. If he looked at her she might think he was pushing for a decision; if he didn't she might think he was embarrassed. Which he was, but not about her condition. He took his glasses off and polished them meticulously.

Jane Moss said, 'It's crazy. The police stopped looking for the necklace after a month. The insurers paid out rather than keep looking. What makes you think that you can find it?'

'Inexperience, mostly,' Daniel admitted honestly. 'I thought if I asked a few questions, and let it be known that the police were no longer involved, and made it clear that we were willing to buy it back, sooner or later someone would come on the phone offering a deal.'

'And did they?'

'No. They came round to my house and bounced my face off the wall.'

Jane had noticed the bruises. She'd thought he'd probably bumped into a door. He seemed the type. He did *not* seem the type to be wrestling with jewel thieves.

'Then…what are you *doing* here?'

'Plan B,' confessed Daniel. 'Miss Moss, Mrs Carson didn't ask me to find your necklace because she thought its loss had left you out of pocket. This isn't about reparations. I suppose it's about reconciliation.

'I don't think I can find the necklace. Everybody told me that before I started. I thought they were wrong, but it turns out they knew more than I did. I came here because I'm wondering if we can achieve some kind of reconciliation that isn't dependent on the sapphire.'

The girl was catching up on where this train of thought was heading. 'You want me to meet her. Margaret Carson. Bobby Carson's mother. You want me to give her a hug and tell her everything's all right.' Any more ice in her voice and the windows would have frosted over.

Daniel shook his yellow head. 'It's asking too much, isn't it? Plus, it wouldn't be true, and I don't think there'd be much peace for either of you in lies, even well-meant ones. But you're half right. I would like you to meet her. I think –

I hope – you'd both get some kind of solace from it.'

'*Solace?*' exploded Jane Moss. Daniel felt himself duck.

'Sorry…bad   word.   Er…catharsis?   Understanding?
Closure?'

There was another pregnant pause, the kind of
breathing space you get before a volcano erupts. Daniel
waited. He hadn't expected this to be easy. Margaret
Carson had hired him to do a job; and this wasn't the
job she hired him for so he probably wasn't going to get
paid; in spite of which, he thought it was the right thing
to be doing.

If Brodie caught him thinking like that he'd wake up
with a crowd round him. But he could only toss the ball
into the air – for anything meaningful to happen, this
damaged girl had to grab it and run. If she could; if she
was prepared to. He didn't want to bully or wheedle Jane
Moss into doing anything she'd regret. He did want to
help her see that it was an option.

'Understanding?' Jane said at last. She sounded almost
shell-shocked. 'The mother of the man who murdered my
fiancé wants my understanding?'

'I don't know if she wants it,' said Daniel carefully. 'But
she certainly needs it. It isn't her asking for this – it's me.
She doesn't know I'm here. She'll be horrified when I tell
her. She wanted you to have the necklace back. I don't
think she ever imagined meeting you – I think she meant
to leave it in a Moses basket on your doorstep, something
like that. If I could have found it, that's probably what
would have happened.

'Since I can't, I need to find another way forward. Mrs

Carson's my client, but this has to work for both of you. It would be a difficult meeting. You'd be brimming with anger and she'd mostly be in tears. But I think it might be worth doing, for two reasons. It would give her the chance to apologise. And it would let you see that she's really a very ordinary person who didn't deserve what happened any more than you did.'

'And that's going to make me feel better, how?' demanded Jane coldly.

It was hard to put into words but Daniel tried. 'Carson's in prison, and he's going to be there for the next fifteen years. There's no point staying angry with him. But you've lost so much, suffered so much, that the anger won't just go away. You're going to be looking for somewhere to pin it. You're bound to feel that, if Carson's mother had brought him up better, if she'd instilled some sense of right and wrong into him, none of this would have happened. So you could blame her. It wouldn't be unreasonable.'

He risked a quick look. Her jaw was clenched hard, as if it required a physical effort to hear him out. 'But if you keep thinking that way you'll stoke a furnace of rage and bitterness that may never subside. You'll end up feeling that she was responsible for what happened, and she hasn't paid for it and never will. And feeling like that, year after year, will do you terrible harm.

'I think if you met her, if only briefly, and heard her apology even if you didn't want to accept it, you could let go of those cancerous feelings. She's a nice woman. I don't think there was anything she could have done to prevent the attack on you. I think, if you met her, you'd recognise that. And it would make it easier to let go of the anger.'

'And what,' asked Jane Moss waspishly, 'if I don't *want* to let it go? What if it's all I have left of the man I was going to spend my life with? What if I want to be angry, and stay angry, and hate everyone who had anything to do with producing Robert Carson, up to and including the midwife who slapped his bum? What if I don't want to come to terms with what's happened?'

Daniel felt his heart twist inside him. Of course she felt like that. She'd been crucified by pain and loss; of course she wanted to hit back. To hurt someone. To nurse her hatred and resentment until they grew big and strong. He could empathise with every word she'd said. But if she couldn't get past feeling this way she was going to waste her life as much as Carson was. Anger that deep, that all-consuming, was profoundly damaging. Ultimately, it would ravage her. Daniel knew this for a fact.

'Then it'll destroy you,' he said quietly. 'And that won't actually be Robert Carson's fault. He killed Tom. He put you in a wheelchair. Those are about as heinous as crimes come, and if he pays for them every day he still won't live long enough to settle the debt.

'But this isn't his doing. You have a choice about where you go from here, and if you won't build a life worth having on the ruins of the old one, that's not entirely his fault. You're strong enough; we both know that. So it comes down to what you want. Essentially, whether you want to serve a life sentence too, or if you're prepared to take the pain and try to fashion something worthwhile out of it.'

He made himself meet her hot and angry gaze. 'I'm not saying that necessarily means meeting Margaret Carson. But if you decide not to, don't let it be because you're afraid of losing the capacity to hate.'

For a long time Jane Moss said nothing at all. The tense silence stretched. Reviewing his performance, Daniel was pretty sure he'd said too much – though he could be wrong, he might have said too little. In any event, he didn't think he'd persuaded her. If he had, she'd have found something to say by now.

At last she whispered, 'Get out.'

Disappointed but not surprised, Daniel nodded and stood up. 'All right. I'm sorry. But throwing me out won't resolve anything. I'm not the problem.'

'What is the problem?' she gritted.

'I suppose, how you see the rest of your life. Whether it's going to be blighted by what happened to you, or if you're going to grab it with both hands and make it work for you. I know this is nothing like the future you expected. But one way or another you have to deal with it. What happens next is up to you. You're the only one who can claw something worth having out of the flames.'

'Get out,' she said again, more forcefully.

'I'm going.'

She didn't see him to the door. She sat where she was, immobile, intransigent, and her eyes were like knives in his back. Daniel said nothing more. Perhaps she'd think about it later. Either way, he'd given it his best shot. He felt a weight lift off his shoulders as he closed Mrs Sanger's front door behind him.

The path through the front garden ended in steps down to the pavement. A new path off the drive had been created for the wheelchair. Though he thought he'd probably failed in his mission, Daniel was glad to be back on the public thoroughfare. Almost the worst part of Brodie's business was invading people's privacy. It embarrassed him dreadfully. He was sorry he hadn't achieved what he came here for, but he was glad to get away.

He didn't take an incautious step into the road. He was walking on the pavement when the car came from behind and mounted the kerb, and scooped him up on its nearside wing and flung him into Mrs Sanger's garden wall. He didn't even roll. He lay, unmoving, with his face in the dirt and one arm twisted up his back, and the car raced away down River Drive in a roar of pistons and a squeal of tyres.

Chapter Fifteen

Jane saw it happen. She wouldn't have done if she'd held firm to her resolve, turned her back and never watched him go. But at the last moment some impulse of curiosity made her hesitate, and she opened the door again a crack and peered out. Afterwards she could never say why. She wasn't interested in the kind of cars people drove. And everyone leaving here turned towards Dimmock because River Drive was a cul-de-sac.

But for whatever reason she did open the door a little to watch her visitor walk down the front steps. And the sudden roar of the car that came from nowhere kicked her in the gut like a mule, landing her in the road outside The Cavalier nine months and a lifetime earlier.

People who've never had them imagine that post-traumatic flashbacks are just a rather full-on memory. But they're more multidimensional than that. A flashback is so distressing, so disruptive to recovery, because it's exactly like reliving the experience. Typically the worst moment of someone's life, and their own mind condemns them to suffer it in all the original detail, the fear and pain undiminished, over and over again. You can't turn it off.

You can't wake up. Many victims find it more distressing than the original incident because the one thing it lacks is the element of shock that made the actual episode seem less than real. Flashbacks always seem utterly real.

It wasn't the first time Jane Moss had found herself cannoned back to the nexus between the best and worst moments of her life. It *was* the first time that she couldn't afford to give in to it. Before there had been no one in the nightmare with her. This time the flashback had been triggered by the sight of a man being hit by a car and flung into a brick wall, and he hadn't got up and he wasn't sitting out of sight yelling for help. He could be dead, or so badly injured that he would die without immediate assistance. River Drive wasn't the sort of place where people watched the street from behind lace curtains, so probably only she and the driver of the car knew what had happened.

She hadn't time for a flashback now. She hadn't time to seek help. If Daniel Hood wasn't breathing his life expectancy was about three minutes, and in a town of sixty thousand people he was probably the only one in a position to help him that quickly.

Even so, it was important to do this right. She took the few seconds necessary to think it through – what she would need, what she would need to do. It would be impossible to run back if she forgot something. She grabbed the phone and crammed it into her back pocket. Then she threw open the door and set the wheelchair at the ramps like a jockey tackling Becher's Brook.

Still thinking all the time, she headed not for the drive

but for the steps at the garden gate. She couldn't get down them in the chair, but if Hood was badly hurt she'd need to get down to his level anyway and this way was quicker. She left the chair at the top of the steps and came down them on her belly, like a seal, clawing her way on strong arms, the phone safe in the hip pocket of her jeans.

She found him spilt along the foot of the low wall, face down, the bright hair dusty with road dirt. He wasn't moving. Jane reached his foot first and gave it a tug, and still he didn't stir. She crawled the length of him – it wasn't far – until she reached his shoulder, and she pushed him onto his back. If his back was broken she could make things worse – but if he wasn't breathing they couldn't get any worse so she took the risk.

Either the grip of her hand or the fresh air revived him. Jane felt his narrow frame shudder as he drew a succession of uncoordinated breaths, and she vented her own lungs in a heavy sigh of relief. 'Mission accomplished.' She groped for the phone and dialled 999.

By the time she'd explained the situation, Daniel was sitting up with his back to the wall, his arms across his knees and his head resting on his arms. More conscious than not and, as far as Jane could tell, substantially uninjured.

'Police and ambulance are on their way,' she said, her voice gruff with reaction. 'Sit still and wait. You'll be OK.'

Daniel nodded slowly. 'I *am* OK. Thanks to you. How…?'

He was looking straight at her, but she knew he wasn't seeing much. His glasses were in the gutter; she hauled herself to the kerb to retrieve them. One lens was broken. He put them on anyway, and immediately the world started making sense. 'Oh…'

'Don't worry about it,' grunted Jane, hauling her legs into some sort of decorum, 'I'm tougher than I look. Anything broken?'

Daniel had gingerly untwisted his arm, and everything that should bend was bending and nothing was that shouldn't. 'I don't think so. Can I…?' But when he saw where the wheelchair was, where Jane was and where he was, he didn't bother finishing the sentence. 'No, I don't think I can. Not for a minute. Sorry.'

'Stop apologising. It wasn't your fault. You didn't step out in front of that car, it came after you.'

'Yes?' He really hadn't known what happened. 'I wonder why.'

She regarded him critically. 'You don't look worth robbing. Who've you been annoying?'

'Recently? Only you.' But of course that wasn't true. The man at the netting shed wasn't exactly annoyed, but he was pretty clear about what he wanted Daniel to do. And he hadn't done it.

The ambulance and the area car from Battle Alley arrived together. Constable Reg Vickers, who knew him, stood looking speculatively down at Daniel. 'All right, what's the story this time?'

Daniel tried a careful shrug. 'Someone hit me with a car.'

'Who?'

'I don't know. He didn't stop to introduce himself.'

Vickers considered the location. River Drive wasn't

on the way to anywhere; residents and tradesmen were
the only ones who came here, making it an unlikely spot
for a hit-and-run accident. 'I don't suppose you got the
number.'

'Sorry. Too busy headbutting this wall.'

'Miss?'

'I saw it, but it was over too quickly.' Jane described the
incident and also the car, but Vickers reckoned there were
probably a thousand like it in Dimmock alone.

'You're not making it sound like an accident,' he said.

'It wasn't.' She gave him a grin containing no mirth
whatever. 'Trust me – I know what I'm talking about.'

Only then did it strike him who she was. He'd
supposed – foolishly, he realised – that she was sitting on
the pavement to keep Daniel company. 'I'd better let Mr
Deacon know.'

'And we'd better get Daniel down to A & E,' said
one of the paramedics. 'Stay where you are, we'll get the
stretcher.'

Daniel shook his head. 'I don't need a stretcher. I'm a
bit bruised, that's all. Give me a hand up. I'll be fine.' He
tried to remember what Jane Moss had said that impressed
him. Oh yes... 'I'm tougher than I look.'

The policemen and the paramedics exchanged a
surprised look. Then, as a man, they burst out laughing.

Deacon picked him up from A & E. Partly to garner more
detail, partly to ensure that nothing more happened to
him on his way home. Whatever else there was between
these two men – and there was a lot, both good and bad,

from conflict of ideologies to personal rivalry – there was now a kind of friendship. They would never exchange birthday cards. But somewhere in the stony heart of him Deacon would have been sorry if this attempt to distract Daniel from his inquiry had proved more permanent than the first one.

He headed not for the shore but for Chiffney Road. Daniel was surprised. 'Why Brodie's?'

Deacon scowled. 'Because she said so.'

'Ah.' There seemed nothing else to say.

'Did you see the car before it hit you?'

'I didn't even see it after it hit me.'

'So you don't know if there was one man in it, or two, or half a rugby team.'

'If Jane hadn't seen it I wouldn't have been sure it was a car.'

Deacon sniffed. 'Some witness you are. OK. You walked up to River Drive?' Daniel nodded. 'Were you followed?'

Behind the crazed lens of his second-best spectacles Daniel's eyes were astonished. 'Who'd follow me?'

'Duh?' sneered Deacon. 'People who wanted to smear you along a wall? They followed you because they wanted to know if you'd taken their friendly warning to heart. If you had – if you were taking Mrs Campbell-Wheeler another bit of that pink glass – they'd have let you get on with it and you'd never have known they were there. But you went to Mrs Sanger's and talked to Jane Moss. That's why they hit you.'

'Because of the necklace.' Daniel was confused. 'But they must know I'm never going to find it. So why do they care if I talk to Jane? What do they think she might tell me?'

'Somebody's very nervous about this whole business,' said Deacon, lips pursed. 'Nine months after the event, with Carson doing his time in silence, anyone who might have been implicated should have drawn a line under the whole business. But someone's still anxious enough to keep tabs on what's happening. And when he learnt that you – not even me,' he added with unconscious hubris, 'but *you* – were sniffing around, instead of giving a shrug and getting on with his day he thought he had to stop you. And I have to ask myself why? What danger could you possibly pose to a man like that?'

'A man like what?'

It was a good question. 'Well, he's not the blagger – we know who that was. Even if Carson had a partner we never heard of, he'd have been in the same league. Small-time. Vicious, but essentially small-time. This business of watching you, putting the frighteners on you, trying to distract you with a few broken bones – that smells… bigger. Like someone with more clout.'

'Broken bones,' echoed Daniel weakly. 'They weren't trying to kill me then?'

Deacon shook his head. 'You'd be dead if they were, or at least in ICU. This was like the thing at the netting shed, only more so. Carson was willing to kill people in order to line his pocket. This guy's more worried about protecting himself. But he'd rather not kill you in the process.'

'That's…reassuring,' murmured Daniel.

'Don't get smug,' warned Deacon. 'If you push him, he'll push back. He wouldn't have started this if he wasn't prepared to finish it.'

'I'm not pushing anyone,' protested Daniel. 'I don't know *who* to push. I'm not sure I'd know how to. Jack... if he's feeling so vulnerable that my bumbling about is making him paranoid, he's in this up to his eyebrows. And he knows there's a trail linking him to Carson and the necklace, and that if you get wind of it you'll follow it all the way to his door.'

The car had come to a standstill. Deacon was staring at him as if he was talking in equations. But though his first instinct was always to slap Daniel down, the detective in him – and Deacon was nearly all detective – was already racing ahead. He might not like being beaten to an inference by a teacher of mathematics, but he was too good a policeman to ignore it out of pique. He knew that, along with the other traits that drove him mad – the quiet obstinacy, the self-righteousness, the fundamentalist approach to the truth – Daniel possessed an incisive intellect. He was the original class swot; and though nobody likes a know-all it's just plain stupid to ignore what he has to say.

All the evidence had pointed to Robert Carson as a lone gunman. His brief had told the court he was acting alone – that he'd hung around The Cavalier on spec, picked a likely target and been startled to find himself in possession of some valuable bits of jewellery. But if that was true, who was so worried about Daniel Hood's *Boy's Own* investigations? It was beginning to look as if, after all, someone had been standing on the grassy knoll.

He was still staring speechlessly at Daniel when Brodie tapped red talons peremptorily on the window. 'What are you waiting for – a kiss goodnight? Come inside. I want to talk to you.'

Chapter Sixteen

Deacon declined her offer. 'I need to get back. There's something I have to do.'

Brodie didn't argue. The invitation hadn't been aimed at him. And it hadn't actually been an invitation.

All the same, the sight of Daniel with mud on his clothes jolted her. She installed him on the living room sofa and surveyed him critically. 'Are you all right?'

He nodded, a shade gingerly. 'Jack reckons it was mostly meant to scare me.'

'Did it work?'

'Oh yeah.'

'*Who?*' she wanted to know.

'That's the mystery. It's beginning to look as if someone was pulling Carson's strings all along.' Daniel eased his bruised bones against the softness of the cushions. 'Was that what you wanted to talk about? I know I'm not making much progress. But I'm not ready to give up just yet.'

For once she wasn't thinking about the accounts. 'Someone hit you with a car because you went to see Jane Moss. What are they going to do when they realise even that hasn't put you off?'

Even when he was being stubborn, Daniel wasn't stupid. He knew he was in danger, and that not knowing quite why made it difficult to protect himself. But like a stubborn horse, the harder he was pushed, the more he dug his heels in. 'I'll be more careful. And I think Jack's got interested in what's going on. When whoever's doing this finds out, the last thing he'll be worrying about is me.'

He had a point. 'All the same, you have to remember this is a business,' said Brodie, 'not a crusade. People pay us to find things. Nobody pays us enough to risk our necks.'

Which was a bit rich, coming from her. 'You've risked yours often enough.'

She scowled. 'Not intentionally. I mean it, Daniel. We can't afford to get emotionally involved. When it starts looking it could cost us more than we're going to earn, we walk away.'

'I'm not emotionally involved,' he said firmly. Then, with just a little doubt, 'At least, I don't think so. But I don't want to walk away if I can help these people. Not just the client – Jane Moss is desperately in need of some kind of closure too. She's so angry... Well, of course she is, she's been terribly hurt. She tries not to let it show. She won't let people help her. But she needs to let go of the anger. I think I can help her find a way. I think, at some point, she might let me.'

Brodie's lips sketched a tiny smile. 'You like her.'

'I admire her,' Daniel said, choosing his words carefully. 'She's been through hell and come out the other side, and though I didn't know her before I bet she's still pretty much who she always was. It hasn't broken her.' He shook his head in wonder. 'How could you not admire someone who's been through all that and emerged essentially intact?'

Brodie nodded agreement. 'And you like her.'

'She crawled on her belly to help me when she thought I might need it.'

'And you like her.' Brodie chuckled. 'Don't bother denying it. It might be unprofessional but that's not why I wanted to see you.'

'No?' His muddy cheek paled. 'Is it Jonathan? Has something happened?'

'No,' she said quickly, reassuringly. 'Or rather yes, but not a bad thing.'

They went into the kitchen. Difficult things, important things, they always discussed at the old deal table rather than in the comfort of the living room. Daniel took the mug he was offered, noting how it had stewed as she'd heated and reheated the coffee while she waited. 'Tell me.'

So she told him. About Hester Dale and how they met in the hospital chapel. About faith and the strength some people drew from it in adversity. About Hester's kindness, and how she wanted to use the strength of her faith to try to help Jonathan.

Daniel listened in silence; more than that, in stillness. Every word grated on his conscience. It wasn't merely nonsense to him – it was offensive nonsense. The same nonsense that made people fear, despise, hate and finally kill other people exactly like them except for the shape of the symbol they worshipped under. It was the same nonsense that made people who would resist any other form of oppression set about oppressing themselves. It was the ultimate get-out clause, that sanctioned anything, however terrible – even better than *I was following orders*. A man might burn another man because his superiors commanded it, but only belief in a god could make him sing as he did it.

Yet he understood how watching her child sicken beyond the aid of medicine would make Brodie look for miracles. Try anything that might offer any hope, however remote, of halting the decline. He'd understood when she trailed Jonathan across continents in pursuit of a solution. As time went on and he saw what the quest was taking out of both the baby and his mother, Daniel had stopped thinking it was the right thing to do, but he hadn't said as much to Brodie because it was her decision to make and hers to live with.

He still felt that way. The very idea of faith healing – intercession, remote prayer, whatever snake-oil name you cared to give it – might light a brimstone fire under his temper and make this gentle man want to bang heads together. But that was his creed: much as he might want to, he hadn't the right to impose it on others. Not even Brodie. Perhaps especially not Brodie, and especially not now. So he listened; and the stillness was that of someone using half the strength of his body to stop the other half throwing things.

He waited until he thought she'd finished. Then he spent a little longer working out what he wanted to say. Finally, quietly, he responded. 'You don't need my approval to do anything you think might help Jonathan. Not for a surgical procedure, not for a medical treatment, not for this. If it's my opinion you want, you can have it. But I'm pretty sure you know what it is already.'

She was nodding, almost nervously. Almost as if there was something more. 'I know. To you this seems like primitive superstition. You're a scientist, you want proof. You want a hypothesis that can be tested. Faith has no appeal for you. You don't want to put your trust in anything you don't know to be true.

'But Daniel, what if you're wrong? What if there is something more? What if there's a power – don't call it God if you don't want to – operating above the laws of science? What if enough people believing in something strongly enough for long enough can make it real? Couldn't that mean there's a way of helping Jonathan when even the best doctors and surgeons can't? I know, there's no proof. But absence of evidence isn't evidence of absence.'

'On that basis,' murmured Daniel, 'you might as well trust to advanced aliens beaming Jonathan up to their spaceship to fix him there. We don't *know* there aren't people cleverer than us jetting round the galaxy. There seems every chance that there are. We're starting to find planets capable of sustaining our kind of life - it's reasonable to suppose some of them may be older than ours, their civilisations more advanced. That strikes you as fanciful. But an invisible, intangible, undetectable but still omnipotent God doesn't?'

'People have believed for generations,' Brodie reminded

him. 'Strongly enough to die for their beliefs.'

'They died from measles, septicaemia, bad water and childbed fever as well,' said Daniel promptly. 'Mostly, as cultures progress, they learn to manage their affairs better and stop dying unnecessarily. A thousand years ago, when there was so much about the world that people didn't understand, maybe there was an excuse for believing in God as an explanation for events that were beyond their comprehension.

'But we are no longer those people. We've grown, and we've learnt. We can look into the depths of the galaxy where the stars are not only impossibly far away, they're also impossibly old. We can look into the core of living material and see the moment at which conception takes place. But wherever we look, however powerful our lenses, we never find the fingerprint of deity. Certainly we find new mysteries – but if we can't solve them, our children will. Or their children will. If there was something like a god in the universe, don't you think we'd have found *some* proof by now?'

Brodie was still nodding anxiously, nervously. 'You're probably right. Daniel, I admit it – you're probably right. It's probably just a primordial instinct that's somehow survived the Age of Reason the way our appendixes survived evolution. But *what if you're wrong*? What if there is a power, and it can be reached? What if it could help Jonathan, and we didn't ask it to?'

Daniel ran distracted fingers through his yellow hair. 'I don't want to persuade you of anything. If this makes sense to you – if you think it might help – do it. If Jonathan starts getting better, we aren't going to know or even care why. We can send flowers to Hester Dale, his doctors, the Archbishop of Canterbury and the Dalai Lama, and I'll pay for them. I don't need to believe. Do what you think is best. You know I'm behind you.'

'Are you?' Brodie asked, her head tilted to one side like a troubled bird's. 'Really?'

He didn't understand. 'Of course. I always have been. I always will be.'

'Then there's something more I have to ask of you.'

'Anything.' When he said it, he thought he meant it. Then, in her face before she got the words out, he saw what she was about to say. The demand she was about to make of him. The pit fell out of his stomach. He felt the blood drain from his face. 'Brodie…'

'I have to,' she said, dogged with despair. She knew exactly what she was asking of him. She had before she started. 'It's part of it. There have been studies – they keep a record of results. Sometimes the statistics seem pretty significant. Hester said her group was convinced that involving those nearest to the patient made a difference to the outcome. That the group praying could improve someone's chances by maybe ten per cent – but if family and friends were praying as well, that figure could jump to fifteen per cent. I know, fifteen per cent is still only fifteen per cent. But it's so much more than nothing. This is the only chance he has left, Daniel. You can't refuse.'

There were statistics on that too. In the four years they'd known one another, both of them would have struggled to remember a time he'd refused her anything. Brodie was counting on it. She couldn't believe he'd choose now to start.

Daniel had risked his life for her. He'd risked his liberty, his future, his sanity. She'd never asked him for his soul before.

He didn't think she understood that. And if after four years she still didn't, he doubted he could find the words to explain. He said, gruff and a little breathless, 'Brodie – what possible good could the prayers of an unbeliever do? Even if there was something in it, which I know and I think you know there isn't. I understand that right now even the long shots seem worth taking, if only so that you know you've tried everything. If it'll do even that much good, do it. But don't ask me to join in. It would be a mockery. Of everything I believe in, and everything Hester Dale believes in.'

'But what harm can it do?' demanded Brodie, caught between anger and tears. 'So it's a mockery. So it'll make you feel stupid. So what? Are your beliefs *that* important? This is my child's life we're talking about! I don't *care* if it makes you feel like an idiot. Do it anyway.'

He didn't think she knew how much she was hurting him. But if she had known, he was pretty sure she'd have gone on hurting him if it meant getting what she wanted. All mothers are single-minded when it comes to their children. Brodie Farrell could be single-minded about the precise colour of paint she wanted on her front door. She didn't compromise. If she was going to start compromising, it wouldn't be over something that mattered as much as this.

And in a way he could see that she was right. Compared with Jonathan's well-being, his conscience was of no importance. If giving the child a kidney would have saved him Daniel would have done it. The difference wasn't that what she was proposing seemed unlikely to work. Many medical procedures are begun more in hope than expectation. The difference was that the horns of this particular dilemma were the two principles he'd cherished, to exactly the same degree, all his adult life.

He believed in what he could see, or experience, or logically infer, or trust to the genius of better brains than his. He didn't buy a can of beans without knowing where they came from, who made them, what they put in them and how the price compared with beans canned by other manufacturers. He wanted information, not dogma. He took nothing on faith.

And he told the truth. He didn't lie, even when the cost of honesty was greater than the value of what it was protecting. The truth itself was his holy grail.

To do as Brodie asked would mean abandoning one of those principles. Either persuading himself that the scientific rigour he applied to every other aspect of his life should be put aside on this one occasion, or going through the motions with his fingers crossed behind his back in a pantomime of belief.

For Brodie, for Jonathan, he could have bent to the need if either of those principles had meant a little less to him. She wasn't asking him to do something wicked. What he was being asked to believe was believed in by millions of people all over the world; many of them seemed to suffer no obvious harm and most insisted it was good for them. Or he could tell a little white lie. Recite the words in the sure and certain knowledge that they meant nothing because there was nothing out there to pray to. The only difference between his prayers and Hester Dale's would be that Daniel knew that. The snowiest of white lies, that hurt no one and made someone close to him feel a little better.

If he did as she asked, all it would cost him was sleep. He'd done things that had troubled his conscience more. It was a burden, but one he could carry. For Brodie? – of course he could. It wasn't as if there would be any consequences. There *would* be consequences if he refused. Because then, when Jonathan died – as die he was going to; Daniel knew that even if Brodie was somehow still in denial – it would be like a wall between them, denying them both the comfort they should have found in one another. Just a little bending could save them that.

He mumbled, 'Please don't ask me…'

'I have to.' Brodie's voice was as hard as steel. 'It matters too much. I need every weapon in the armoury. I need everyone who gives a tinker's damn about Jonathan to pray for his recovery.'

'But I'm an *atheist*…'

'And I'm desperate,' snarled Brodie. 'Daniel, you're going to do this for me. I don't *care* what it costs you. In fact, maybe that's the point. If you're wrong, if there really is a God, maybe the prayers of an atheist are what He wants to hear above anything else. Think of it as your sacrifice. Maybe you can give Jonathan something no one else can. Maybe the sacrifice of your principles is what it's going to take to save him. And anyway, we're going to find out.'

They'd reached that point where there was no room left for compromise. Either he did as she demanded or he refused. They looked at one another in shocked silence as an awareness of the significance of the moment grew in each of them. Right here, right now, something changed and would never be the same again. It wasn't the end of their friendship – it was too big a thing in their lives – but there was a paradigm shift in its nature, and both of them felt it. It would take time, and a calmness they couldn't currently command, to work out what it meant – how they went forward from here. Knowing that they would, but that nothing would ever be quite as it had been.

But they weren't wondering who'd blink first. Brodie couldn't afford to blink. It wasn't mere rhetoric when she said she was desperate. Principles? She'd have flayed him alive if she'd thought it would do any good. He was her best friend, but she'd have lit a bonfire under him to save her child. In the gauntness of her expression was a kind of horror at what she was reduced to.

In Daniel's misty grey eyes, behind his third-best spectacles, were pain and compassion. All the times he'd said – to her, to Deacon, mainly to himself – that he'd do anything for her came back to haunt him. Or not that, because he'd meant it when he said it and it still held true today. But he'd never expected that keeping his word would cost him his self-respect. Most people would have thought it a modest enough price to pay. But Daniel didn't, and

Brodie didn't. She knew what she was asking. Only an inner despair she could deal with no other way would have brought them to this. She felt to have no alternative. Only Daniel had a choice.

His voice was a mere murmur of sound. But it filled all the space between them. He said, 'All right.'

Chapter Seventeen

'Lionel who?' said Terry Walsh, his wind-tanned face wrinkled in well-feigned puzzlement. It was Sunday afternoon, and he'd gone to the marina to enjoy a bit of quiet pottering aboard *Salamander*. He'd looked up from greasing a winch to find a detective looking down at him.

At which point he'd done the only civilised thing: invited him aboard and offered him a beer.

'Littlejohn,' said DS Voss again. He had the policeman's patience that Deacon had never been able to master. He didn't mind how often he repeated a question as long as he got the right answer in the end. 'Lionel Littlejohn. He used to work for you.'

Walsh gave a friendly, confident smile. 'He may have done, Sergeant. A lot of people have, down the years. Give me a clue. What does he do?'

Voss considered. 'I believe he's done a few different things in his career. Driving. Lifting. Oh…and time.' He'd accepted the beer out of politeness but he wasn't drinking it. He needed all his wits about him.

Walsh's smile went impish round the corners, his voice

reproachful. 'Sergeant Voss! You know I don't employ criminals. At least, not knowingly.'

'At least,' murmured Charlie Voss, 'not those *we* know are criminals.'

Terry Walsh enjoyed the relationship he had with Dimmock CID, in the same way that a dog enjoys dancing just out of reach of its handler. He'd known Jack Deacon on and off since they were boys; he was pretty sure he was smarter than Deacon. Voss was smart too, but Voss was handicapped by wanting to do things by the book. He *believed* that stuff about protecting and serving. While Walsh wasn't getting any younger, his mind was as nimble as ever. A day might come when bad luck or bad judgement allowed them within grabbing range of his collar, but it wouldn't be today.

'Describe him, then.'

'Big man. Late fifties now. Walks like he's just sailed round the Horn on a tea clipper.'

'Mm...yes,' said Walsh, as if that rang a bell. 'Littlejohn? Maybe that was his name. I think he worked for a time as a doorman at The Dragon Luck. But you're going back a few years. And – as I believe you know, Sergeant Voss – it's not me but my wife who's part owner at the casino.'

'According to my information, he did odd jobs for you as well.'

'That's always possible,' conceded Walsh. 'He'd work to whichever of my managers took him on – I probably saw very little of him. Listen, if it matters I can find out for you...'

It did matter, but Voss knew that no account Walsh had

even five minutes to fabricate could be either relied on or broken. 'Maybe later. Have you seen him recently?'

Walsh shook his head pensively. 'I don't think so. Didn't he…I may be thinking of someone else…it runs in my mind he went up north. Years ago – four, five years ago.'

'That's what we thought too,' nodded Voss. 'Until he let himself into Daniel's house and bounced his head off the wall a couple of times, and then ran him down in the street.'

Walsh's eyes widened. 'Daniel Hood? Is he all right?' Voss nodded. 'Whose toes has he been treading on now?'

'He didn't know he had,' said Voss. 'But what he's been working on is the Carson case. You know – Bobby Carson? Ran down a young couple outside The Cavalier in order to rob them? Daniel's been trying to find the girl's necklace. He didn't think he was making much progress, but he must have been. Lionel Littlejohn didn't come all the way down from Carlisle to put the frighteners on someone who was stuck up a blind alley.'

'Quite,' agreed Walsh pensively. 'So Daniel's looking for the jewellery, is he? Because Mrs Farrell's otherwise engaged. Is there any news, Charlie? Is she making any headway?'

Dimmock was a small community. No one here had many secrets, even from their worst enemies. And Terry Walsh was far from Jack Deacon's worst enemy. 'No,' said Voss, taking a moment off from the business in hand, 'I don't think she is. It isn't looking good.'

'I've said this to Jack,' said Walsh with a kind of quiet insistence, 'and now I'm going to say it to you so you can remind him. If there's anything I can do, I want to know. I've a stake in a number of different businesses, including biomedical ones. There's a clinic in Sweden that's working on my research grant. Maybe they think they've talked to enough experts, but if they want to see another one I can arrange it. It's a fast-moving field – there are a lot of studies being done...' He gave a tight smile. 'All of which, of course, they are aware of. It's just... If Jack's kid dies, it isn't going to be because I or anyone I know could have helped and didn't.'

'I think the superintendent knows that,' said Voss quietly. 'But I'll make sure. Now, if you don't mind, Mr Walsh... Lionel Littlejohn.'

'He denied all knowledge of Littlejohn's whereabouts or activities,' Voss reported on Monday morning. It was eight-thirty, and already the CID coffee machine was on overload.

'Did you believe him?' asked Deacon, breakfasting on biscuits.

Voss considered. 'No. He knew who I was talking about. He also knew *what* I was talking about. He admitted that Littlejohn used to work for him, but only because he knows we can prove it. He thinks it's all we can prove.'

'You think Terry Walsh hired Lionel Littlejohn to come back here and put the fear of God into Daniel because Daniel's looking for the Sanger necklace.' It was impossible to tell from Deacon's expression whether he liked the idea.

All Voss could do was give his opinion. 'Yes.'

'Walsh didn't steal the necklace. We know that. Do you

think he hired Carson to steal it?'

'No, I don't,' said Voss. 'It isn't his style. And if he'd wanted it that much he'd have hired somebody better to steal it. Someone who wouldn't have left a trail of bodies, and wouldn't have got caught.'

'Someone like Lionel Littlejohn.'

'Well…yes.'

'Suppose,' Deacon ruminated. 'Just for a moment, suppose you're right, and it's Terry pulling Lionel's strings. Why?'

'If this isn't how he does business, maybe it's personal.'

'You think he had a grudge against Tom Sanger and Jane Moss?' Deacon asked sarcastically.

Voss didn't dignify that with a reply. 'Could he be protecting someone?'

The heavier of Deacon's eyebrows lifted. 'I doubt it. For one thing, it's too late – Carson's already admitted the offence and gone down for it. For another, he's a nasty vicious little amateur, exactly the kind of local thug who muddies the water for pros like Walsh. Walsh wouldn't help him for the same reason he wouldn't hire him.'

Voss concurred. 'How about the fence? Somebody took those pieces of jewellery off Bobby's hands. If we knew who he was, he'd go down too. Maybe Walsh is covering for him.'

Deacon shook his head. 'People like Walsh don't take risks to protect fences. Fences protect people like Walsh.' He scowled. 'There's something we're not seeing here. Or seeing but not understanding.'

Lacking inspiration, Voss shrugged. 'Maybe I'm wrong.

Maybe Walsh wasn't involved. He isn't the only target criminal Littlejohn worked for. Maybe Lionel's helping out another of his old mates.'

'Maybe.' Deacon gave a sour sniff. 'I hope not.'

'Why?'

'Because if it is Terry he'll draw the line at slitting Daniel's throat. He'll try to scare him off, he'll try to put him out of commission, but he won't kill him. At least, I don't think so.

'Plus, the reason he's doing this is that he feels exposed – out on a limb. He thinks that if Daniel keeps shaking the tree he could fall out. I may not know exactly how, but I know *he* knows he's vulnerable.' He gave a slow smile like a crocodile spotting the first migrating wildebeest. 'All I have to do is work it out and I've got the bastard.'

Daniel was not unaware of the risk he was running, but he'd put it to the back of his mind. Even the Carson commission seemed less important to him than it had. He went to see Margaret Carson more in a spirit of clearing the decks, freeing his mind for the even more difficult task that lay ahead.

She ushered him anxiously inside, her expression an inseparable mixture of hope and dread. 'Have you found it?'

'No,' he said immediately. He didn't want to mislead her, even for a moment. 'I'm sorry. Everyone I talk to tells me it's gone – that I won't be able to find it. That it'll have been broken up by now and the stone reset in another piece of jewellery.' He gave a regretful little lopsided shrug.

Since he broke his collarbone, one shoulder didn't go as high as the other.

The disappointment in Mrs Carson's face was like a little death. There could be no doubting either her commitment or her sincerity. She desperately wanted this to succeed, whatever the cost to herself. 'What are you saying, Mr Hood? That you're giving up?'

He bit his lip. 'Not exactly. But I think it's time we looked for a Plan B. I know you wanted to return Jane's necklace. But if that isn't going to be possible, is there something else we could do to help you feel you'd made some kind of reparation?'

Margaret Carson had no idea where he was going with this. Her eyes went from puzzled to cold. 'You're not suggesting I write her a cheque?'

'No,' said Daniel, appalled at the notion. 'She wouldn't take it. She's already slapped my face once – if I offered her money I think she'd knock me down. No, that's not what I was thinking. How would you feel about meeting her? You could tell her what you told me – how devastated you were by what Bobby did, how helpless you felt to stop him. It would make you feel better. It would also make Jane feel better, which is even more important.'

In the dark watches of the night we weigh all kinds of possibilities that aren't even genuine possibilities. Things that make winning the lottery look like an each-way bet. In the dark recesses of the soul we contemplate deeds that we wouldn't admit to knowing the names of. Even Daniel, who policed his soul like a man who believes in God, had toyed with murder in the place where neither conscience nor consequences rule. In the privacy of your own head, anything is an option.

But Daniel knew from the way her face fell, from the way her eyes hollowed and comprehension crashed through them, that Margaret Carson had never for a moment thought she could meet Jane Moss – not in any forum, not in any circumstances. He might as well suggest that she raise Tom Sanger, Lazarus-like, from the dead. She couldn't do it. Her lips rounded like her eyes, grey in the white of her face. 'No...!'

'If you like,' he pressed diffidently, 'I could be there. I've already sounded Jane out on this. She wasn't keen on the idea either but she agreed to a meeting, to see if you could lay the ghosts between you. It's absurd to talk of moving on from something like that, but it's still necessary at some point to draw a line under it. I think meeting you would help her do that.'

Mrs Carson struggled to string a sentence together. 'How could it *possibly* help her? How could she bear to be in the same room with me?'

But Daniel was speaking about something he knew. How runaway emotions cast shadows both forward and back, tainting past and future alike. Quietly, he tried to explain.

'She must have wondered what kind of a home he came from, a man capable of doing what Bobby did. Her imagination will have run riot. If she meets you she'll see she was wrong. That he came from a decent home, and a mother who cared about him and was appalled at what he became. Who tried to stop him and couldn't. Somehow he was born to do what he did. No one could have stopped him – not you, and if she'd been his mother, not her. I think she'll find a little comfort in that. Bobby was wholly responsible for his own actions, and now he's paying for them. End of story.'

But Mrs Carson's eyes were wild with fear. The mere suggestion that she meet Jane Moss had sent her into a blind panic. She'd found a way of dealing with the unbearable. Events which could have destroyed her had been sublimated into a cause. While she was driving the search for the star sapphire, and working out how to fund it, and wondering if she could manage by remortgaging her house or would have to sell it, she could live with the shades of the murdered boy and the broken girl. There wasn't much she could do about Bobby's crimes, but there was this, and she could do it with all her resolve, all her energy. If she did that, at the end of the day she might just be able to sleep and, if she did, to bear the dreams that would come.

Now this man she'd risked trusting, a man she'd opened her heart to, was telling her it wasn't an achievable goal – that she'd been fooling herself. That she couldn't restore the stolen necklace to its rightful owner, and would never be able to however long she kept trying. That the best she could do was face the maimed girl and tell her so. It was a flimsy hope from the start, that she could buy back the only thing Jane Moss had lost that money might find. When it collapsed, so too did the defences she'd built to shield herself from the unbearable facts. Exposed to the full force of them, she knew she would wither and die inside. A terrible moan whispered in her throat. 'No...'

They were in the living room, facing one another across an occasional table supported by a wooden elephant. There were more elephants on the mantelpiece, in a range of sizes like flying ducks. It was that kind of house – not the smartest, not at the cutting edge of interior design, but serviceable and comfortable and tidy. A nice home; a good place to raise children. Margaret Carson was a woman who, in another life, would have prided herself on her baking and her ability to find a reliable plumber. She was not someone who would have contemplated buying a sapphire. The jewellery box on her dressing table contained a modest engagement ring, a string of cultured pearls and some gold stud earrings. When you lifted the lid it played a tune and a ballerina in a tutu pirouetted *en pointe*.

Afraid she was going to faint, Daniel reached out a hand. 'Mrs Carson, the last thing I want to do is upset you. I'm trying to help.'

Bobby Carson's mother gritted through ashy lips, 'Then find the stone...'

'I don't think I can.'

'Then I'll find someone who will.' She straightened her back determinedly. 'Let me have your account.'

Chapter Eighteen

Deacon always had leave owing. It was one of the anchor points in the uncertain world that was Battle Alley Police Station. He'd never quite got the point of holidays. Every so often Superintendent Fuller would insist, and he'd grumble and argue but eventually and with a bad grace he'd pack a bag and drive somewhere virtually indistinguishable from Dimmock. But as likely as not, before he'd got his trousers rolled up and his knotted hanky in place he'd have stumbled on a crime, solved it and arrested the criminal, leaving Fuller to liaise apologetically with whatever manor he'd trespassed on and tear up and throw away the record of his senior detective's time off.

Fuller had assumed, as Jonathan's condition deteriorated, that Deacon would call in all the weeks – indeed, all the months – he was owed to take his partner and their son wherever they could glimpse a glint of hope. He got as far as wondering who he could get in to head up CID in his absence. But when Fuller broached the subject, Deacon cast him an armour-piercing shell of a glance and said – growled, rather – that it wouldn't be necessary. He didn't elaborate. But Fuller had been a policeman for as long as

Deacon had, and he knew the parties involved, and he inferred that they'd already discussed the possibility of Deacon travelling with her and Brodie had vetoed it.

Fuller was less surprised than Jonathan's father had been. Deacon wouldn't have been his companion of choice for a long and trying journey either. Everything he knew about Brodie Farrell suggested she'd want to do this her way, and if that meant carrying the luggage she'd do that as well.

So when Deacon stuck his head round the senior officer's door to say he'd be taking a few days off, and there was nothing going on that Detective Sergeant Voss couldn't handle but if anything strange or startling came up he could be back at his desk in an hour, Superintendent Fuller was confused. He'd heard about the trip to Switzerland that ended at Crawley, had understood there would be no more foreign expeditions. He couldn't imagine Deacon sitting in a darkened room waiting for his son to die.

But Deacon didn't owe him an explanation so Fuller just nodded and said, 'If you need anything...' and Deacon nodded too and said gruffly, 'Right.'

When he told Brodie he wasn't going to the office for a few days, she too was surprised. But, preoccupied with what she was increasingly thinking of as Jonathan's last best chance, she supposed he was leaving himself free for the intercession. She appreciated the thought, she just hoped he wouldn't get under her feet.

'You could go and see Daniel. He might need some moral support.'

Deacon frowned. '*Daniel* might? Why?'

'The whole praying thing. He said he'd do it. My guess is he's still trying to square it with his conscience.'

Deacon's frown turned to a scowl. He hadn't taken time off work in order to hold Daniel Hood's hand, even metaphorically. 'I'll look in on him later.' He made his excuses and left before she could ask what he meant to do first.

If she'd had less on her mind, Brodie might have realised that the only thing that would make Jack Deacon turn his back on the work he should be doing was work he shouldn't be doing.

Disconsolate, Daniel walked across town once more to deliver his news to Jane Moss. Mrs Carson lived off the Brighton Road and Mrs Sanger's house was in River Drive, so the walk took him forty minutes each time. This time it took him thirty-five of those minutes to work out exactly why he was so dismayed.

It wasn't because the commission was coming to an end. Like a minor royal, Daniel didn't concern himself overmuch with money, even Brodie's. He wasn't doing this to protect her bank balance, he was doing it to keep her business alive, so it would be there when she needed it. If he could generate a little income in the meantime so much the better, but he didn't lose sleep worrying over it. Brodie had had some good years before Jonathan came along; there was enough in reserve to cover the fact that Daniel would never have her business acumen, however long he occupied her chair.

In part his disappointment arose from his belief that a

meeting represented the best way forward for both women. He'd expected that Jane Moss would need convincing, and indeed she'd thrown him out for suggesting it. But after his close encounter with the car she gave it a little more thought.

He took her flowers on the Sunday afternoon, wanting to thank her for her help and check that she hadn't injured herself. She said not, but he noticed the scratches along her forearms where she'd dragged herself. She kept looking at the flowers. It occurred to Daniel, belatedly, that probably the only flowers she'd received since Tom's death were the ones from his funeral. He winced, afraid that he'd hurt her again.

But apparently not. She cradled them in her lap like something precious, and thought for some time, and then said, 'If you still want to arrange this meeting between me and Margaret Carson, go ahead.' She didn't sound wildly enthusiastic. Her manner was terse, her expression pinched. She wasn't looking forward to it, wasn't convinced it would help. But she was willing to give it a try.

And Daniel had thought it was a done deal. It didn't occur to him that a woman who was prepared to sell her house in order to make amends for someone else's crime would baulk at apologising instead.

But even that didn't explain the extent of his regret. He puzzled over it all the way up from town. Only as he caught sight of the cul-de-sac sign at the end of River Drive did the truth begin to dawn on him. He was sorry not because he thought Margaret Carson had made the wrong decision, although he did; and not because Brodie would think he'd lost a nice little earner, although she would; but because once the file was closed he'd have no reason to see Jane Moss again.

The thought was enough to stop him in his stride. What can only be described as a foolish smile stole across his face. It was that simple? He liked the girl and wanted to see more of her? He didn't need an excuse – all he had to do was phone and ask her for a drink. Or, since this was Daniel, if she'd like a look through his telescope.

She could only say no. She probably would say no. But Daniel was familiar with rejection; the prospect wouldn't have stopped him. Nor would the fact that Jane Moss was scarred and a cripple. She was – but in a way so was he. And it wasn't because she might consider herself still bound to her murdered fiancé. One day she'd be ready to move forward; in the meantime there was no harm in a friendly drink, or a galaxy or two. What stopped him asking to see her again – and risking, as men asking for dates always risk, being told that the object of his interest would rather sandpaper her bikini line – was the half-formed sense that it would be a kind of betrayal. Not even of Tom Sanger but of Brodie Farrell.

He continued walking, slower now, trying to feel his way round the dilemma. Daniel was not an emotionless man. He was a private man, but he felt passions as strongly as other people. He just tended to feel them for different things. He wasn't a virgin, but somewhere in his heart he was.

It was absurd, he decided. He owed Brodie his friendship, his loyalty, his professional services such as they were, and a willing if inconveniently low shoulder to cry on when the need arose. He did not owe her the kind of fidelity that seeing Jane or anyone else would compromise.

For three of the four years he'd known her, the intensity of his feelings for Brodie had precluded feeling anything comparable for someone else. He knew they had never been, would never be, reciprocated in kind, had come to terms with the fact that that part of her life belonged with Jack Deacon; and if they parted one day, she'd find someone to replace him and it still wouldn't be Daniel.

He didn't blame her for that. It wasn't Brodie who'd moved the goalposts. The manner of their meeting had been so traumatic they should never have been able to get past it. But they did, because each recognised in the other something extraordinary. They described what burgeoned between them as friendship but it was much more than that. It was as if in some part of their souls they were twins separated at birth. It was strange and unsettling, and there really weren't words to adequately describe it, but it was powerful enough to make each of them reassess their attitude to the world.

Daniel had been content as a quiet loner; now he realised his life had been incomplete, that there'd been a hole at the core of his being he hadn't even been aware of. Odder still was the fact that Brodie Farrell felt the same way about Daniel. She had never been a quiet loner. She *had* been happily married, until a divorce she hadn't seen coming turned her world upside down. Surviving, making a new life for herself, brought out unexpected strengths in her but also left her embittered. That was perhaps the best single thing Daniel did for her. He restored her faith in people.

And she loved him for it. But she didn't love him in the way that, over the next several months, he came to love her. He was her best friend, as close as a sister. He was the most important man in her life, even after the thing with Deacon started. But – and it was a big *but*, a huge big insurmountable *but* – she wasn't in love with him. It pained her to know how much she was hurting him, but it didn't alter anything. She told him – begged him, on occasion – to find someone who could feel about him the way he felt about Brodie.

He hadn't even tried. In all his life he'd only felt this way once. He thought – and he thought it was typical of his luck – that he'd finally found the one woman in the world for him, and she was so far out of his class that the only role left to him was that of faithful hound. So he took it. If it was something or nothing, he'd settle for having less of Brodie Farrell than he'd choose but perhaps more than he'd any right to expect.

Now, for the first time and to his absolute astonishment, he found himself feeling drawn to someone else. Not to the same degree, of course. He'd known Brodie for four years, spent a lot of time in her company, knew her intimately in every way but one. Sometimes he thought he knew her better than he knew himself. And he'd only just met Jane Moss, and he'd no reason to suppose she was interested in him in that way either. She'd slapped his face, then she'd crawled on her belly to help him. Men with much more experience of women than Daniel had would have struggled to read the auguries in that.

But even that wasn't the problem. The problem was that he would have liked to explore the situation – but to the part of him that was Brodie's faithful hound it felt like biting the hand that fed him. He'd spent so long wanting something he couldn't have that it felt like adultery to want something else.

Though he was walking slowly and thinking hard, that was a lot of ground to cover. Thirty years' worth, if looked at in a certain light. He failed to reach a conclusion before his thoughtful steps had taken him up River Drive to Mrs Sanger's front gate.

He hesitated. If Jane Moss came to the door now he'd have no idea what to say to her. Right now he couldn't remember why he'd come here. Something to do with Margaret Carson... He thought he'd better turn round and come back another time when his head was clearer.

Fate took a hand. They were in the front room – two of them, the low silhouette of the girl in the wheelchair, the taller one of the woman who should have been her mother-in-law by now. Jane looked out, saw him hovering stupidly on the pavement and raised a hand in greeting. Imogen Sanger came to the door and smiled a welcome. 'Daniel? Do come in. Jane's expecting you.'

He could have turned and run, but then he could never have come back. He did the only thing possible. He went up the steps into the house.

Chapter Nineteen

Deacon had no idea what he was looking for. But then, so often he didn't. He knew there was something to find from the way people were behaving, and that was enough. Usually, if he got hold of the people who were behaving oddly and asked them why, they told him. Not immediately, of course, but by the time he'd loomed over them and threatened to reopen some files they'd hoped had been closed if not lost or buried in concrete…

The problem this time was that he didn't actually know who was behaving oddly. All he could say with confidence was that someone felt sufficiently threatened by Daniel Hood's enquiries to put the frighteners on him.

But that was significant. Though Deacon knew Daniel had a dangerous side to him, casual acquaintances only saw a mild-mannered man with a boring job, a geeky hobby and inexplicably good luck with women. Most people with something to hide would have been happy to learn that the only one showing an interest was Daniel. But someone knew him well enough to feel it was worth sticking his head above the parapet to scare him off. Knew that Daniel was like a dog with a bone – a small, well-trained dog perhaps, the sort that neighbours' children take for walks and strangers pat outside shops, but capable of absolute single-mindedness once he knew there was something to be dug up. Knew that many a well-planned murder has come to light thanks to some little dog rooting round in the undergrowth.

Lionel Littlejohn was the key. Not so much finding, arresting and questioning him, although in due course Deacon would do all three. But Littlejohn would tell him nothing. He was a professional, he'd eat his own left leg first. But even without answers Deacon could make inferences. Someone Lionel had kept in touch with after he left Dimmock now needed his services urgently; and Lionel thought enough of him to risk his well-earned retirement by returning to his old stamping ground and throwing his considerable weight around one last time.

Like Voss, Deacon kept coming up with the same name. You could call it copper's instinct, you could call it experience, but it wouldn't get you laughed out of court because it would never get you that far. The Crown Prosecution Service rolled their eyes despairingly at the mention of copper's instinct. They wanted proof. They wanted signed confessions. If at all possible, they liked crimes to have been committed in front of bus queues.

But the proof was out there somewhere. If it wasn't, why would Daniel's amateur sleuthing have put the wind up someone like Terry Walsh? If it was him. If it wasn't, it was someone *like* him. Powerful, old firm, and worried.

What kind of proof? Something substantial. A witness who couldn't be intimidated, a weapon that couldn't be disposed of, swag that couldn't be fenced even by someone with Walsh's connections. If he'd acquired the necklace before he realised quite what it was, he'd have sent it down deep – locked it in a bank vault somewhere, made a mental note not to open it for fifteen years, and got on with his life. Or he'd have sailed out into the Channel and dropped it over the side. He'd had plenty of time. It was five days before Deacon caught up with Bobby Carson.

If a week is a long time in politics, it's a geological age in criminal conversion. *Anything* can happen in a week. That necklace could have been through a dozen pairs of hands and crossed international borders. It could have had a respectable provenance forged for it and been bought by someone who would never have dreamt of laundering stolen goods. It could have been worn to a society wedding or graced the neck of a king's mistress.

But though Deacon didn't know what had become of it, someone did. Someone knew his own safety depended on people thinking that the necklace was gone and its passage could never be traced. And there was this to be said for Jack Deacon. He liked a challenge.

Voss understood all that. What he didn't understand was why Deacon was taking leave to pursue it. 'It's a criminal matter. You're a detective. *This is what they pay you to do.*'

Deacon glowered at him over the desk he'd been attempting to tidy before going home. 'You'd think so, wouldn't you? Solving crimes, catching criminals. But no. What they pay me for, or what they think they pay me for, is filling in forms. Attending meetings. Listening to windbags who think it's a numbers game, and catching two mobile phone snatchers is better than catching one drug dealer. No, Charlie Voss, I need to give this some serious thought, and then to go talk to some people without having the area car come after me because I've turned my phone off. The only way I can get the time I need to do my job is to go on leave.'

Voss considered. 'You reckon Terry's behind this, don't you?'

'Don't you?'

'Maybe,' said Voss cautiously. 'Some of it makes more sense if he is. Some of it makes less.'

Deacon gave a grim nod. 'I thought that, too. Well, if Division can't pester me for the crime returns for a few days, maybe I'll be able to work it out.'

Voss wondered if he should say what he was thinking. Most people didn't go out of their way to provoke Detective Superintendent Deacon. But then, most of his sergeants hadn't lasted as long as Voss, and the reason for that was a degree of mutual respect between them that bridged the generation gap and even the differences of style and personality. So he said it. 'Then what?'

Deacon indulged himself in a slow, malicious smile. 'Then I nail his head on my wall. I've been trying for ten years. Well, if we're right, this time he's out in the open where I can take my shot. I may not know exactly where I should be looking, but he does. And Terry's got good instincts. He's stayed ahead of me for ten years. If he thinks I can have him now, I'm going to trust his judgement.'

'Or you could let me do it.'

The smile died. The expression in Deacon's craggy face swung between incredulity and indignation. 'Yes, that's going to happen. I'm going to chase someone for ten years, and eat crow every time he gives me the slip, and when the chance finally comes I'm going to hand the collar over to my sergeant. Then I'm going to put on a pink tutu and do the dance of the Sugar Plum Fairy.'

Voss suspected that image would haunt him for the rest of his life. He gave his ginger head a shake to shift it. 'You and Terry have been friends – all right, sort of friends – for rather more than ten years. This may not be the best time to end that friendship.'

Deacon leant back slowly in his chair as he absorbed what Voss was suggesting. If anyone else had said it he'd have been shouting by now. But he'd almost given up shouting at Voss. Too often in the past, when he'd finished shouting he'd had to backtrack, ask Voss to repeat what he'd said and then concede that he was right. So his voice was low but even, like the first rumble of thunder that precedes a storm. 'What are you saying, Charlie? That I might let him get away with murder for old time's sake?'

'No!' Voss said it so fervently he clearly meant it. 'Of course not. He's done a lot of bad things and he needs putting away. But it doesn't have to be you, and maybe it doesn't have to be right now.'

Deacon's heavy brows gathered speculatively. It was a sight that many a criminal had cause to rue. 'OK, spit it out. What's on your mind?'

So Voss told him. About his interview with Walsh, and Walsh's parting comment. 'He meant it. You may not think of him as a friend but he thinks of you as one. If there's a chance he could help Jonathan, maybe you shouldn't put him where he won't be able to. Not right now. You've waited for ten years. You could wait a little longer.'

Deacon rocked deliberately in his chair in a manner that it was never designed to cope with. 'He said the same thing to me. I thought he meant it as well. But you know, and I know, and I think Terry knows, there are no circumstances in which I could accept his offer, however genuine. Perhaps it's as well there's never going to be a moment when it might matter.' His face was the craggy grey of old lava.

Compassion twisted Voss's gut. 'Chief…I'm sorry. I didn't realise things had gone so far. I don't know what to say.'

Deacon forced a smile. 'Nothing *to* say, Charlie. Top and bottom of it is, the poor kid drew the short straw right at the start. Nothing anyone could have done after that would have saved him. I know that, because I know that everything that could be done *has* been done. Which is what the last six months have been about. Brodie said that when we got to this point, we'd want to know that. And she was right. It helps. Not a lot, but it would be worse if we were losing him and thought it was our fault.'

Detective Sergeant Voss wondered if he should be discussing something this personal with his senior officer. But he was aware that Deacon didn't have many people he could discuss it with. 'Have they given you any idea' – he swallowed – 'how long…?'

Deacon shrugged. 'Nobody knows for sure. Best guess is weeks rather than months. Do you know what the worst part is?' He fixed Voss with a steely gaze like pinning a moth to a cork board. Voss shook his head mutely. 'The worst part is, I can't wait for it to be over. Knowing he's going to die, watching him die by inches, and knowing there's nothing I can do about it – it's like there's a cancer eating away at me as well. At me, at Brodie, at whatever chance we have of a life together. And I want it to stop. *I want that badly enough to wish my son would hurry up and die.*'

Chapter Twenty

The woman at the door was as tall as Brodie, with friendly eyes and collar-length curly hair in a pleasant indeterminate shade between fair and grey. 'I'm Imogen Sanger,' she said, showing Daniel to the front room. 'I expect you guessed.'

Jane was waiting for them, her gaze raised expectantly. She wasted no time on preamble or even a greeting. 'Well? What did she say?'

Daniel sighed. 'I'm sorry. She can't face it. When I tried to tell her it would be good for both of you she fired me.'

Imogen had the grace to look faintly concerned. Jane glared imperiously at him. '*She* couldn't face it? I thought this was about making amends? About making *me* feel better?'

Daniel gave an apologetic shrug. 'I suppose everyone reaches a point they can't get beyond. That was Margaret Carson's. Don't…' He let the sentence tail off, aware it might seem impertinent.

'Don't what?' demanded Jane. 'Be unkind? Forget she's had a difficult year?'

Imogen put out a restraining hand. 'Don't shoot the messenger,' she murmured.

But Daniel's metaphysical shoulders were broader than his actual ones. If the girl needed to vent her frustration on someone, he didn't mind it being him. Except that wasn't what she needed. Like Margaret Carson, she needed a way to move forward. However much satisfaction she might derive from snapping at Daniel, it wasn't helping her to do that.

He said quietly, 'Don't underestimate the courage it took to get her this far. She didn't have to do any of this. She could have spent her money moving to a different town, or taken a holiday somewhere till all the papers reporting her son's crimes were chip wrappers and someone else was Antichrist of the Week. She could have sold her story to the Sunday tabloids.

'She didn't go down any of those routes. She put herself in the way of pain, humiliation and expense in the hope of restoring a fraction of what had been taken from you. She didn't have to but she thought she should. She came to me because she was desperate to say how sorry she was, and this was the only way she could manage it. Don't despise her for lacking the strength to do it the way you'd have done it, face to face.'

There he ground to an embarrassed halt, the centre of an astonished silence. He'd done it again. He wasn't a social animal: most of the people he spoke more than a few casual sentences to were friends. They were accustomed to the way he could be quiet and retiring and hardly say a thing all evening, then give a sudden insight into how his mind worked by unleashing a torrent of powerful, passionate ideas. In order to like him – and it was hard not to like Daniel – friends had to resign themselves to a number of odd little ways. This was just one of them. And if they could resist the urge to slap him long enough, often they found his ideas intriguing.

But he tried not to do it in front of strangers. It made them nervous. Eyes lowered, he mumbled, 'Um…sorry.'

Imogen recovered first. She gave a little smile. 'Don't apologise. It was fascinating. Like being in an Ibsen play.'

'I just meant…'

'We know what you meant,' said Jane shortly. 'You express yourself perfectly well. Not succinctly, but well. You want me to walk a mile in Margaret Carson's shoes before I criticise her. You know something, Daniel? I wish I could. Since I can't, and she can't or won't face up to that, we'll have to move on to Plan C. Yes?'

Her directness threw Daniel off balance. He said again, 'Um…'

Imogen gave him a clue. 'Say yes. She'll only bully you until you do.'

'Then…yes,' Daniel said cautiously.

There was a laptop on the table. Jane wheeled herself deftly into position and her hands danced over the keys. 'Guess what I've found.'

'On the internet?' She nodded. 'Cheap flights to Alicante? Half a Royal Doulton tea set? Lord Lucan? How would I know?'

She double-clicked and leant back with an air of triumph. 'I've found my necklace.'

And there it was on the screen. Not in truth a necklace, but a smooth round stone the colour of thunderclouds, with a point of brilliance at its heart from which radiated a dozen thin jets of golden light. It was breathtaking. Just sitting on a piece of white card, with none of the jeweller's art to complement it, just a smoky polished stone perhaps two centimetres across with a star gone nova in the middle of it, it was a thing of startling beauty.

Imogen Sanger's husband had given it to her because he loved her. She'd given it to her son because she loved him. And he'd given it to Jane. It could have been much less distinctive, much less valuable, and still infinitely precious.

Daniel stood frozen, staring at the thing. He couldn't believe she'd found it. He was meant to be the expert, the one being paid to find things, but it was something he'd never thought of doing. It never occurred to him that someone in possession of a valuable, distinctive and above all stolen jewel would think to sell it on eBay. He wouldn't have believed anyone could be that stupid.

Thinking about it now, he still didn't believe anyone had been that stupid. 'Are you sure?'

Imogen touched his arm. 'Sit down, Daniel, you're going to be here some time. I'll make the tea.' She left them alone.

Jane looked contemptuously at him. 'Of course I'm sure. I entered the keywords *star* and *sapphire* and *stolen* and up it came. Don't be so dim. It's a 42-carat black sapphire with a twelve-ray gold star, it was mined in Chanthaburi in Thailand, and a perfectly respectable American dealer is asking the price of a second-hand car for it. Add in the cost of making the mount, and Mrs Carson can buy off her conscience for about three thousand pounds. A bargain, I'd have said.'

Daniel was still struggling to catch up. 'You mean, that isn't actually your necklace?'

'*No*, Daniel,' Jane agreed with heavy patience. 'But if I buy the stone and have the setting copied by a decent goldsmith, and you tell Mrs Carson you've managed to track down the real thing, and she pays you for it and sends it round to me, *then* it'll be mine.'

'But...but...' Daniel was aware he was stammering idiotically. 'What good is that? If it's not the one Tom gave you, why would you even want it?'

'Because I'm a greedy cow and I've seen the opportunity to profit from my misfortune.' The challenge in Jane's eyes was diamond tipped, and it scored.

'I don't believe that,' Daniel said flatly.

The expression in her scarred face softened a little. 'No, you're right. That's not the reason.'

'Then what is?'

She shrugged carelessly. 'I'm not sure I can explain.'

'Try.'

Jane's brows drew together in a scowl. 'Daniel, I don't want to be rude but I don't have to explain anything to you. I don't answer to you. I don't answer to Margaret Carson either. The situation is this. She wants to spend some blood money making me feel better. Well, this would make me feel better.'

'Lying to her?'

Jane's eyes widened in surprised indignation. She wasn't used to having her judgement challenged.

There are plenty of ways in which being in a wheelchair limits your autonomy. Jane had decided early on that needing certain kinds of help made it important to fight for every vestige of independence left to her. She'd been an independent young woman before she was crippled; and before that she was an independent child, curious and adventurous. She'd always believed the word *no* applied mostly to other people.

And most other people learnt to avoid that jolting look of surprised disappointment by letting her do as she chose. They called it *letting her make her own mistakes*. In fact, she made very few mistakes. As well as curious she was intelligent and incisive, and though it seemed she was doing things without much thought, in fact she *was* thinking them through first, just very quickly. Even the mistakes she turned into learning experiences.

More recently people had avoided saying anything that might seem discouraging. So being called a liar by a man she hardly knew came as a bit of a shock. Her head tilted back so she could look down her nose at him. 'That's right, by lying to her. By telling her something she needs to hear before she can draw a line under the whole sorry episode. So she's happy, and I'm happy – and frankly, Daniel, who gives a damn whether you're happy or not?'

'Tea,' said Imogen brightly, returning with the tray.

Daniel took a cup mainly to occupy his hands while he thought. He'd believed he was at the end of the road. Jane was offering him a way forward. But there was no way under the sun he could go along with her deception. He owed a duty of care to his client that would be fatally compromised by selling her a fake stone.

Finally he said, 'I can't lie to her. I can't tell her this is the stone from your necklace when you and I both know it isn't.'

'We don't know that.'

'Of course we do!'

'No, we just know that the odds against it are pretty long. So far as I can see – so far as Imogen can see, and she had it much longer than me – it's identical. If it was in an ID parade it'd be convicted every time. It's the same size, the same quality so presumably the same value as the one Margaret Carson's son stole and she wants to buy back. Nobody's being cheated.'

But it didn't feel like that. Not to Daniel, who lived by the sanctity of his word. Even if the woman hadn't been paying him, he couldn't have told her something which he knew was a lie and which, if she found out, would cause her infinite distress.

Appalled, he looked to Imogen Sanger. He couldn't stop his voice from soaring in a way that suggested the only possible answer. 'Are you comfortable with this?'

She didn't answer at once. She sat down, poured herself a cup of tea, sipped it reflectively. 'Comfortable isn't the word I'd choose. I'm not comfortable with anything that's happened. Not with the death of my son, or the fact that the young woman I was already thinking of as a daughter, who I hoped would give me grandchildren, is now in a wheelchair. Not with the idea that a necklace given to me by the man I loved most in all the world has been sullied, and has vanished into the black market because no decent man would want to own it and no decent woman would wear it.

'Most of all, I'm deeply uncomfortable with the possibility that I triggered these events. That what happened was my fault. I gave the necklace to Tom to give it to Jane. If I hadn't, maybe none of this would have happened. Maybe Bobby Carson wouldn't have noticed them in The Cavalier, would have run some other couple down instead. Comfortable? No, I can't honestly say I am.'

She looked Daniel in the eye. 'But if you're asking whether Jane's proposition makes me more uncomfortable, then no, it doesn't. I'm neutral. We're not going to get my necklace – Jane's necklace – back. I'm not sure how I'd feel about a copy, whether it would remind me more of good times or bad ones. Maybe, in years to come, we'd start to forget its exact history and remember only that my husband and Jane's fiancé loved us enough to give us something beautiful.

'Or maybe not. Maybe it would always have blood on it, and remain at the back of a locked drawer till both of us are dead. I don't know. Anyway, my feelings are immaterial. The decision is Jane's. I'd already given my necklace away before any of this happened.'

Daniel turned slowly back to Jane, waiting expectantly. His voice was low. 'Please. I need to understand. Why do you want to do this?'

Because she wasn't used to being challenged, she wasn't used to arguing her point. Like Deacon, she was better at knowing what she wanted than explaining why. But Daniel kept looking at her, and his pale-grey eyes were unhappy and uncertain but she didn't think they were judging her or, worse, making allowances because he felt sorry for her. After she'd dismissed her first inclination, which was to throw him out again, and her second, which was to go for an easy lie rather than a complicated truth, she knitted her brows and started looking for the right words. She didn't think Daniel would understand but that wasn't why she was doing it. She wanted to explain it to Imogen. To an extent, she still needed to explain it to herself.

'I can't bring Tom back,' she said quietly. 'Nothing, nothing, *nothing* I do or don't do will bring Tom back. If getting out of this thing' – she slapped the arms of her chair – 'and running after him would do it, I'd find a way. Do you believe me?' She was looking at Imogen.

Imogen's eyes brimmed. 'Yes,' she said simply.

Jane swallowed. 'Good. Because I can't prove it. We can't ever have him back. But that necklace meant so much to all of us – you, Tom and me. I only had it for an hour, but what it meant... I can't find words big enough to say what it meant that he wanted to give it to me. That you wanted me to have it. It sounds stupid, but if real, honest-to-God love could be distilled down, poured into a mould and polished up, that's what it would look like.'

She took a deep, unsteady breath. 'But the necklace is gone, and I don't think we can get it back either. Whoever has it, they're keeping it out of sight until their children can enjoy it in fifty years or so. They'll never risk selling it. As far as we're concerned, it's lost.'

Finally, she looked at Daniel. 'Unlike Tom, though, it is only a thing. A beautiful thing, a rare and precious thing, but still only a thing. And though people can't replace one another, things can. I think…I *think*…that if I find a stone that looks like Imogen's stone, and have it mounted in a necklace that looks like Imogen's necklace, though I'll never forget it isn't the same one, when I get it out it'll remind me how much Tom and I meant to one another.

'If there was a photograph of the pair of us with that necklace, I'd treasure it. There isn't. I think that a copy would be like a photograph. I don't think I'd ever want to wear it. I do think I'd like to look at it sometimes and remember.

'Not with bitterness. I *am* bitter about what happened, but it wasn't the stone's fault.' Her eyes, bright with tears now, returned to Imogen. 'And it sure as hell wasn't your fault. It never occurred to me that you thought it might be. Imogen, we *know* whose fault it was. It was a hugely generous gift, and I'll never forget that you thought enough of me to make it. That's another reason I'd like to have it, even if all I can have is the copy. It was yours, and it was going to be mine, and I'm damned if I'll let trash like Bobby Carson deprive me of that too.'

In an instant the women were clinging together, sobbing on one another's shoulders; and for a moment Daniel felt like throwing his arms around them and crying too. He restrained himself. But he no longer doubted Jane's motives.

Imogen produced a handkerchief, mopping her streaming eyes. Her voice was tremulous with emotion. 'My dear girl. Let me buy it for you. It would give me such pleasure. You don't need to have anything more to do with the Carsons. Let me do this, for both of us.'

But Jane wasn't ready to give up her plotting. 'That's so kind, Imogen. If there was only us to consider I'd jump at it.' She extricated herself from the embrace and looked at Daniel, her face streaky and defiant. 'But there isn't, is there? You think there's someone else whose feelings should be taken into account. You think – I'm not sure why – we owe it to Margaret Carson to try to make her feel better. How does that work again?'

Daniel dropped his gaze, embarrassed. 'It's not that I think you owe her anything. It's just that she's hurting too, and I'd like to find a way to help her.'

'And she won't meet me, which would come free, but she will buy the necklace if you can find it?' He nodded unhappily, knowing what was coming next. 'Then what's the problem? She doesn't have to know that the jewel she bought was a substitute. The only thing standing in the way of a solution that'll satisfy all our needs is your delicate conscience. You say you want to help the woman. Well, this is how. You finish what you were hired to do, and never let on that the sapphire you found is not the one Tom's father gave to his mother but its identical twin.'

Terrible things were happening to Daniel's world view. He felt to be at the epicentre of a uniquely personal cluster of earthquakes that were shaking him to his foundations. Jonathan's life – or at least, his relationship with Jonathan's mother – had come to depend on his praying to a non-existent deity. And the contentment of three good women hung on him lying to one of them.

He believed that lying was bad – that lies paved the

road to Armageddon – so he didn't do it. He hadn't done it for so long that, though he was half persuaded that this time he should make an exception, he doubted he could do it convincingly. If there was one thing worse than lying to Margaret Carson about the necklace, it was having her find out that he'd lied. He felt his moral fibre unravelling by the moment.

'Look,' he said slowly, 'I'm not saying I'm going to do this. But if we were to do it, how would we go about it?'

Chapter Twenty-One

Brodie had been growing increasingly anxious all weekend. She phoned Hester Dale several times, trying to find out if there were any ways of doing this that were better than others.

'It's not really like that,' Hester explained gently. 'It's hard to see a pattern. We're talking about divine intervention – if the results were predictable, that would be science. But when science gives up, God keeps going. And we don't know why sometimes He pulls all the stops out to save one individual only to disappoint a dozen others. We just know that He does. We have to trust that He does when He can.'

'It's a funny kind of omnipotence,' grunted Brodie, then flinched as she realised who she'd said it to.

But Hester Dale only laughed. 'That's the bit that passeth all understanding,' she said ruefully. 'There must be a reason. Maybe it's just beyond our comprehension.'

There was a cricket on Brodie's shoulder, and though it looked like Jiminy it sounded like Daniel. It was saying, *And maybe it's because there's nothing there, and it's just coincidence when someone recovers from something he expected to die of.*

She couldn't afford to think like that. She put it behind her. 'I'm sorry, I'm all twitchy. I keep thinking there must be something more I could be doing.'

'You asked your friends to support us?'

'Oh yes.' There was a shortness to the reply that Hester found puzzling.

'Well, that's about it. We pray. We go on praying. And we hope.'

'We could – I don't know – make a donation?'

'If you want to later, fine,' said Hester firmly. 'Not at this point. It's not about money. We don't have much in the way of expenses. It doesn't even take much time. We think of it as a gift of love. The only cost is that, sometimes, we get people's hopes up only to see them dashed. We try not to do that. We try to be sure they understand the statistics. At best, we seem to throw a bit extra into the balance. Improve the odds, just a little. Sometimes it's just enough, but more often it isn't. You do understand that, don't you?'

'Yes,' said Brodie. She knew there were no guarantees. She knew that there wasn't even much hope. But it was Jonathan's last hope. She had to hang onto it with everything, including her fingernails. 'What about meeting him? I could bring him to your – what do you call it? – your prayer meeting. Would that help? *Might* that help?'

'Something else we're not sure of,' admitted Hester. 'It certainly can't hurt. But it isn't usually practical. What you call our prayer meeting is actually twelve or fifteen people scattered all over southern England. We agree a time to pray, and some people like to get together with one or two others in the same area. But it's all very informal.'

'Well, where are you going to be? I could bring him to you…'

Hester hesitated. 'If you feel in your heart that it's going to help, I'm not going to tell you different. The truth is, I don't know. But better than bundling Jonathan into the car, why don't we come to you? There's four, maybe five of us within an hour's drive of Dimmock. Let's get together at your place, just for the first time.' She smiled down the phone. 'See if we can't grab His attention.' She didn't mean Jonathan's.

Monday evening was a good time for everyone who was coming. Brodie had done an inordinate amount of housework during the day, as if prayers offered up in a clean environment were more likely to be efficacious. She'd also done some baking. When she caught herself going to the shed for the hedge-trimmers, she put a stop to it. A god with the power to save a dying child couldn't possibly care about the state of its mother's privet.

And she'd called Marta, and Deacon, and Daniel. Marta Szarabeijka, Brodie's upstairs neighbour, had no problems at all with prayer. She came from a milieu of Middle-European fervency in which faith was so all-pervasive that it was easy to not notice it at all, the way fish don't think much about water. Even at the height of Communism, even among those who most firmly embraced it, the attendant atheism never really caught on. People paid it lip service, but an awful lot of them still went to church.

Deacon wasn't so much an agnostic, someone who didn't know if there was a God, as someone who didn't care. If there was, He didn't interfere much in the day-to-day running of a criminal investigation department, which suited Deacon fine. He could get on with a God who minded His own business. Except that right now he hoped God considered Jonathan His business. Deacon would pray with the best of them, even if he couldn't remember the last time he'd done it and would probably never do it again.

And then there was Daniel.

Brodie had been trying to speak to him since lunchtime. But the answering machine was picking up the office phone and Daniel's mobile was switched off. However often she told him not to do that, that she needed to be able to reach him, he persisted. It was one of his little obstinacies, his way of saying that tools and gadgets were at his disposal, he was not at theirs.

So six o'clock came, and she still didn't know if she could count on his presence tonight. She left messages on the office phone and his home phone, and texted his mobile. Then she waited for him to get in touch. And waited, and waited some more; and her temper did not improve with the passing hours.

Deacon arrived at quarter past seven. He looked round suspiciously. 'Where are the God-botherers?'

'Not here yet,' said Brodie. 'And if you call them that to their faces, I will kill you.' She sounded as if she meant it.

'And, um...?' He was still looking, still failing to find anyone.

'Paddy's upstairs with Marta. They'll come down when we're ready to start. Jonathan's in his cot. Last time I looked he was asleep.'

Deacon hadn't meant any of the three of them. 'What about Daniel?'

The sparks in Brodie's eyes would have been lethal in a dry forest. 'I don't know where he is. I can't get hold of him.'

'Do you want me to fetch him?'

'I don't know where he is!' Behind the anger he could hear a terrible anxiety. She so desperately wanted this evening to go well.

'He's on his way. Being Daniel, he's walking. I'll go meet him at the bottom of the hill. We'll be back here in five minutes.'

'How do you *know* that?' demanded Brodie distractedly.

Deacon gave an oddly gentle little sigh. 'Brodie, you asked him to come. That's how I know. He can't refuse you anything. He never could. Even something as hard for him as this.'

But Brodie was too fretful to acknowledge that. She remembered only how reluctant Daniel had been to cooperate. 'Go see if you can spot him. Maybe he's gone home, just isn't answering the phone. Hester will be here about eight. Try and get him to come. Tell him, even if it makes no difference to Jonathan, it'll make a difference to me.'

Deacon went out by the door he'd just come through. 'Back in five,' he repeated wearily.

As soon as he turned onto the Guildford road he saw the small blond figure trudging up the hill quarter of a mile away.

Finding that Daniel had made it to the prayer meeting

did nothing to soothe Brodie's humour. In truth, it wasn't much to do with Daniel, and it wasn't genuine anger so much as worry following the path of least resistance. 'Where the hell have you been all day? You know I was counting on you for this evening. You said you'd be here.'

'I am here,' Daniel pointed out mildly.

'Only because Jack dragged you here kicking and screaming!'

In all honesty Deacon felt obliged to contradict. 'He was on his way. I told you he would be, and he was.'

'Took the scenic route, did you?' demanded Brodie nastily. 'Needed a bit of Dutch courage first?'

All the time they'd known one another Brodie had used Daniel as a kind of depository for her fears. Sometimes she talked to him as she dared talk to no one else, with a searing honesty that flayed her soul. And sometimes she dumped on him a coarse-gravel mix of rancour, sarcasm and something bordering on malice as if she despised him. She did it because there were times when she needed help carrying her burdens and hated to ask. Experience had taught her that most people would take her flak for longer than was reasonable, and Daniel would take it longest of all.

But not for ever. Paler than usual, his grey eyes glittered like steel. 'Brodie, I'm doing what you asked. I'm *going* to do what you asked. Don't talk to me as if I make a habit of letting you down.'

It was as if Lassie had bitten her. Even the anxiety went on hold while she stared at him in astonishment. If only she'd apologised then. She knew she was being unfair. He knew why she was so tense. If only she'd said, 'I'm sorry.

This business with Jonathan has got me bouncing off the walls. Forgive me?' He would have done – of course he would, instantly, totally.

But she didn't. When she got over the surprise she did what she always did: came back fighting. It was who she was these days. Often it was a source of strength, that got her through situations that should have defeated her. But there were times, and this was one, when it was a weakness, a way to avoid an unpalatable truth. She was quick with words. She'd discovered that being quick with words could make you seem right when in fact you were wrong.

'Oh Daniel,' she said impatiently, 'don't whine like a little girl! I swear to God, sometimes I don't know if I'm talking to you or Paddy. I've been looking for you half the day. Don't tell me you weren't avoiding me because I know you were. I know you don't want to be here. I'm sorry, but I need you. Your delicate conscience matters a good deal less to me than my son's welfare.

'You're doing this for me, Daniel. Will you at least try to do it with a good grace, and save your Joan of Arc impression for some time when we're not too busy to enjoy it?'

Even Deacon winced. Daniel went white. The shabbiness of her attack left him speechless. He'd taken some injustice from her over the years, and made allowances because of the circumstances, or the history, or simply because he loved her. This was different. It's one thing to make yourself someone's dog, another to have them produce the collar, the lead and the rolled-up newspaper. He couldn't believe she'd spoken to him like that when he was pawning his soul to do what she wanted. Though in fact it was hardly out of character. She behaved like this primarily because people, Daniel included, let her. Even so, the magnitude of the betrayal stunned him. He stared at her open-mouthed, too shocked to reply.

She turned her back as if he was something dealt with. 'Now,' she said briskly, 'there's wine in the kitchen. I'm not going to offer it up front in case it's not the right thing to do...'

Daniel's mouth was dry, his voice a husk. 'You mean, in case you cause offence?'

Brodie looked round exactly as if the dog had spoken back to her. 'What?'

Deacon muttered, 'Daniel...' and his tone was low with warning. Not menace; he had no thought of protecting Brodie's feelings. But he saw a moment coming that, if they didn't take care, would sunder them – would cleave this strange bond they had, that he would never understand but which he knew was massively important to both of them – as an adze splits wood. He knew what the loss of it would mean, not only to Daniel who wore it on his sleeve but also to Brodie who affected sometimes to have outgrown it. If this exchange continued to its logical conclusion, he thought that the woman he still cared for, the mother of his son, would regret it for the rest of her life. He flagged his warning to Daniel because he didn't think Brodie would listen.

But Daniel was too hurt to heed him. The sting of her words made him reckless. 'I love Jonathan too! I wouldn't be here if I didn't. I wouldn't be ready to give away something that matters to me. Jonathan, and Paddy, and heaven help me but even you, are the closest thing I have to a family. I'd do anything for any one of you – you know that.

'But don't presume on it. It's not something you have a right to expect. Commitment is a two-way thing, Brodie, not just something that other people owe you. It's time you stopped expecting so much more than you're willing to give.' Distress thrummed in his voice.

'I know you're worried out of your mind. I've tried to make allowances for that – we all have. But a sick child isn't a get-out-of-jail-free card: it doesn't entitle you to ride roughshod over everyone else, and not even notice the damage you're doing. I've given you all the help I could. I'm sorry if it wasn't enough. I'm sorry if you think I could have done better. Tell me what you want and I'll try to do it. Not because I think you'll return the favour some time. And not, in fact, because I want your gratitude. All the same, a little gratitude wouldn't go amiss.'

Brodie's fine, dark eyes were vast with indignation. 'Daniel! You want a sticker for your star chart! Of course I'm grateful. Without you I'd have had to wind up the business instead of watching it die by inches. On the other hand, I'd still have a professional reputation in this town, and clients who'd want to know when I was in a position to start up again. Right now Looking for Something? is a public joke. Your antics have got half Dimmock laying bets on whether it's Bobby Carson's mother or Tom Sanger's fiancée you've got the hots for. And which of the three of you is the most pathetic.'

'Brodie!' growled Deacon, scarce able to believe what he was hearing. He *knew* how Brodie felt about Daniel Hood. It had irritated him almost beyond bearing for four years. Though he understood that she had more pressing matters on her mind right now, still he was sickened at the way she'd turned on her friend.

And he knew that tomorrow she'd be sorry. By tomorrow, though, it would be too late. You kick a dog once too often and it runs away. Daniel was hard up against the limit of what even his devotion could take. Deacon saw it in the ashy pallor of his cheek, the glassy stretch of his eyes. She'd pushed him before now, pushed hard – an unthinking cruelty, or because she was hurting and needed to unload some of it. And he'd loved her enough to take it. But Deacon didn't think anyone could love anyone enough to take this.

There's nothing intrinsically impressive about a grown man drawing himself up to his full five foot seven. But it isn't always the biggest volcanoes that erupt. Daniel stood still, utterly still except for a fine trembling, his face as white as bone, his jaw clenched. Behind the thick glasses a steely resolution had replaced the pain. He felt in his pocket, put her office keys on the coffee table – not violently but with a rigid control that was much more awesome.

His voice was quiet but every word was clearly audible. 'You'll find everything in order. If there's anything you don't understand, call me.' He headed for the door.

And it seemed that only then did Brodie realise what she was doing, how profoundly she'd hurt him. She reached out a hand – but not far enough to touch him, as if even then she baulked at admitting the enormity of her offence. 'Daniel! Don't go off in a huff. Talk to me.'

He didn't look at her, just paused in the doorway. 'I don't think we've anything left to say to one another.' Then he was gone.

Deacon was looking at her in appalled incredulity. When she felt his gaze Brodie sniffed and gave a little shrug. 'I knew he'd get out of the praying thing somehow.' Then she went into the kitchen to turn down the oven.

A minute later the doorbell rang. Deacon stayed where he was because he wanted to see what Brodie would do.

She didn't run. She walked out into the hall and opened the front door. If she had an apology ready it didn't show in the set of her shoulders.

But it wasn't Daniel. It was Hester Dale and two of her friends. When Brodie looked past them, there was no one else in the drive.

Chapter Twenty-Two

The house on the shore was in darkness by the time he returned. Daniel climbed the iron steps on automatic pilot and let himself in without turning on the lights. It was as if he was afraid what he might see. Not the end of the world, but perhaps the end of his.

It had taken him two hours to get home. Normally he could walk down the hill from Chiffney Road in twenty minutes. This evening he'd taken a detour that took in the park, Fisher Hill, the undercliff and other places he didn't actually remember being. He'd always walked a lot. He did much of his thinking on his feet, but not tonight. His brain was paralysed by the turn events had taken. He wasn't distraught so much as numb – the kind of numbness you get if you lose a limb in an accident. For just a few seconds, before the nerves recover enough to start screaming.

It wasn't a big living room. There was a sofa and a chair. He sat in the chair. He hadn't drawn the curtains as he came in so he could see down the stony beach to the faint line of luminescence where the Channel began. It was a calm night, everywhere but inside him, so the glassy swells reflecting the sinking moon made a silver highway to France. Pinpoints of light miles away marked the passage of ships. Higher and brighter were the stars, light years away, swinging above the horizon in an endless silent carousel.

As always, the sheer timeless scale of it amazed him. For all he knew, any one of those distant blazing suns was history now, exploded or cold and shrunken, news of its demise patiently trudging across the void at a hundred and eighty-six thousand miles a second. It made his problems seem paltry by comparison. Except for one of them, which was immediate and unavoidable.

After a while he got up and went outside, onto the gallery. The telescope – the ugly love child of a tin bucket and a bit of garden trellis – was tucked away in its corner. He let it be, instead pulled up a deckchair and leant back, gazing and gazing.

If the psalmist had spoken of lifting up his eyes unto the *skies*, he might have made a convert. Or perhaps not. Daniel had spent his life trying to make sense of things. He was a mathematician because numbers are quintessentially logical, not open to interpretation. He was an astronomer because the cosmos is maths' grandest stage. So much, and yet still measurable; so far, and yet still in some measure knowable. Studying the stars had taught him two remarkable truths. That there is so much more out there, and much of it so much stranger, than anyone could have imagined for most of human history. And that people in his generation and the couple preceding it had been smart enough to find out. People. Extraordinary people perhaps, giants standing on the shoulders of giants, thinking brilliant thoughts and devising ways to test them, but people nonetheless.

And if people could work out what was happening on the furthest edge of the universe, which is in any event receding so fast that it's vastly further away now than when you started reading this sentence, Daniel simply couldn't see what need there was, what room was left, for a god. It seemed to him that all the attributes believers used to define deity were being steadily assumed by people who were curious enough to ask questions and clever enough to find the answers.

But still not clever enough to save one small boy from the ravages of a disease he was born with.

He'd promised to do something to try to help. He'd made the promise most unwillingly, feeling foolish and sure it would accomplish nothing, before the child's mother had made him the butt of her anger and frustration. Before she'd pulled out every stop she could reach to humiliate him. Before he'd left her house bleeding invisible rivers from the wounds she'd inflicted, knowing that a place where he'd found ease in his own hopelessness was somewhere he could not now return, and would not be welcome if he did.

It altered nothing. He'd given his word. Nothing that had happened since could erase the promise. He'd said he'd pray for Jonathan's recovery, and pray he was going to have to. Not because he thought it would help, and not because he thought Brodie would check, but because he'd promised and he'd rather break his right arm than a promise.

Well, the night sky was Daniel's cathedral. Anything he could achieve with a bunch of earnest devotees in a suburban sitting room, with wine waiting in the kitchen in case it might cause offence, he could certainly achieve here, alone, under the spangled dome of the cosmos. He gave his yellow head a fractional shake, incredulous at where events had brought him. Then he made a start.

Briefly he considered, and dismissed, the agnostic's prayer: *Oh God, if there is a God, save my soul, if I have a soul.* He wasn't an agnostic. He'd never sat on a fence in his life. If he was going to do this he was going to do it honestly. Alone on the iron gallery above the beach, the only sound the whisper and chink of the tide among the stones, the nearest human activity a hundred metres away on the Promenade, his lips moved on words he'd never thought to utter.

'If I'm wrong about this,' he murmured, 'and there's somebody out there listening, I suppose what I want to say is, Please can you help?'

It seemed only polite to wait for a response. But no comets flashed across the sky so he continued. 'I wouldn't ask – I don't have any right to ask – but there's a little boy who's going to die if you don't. Maybe that doesn't mean much to you. Children die all the time for want of a miracle. And a miracle's what we need. If there was a medical treatment that would save his life, his mother would have found it. She's good at finding things.'

The problem was, he had no frame of reference. He wasn't sure how you were supposed to do it, and whether how you did it was supposed to matter. He vaguely remembered RE lessons at school, the general import of which was that there was a beard in the sky watching everything that little boys did but not usually stopping them, or at least not in time. All the same, the beard gave him an idea. The grandfather who raised him did not in fact have a beard, but he was a kind, gentle, thoughtful individual who had given Daniel much of his moral code and to whom Daniel had continued turning for advice until his death six years before. He could do worse than talk to God as if he was his grandfather.

'She thinks this is his last chance. Brodie – the child's mother. She's a friend of mine. More than a friend, actually.' He gave a wry little snort. 'Being omniscient I guess you know that. And she thinks that getting the two of us talking about it might somehow help. I wasn't keen. But…'

'Do you remember a man called Cromwell?' he asked, apparently changing the subject. 'He killed a king and overturned an order that had been established for a thousand years – so long that most people considered it an expression of divine will – because he thought it was the right thing to do. Not a terribly attractive man in many ways, but he said one thing I've never forgotten. He said: "In the bowels of Christ, think it possible that you may be mistaken."'

He flicked an uncertain little grin into the darkness. 'I'm guessing the oath isn't one of your favourites, but for what it's worth, that's what I'm trying to do now. To consider the possibility that I've been wrong. That everything I've reckoned to know for the last twenty years was based on a fallacy. That it was arrogant, conceited and wrong. That those who've clung to essentially the same belief for the last four thousand years, whose faith is stronger than sense, stronger than science, were right – you were there all along. You don't show yourself openly because you choose not to, and you make the rules. Absence of evidence, as someone reminded me recently, is not evidence of absence. Oh… sorry. I guess you were there when she said it.'

He hesitated. He rather suspected this wasn't how prayers normally proceeded. He just had to hope that the form was less important than the content and that sincerity counted for something. He was doing his honest best.

'I don't suppose this is the first time someone's tried to strike a deal with you. "Please, Lord, save my child and I'll…" – whatever. I imagine it happens a lot. You'd think that if it worked nobody's child would ever die. But maybe it works sometimes. And if it works sometimes, maybe it can work for Jonathan.

'I hope it doesn't come down to what the supplicant can offer. "Save my child and I'll build a church." *Yeah, OK.* "Save my child and I'll plant a tree." *No, sorry, got loads already.* I hope it's the value of the sacrifice to the person offering it that counts. If it is, maybe I'm not wasting your time. Because there's something I can offer that you won't get every day.'

He paused a moment, aware of what he was doing. He was about to make a commitment to do something he absolutely didn't want to do. And in a way it hardly mattered if there was someone listening or not – if Daniel made a promise he was going to keep it. If Jonathan lived, he was going to have to find a way of keeping this one.

If Jonathan lived. That was the prize, and it was worth any effort to win it. All he had to do was hold on to that thought. He took a deep breath and jumped in.

'I need you to believe that atheism matters as much to me as faith does to worshippers. I don't know if I could die for it, but I've lived by it since I was old enough to make a rational choice and it's reflected in every aspect of my life, of who I am. So this is the deal. Save Jonathan and you get me too.' He gave an unsteady little chuckle. 'I don't know if that seems much of a bargain to you but it's the best I can do. I don't have anything else to offer. If you accept, I won't be the best-schooled believer you have but I will be trying hard. I won't just go through the motions. I'll give it everything I've got.'

Again he waited. Somewhere along the Promenade a dog barked. He didn't think it was a sign of anything, unless the proximity of a cat. He couldn't think of anything else to say, anyway, to sweeten the pot. 'OK. Well, that's about it. I look forward to hearing from you. Oh…and, give my love to Grandad.'

Though he'd gone along with it in a spirit of *anything's worth trying*, the prayer meeting left Deacon vaguely disappointed. If the intercessors had stripped naked and daubed themselves with woad he'd have been the first to mock, but at least he'd have felt they were giving it a bit of welly. But a bunch of middle-aged, middle-class, middle-income people sitting in a suburban living room sipping wine were somehow less convincing than the zealots he was expecting.

Brodie produced a small buffet and the wine – which proved entirely acceptable – and they sat making polite conversation for half an hour. Marta brought Paddy down from upstairs. Then Hester Dale suggested they make a start.

Brodie asked if she should bring Jonathan in. It didn't seem to be necessary, but the intercessors were generous enough to say they'd love to see him anyway. Jonathan was wan and barely stirred, and after the visitors had made the requisite admiring noises – Brodie appreciated their kindness though in truth there wasn't much to admire – he settled on his mother's lap and made no further contribution to the proceedings.

They didn't form a circle. They didn't chant, or touch the child. They didn't stand, or kneel, or even hold hands. They sat quietly, eyes lowered, and Hester Dale said softly, 'Lord, this is Jonathan, who needs your help. This is his mother, and his father, and his sister, and they love him dearly. And we are their friends, and we ask a blessing for them all. We ask that you make him well again, to enjoy the life you gave him. But whatever your plan for him, we accept your will.'

A man called Steven spoke in a similar vein; others just sat, eyes lowered, occasionally murmuring, 'Amen.' When Hester asked if Brodie wanted to say something she started but then choked up. Hester patted her hand reassuringly. 'It's all right. He knows what you wanted to say.'

'I'd do *anything*,' mumbled Brodie, her voice cracking.

'He knows that too. Mr Deacon?'

Deacon cleared his throat like a bullfrog preparing to

sing. Deeply embarrassed, he kept his eyes on his son. 'This is my only child. I don't want to lose him. Down the years I've done some good things. I've helped other people's children – I've even saved a few. I'd like to think it's my turn.' He trailed off, afraid – for possibly the first time in his life – he might be causing offence. But Hester only smiled encouragingly.

She turned to Paddy. 'What about you, honey? Do you want to speak to God?'

Paddy nodded solemnly.

'What do you want to say?'

'I want Jonathan to get better,' she whispered, shy in front of the strange adults. 'I could give up riding...'

'I'm sure God appreciates the offer,' said Hester gently. 'But then, who'd look after His ponies? I think you should keep riding unless He tells you to stop.'

After they'd gone, after Brodie had put Paddy to bed, Deacon helped her to tidy up. 'How do you think it went?'

Brodie shrugged tiredly. 'No idea. We're not going to know until either he dies or he doesn't.'

'You think, if he dies that means we did it wrong?'

She shook her head. 'I shouldn't think so. That would make Him a pretty petty God, wouldn't it? Oh Jack, let's be realistic here. It was always a long shot. But if a long shot's all you've got, you take it. We've taken them all – tried everything. Now we wait.'

There was something else he needed to ask. He knew she'd be annoyed, but he didn't feel he could let it pass without comment. 'Brodie...what was all that with Daniel?'

She tossed her hair contemptuously. 'I know. He promised he'd be here. I know he wasn't happy with the idea, but still…'

'That's not what I meant,' said Deacon, though he was pretty sure she knew already. 'Why are you treating him like this? Why are you so angry with him?'

Brodie turned on him sharply. 'You know how much this meant to me. So did he. But he couldn't put his precious principles aside for the half-hour it would have taken to do what I asked.'

But Deacon knew about dishonesty, dealt with it every day; recognised it in himself sometimes and recognised it in Brodie now. 'That's not fair. Daniel did exactly what you asked. He came here ready to do what you wanted. As ready as I was, though it was going to cost him more. But even that wasn't enough for you. You ripped him to shreds. You tore his heart out. Why?'

For once, the temper which was always her first line of defence wasn't up to the task. Great rents appeared in it, and her face crumpled and suddenly tears were flooding down it. Her voice was thick with them. But all she would say was, 'Because he deserves it!'

Chapter Twenty-Three

Criminal detection is like algebra. You start off with a few facts and a lot of unknowns, and set about replacing the question marks with true values. Mathematicians do this with formulae – the degrees in the angles of a triangle always add up to one hundred and eighty, that sort of thing. Detectives are supposed to do it by numbers too, but Deacon preferred his own methods. They could be summarised as three laws:

Everyone is guilty of something.

There is no such thing as the perfect crime.

Leaning heavily on the wrong person will not solve today's crime but may very well improve the overall clear-up rate.

The morning after the prayer meeting he took his son for a drive in the car. The doctors had said that little outings would do nothing but good, getting a bit of sunlight onto Jonathan's skin and fresh air into his lungs. And they were a chance for his parents to enjoy something approaching the normal experience of having a baby. Also, Brodie had to open the office.

Deacon drove up onto the Firestone Cliffs and parked

with a panoramic view of the Channel before him. The sea was bright blue. He settled Jonathan on his knee, and the frail child drifted between sleep and blowing contented bubbles while the detective thought.

The view wasn't the only reason he'd come up here. Terry Walsh had a house on the Firestone Cliffs, one of just half a dozen sharing the best address in Dimmock. He wasn't planning on visiting Walsh today, but it pleased him to plot the man's downfall while sitting on his doorstep.

The more he thought about it, the more convinced he was that Walsh was involved in the Carson case. He had no evidence. He had a theory of a kind, but it fell far short of a case. All he really had was a well-honed instinct that zeroed in on criminality as a sniffer dog zeroes in on hash. He *knew* Walsh was up to his neck in this. He'd find a way to prove it.

For once, though, the three laws offered little help. Of course Walsh was guilty of something – he was the nearest thing Dimmock had to a Godfather, even if Deacon hadn't yet been able to prove it. Walsh was a free man because he'd been both clever and careful every day for ten years. Having dealings with Bobby Carson would have been an uncharacteristic error of judgement. Then he'd tried putting the frighteners on Daniel Hood when he'd have been much safer trusting that Daniel's lack of skill meant he'd hit the buffers sooner rather than later anyway.

There was, of course, the possibility that it wasn't Walsh but someone else, making the same mistakes for the same reasons. This should have been a cheering thought, because Deacon had a better chance of catching someone else. But he wanted it to be Walsh.

That was why he'd taken leave. If he was detecting on public time he had to do it properly – work from the facts of the crime towards the identity of the criminal. If he was on his holidays he could please himself how he established Terry Walsh's guilt.

He didn't usually think aloud. But there were only the two of them here, and Jonathan didn't know what most of the words meant but he liked the sound of his father's voice. So Deacon discussed the matter with him as he would have done with Voss.

'Points in favour of Terry Walsh being behind all this,' he observed to the top of the slumbering infant's head. 'One, Lionel Littlejohn worked for Terry. All right, he worked for other people as well, but he wouldn't have come out of retirement for all of them. He would for Terry.

'Two, most of the people Lionel might have done this for wouldn't have been so considerate. If they were worried enough to need Littlejohn's help, they wouldn't have settled for giving Daniel a bloody nose as a warning – they'd have wanted him in the hospital, or the morgue.

'Three, Bobby Carson went to prison on the basis that he was acting alone. If he was working for someone, he kept it quiet because he knew that nothing the law could do to him was as bad as what would happen if he grassed up his boss. Terry Walsh isn't the only man on the south coast that you'd give years of your life to avoid upsetting, but he's a front runner.'

Jonathan gave a sleepy hiccup. It might have been agreement or wind.

'And lastly,' said Deacon, his voice a soft rumble where his jaw rested against Jonathan's bald spot, 'I *want* it to be Terry. This probably isn't as good an argument as the others, but there is such a thing as poetic justice. It *ought* to be Terry. It ought to be me that proves it.'

He was so deep in thought that he didn't notice the big 4x4 drawing up behind him. The first he knew was the rap of a polite knuckle on the window by his ear. Jonathan woke just long enough for a gummy yawn before falling asleep once more.

Deacon lowered the window, and Caroline Walsh said, 'Are you all right, Jack?'

These days, when Terry Walsh was a wealthy entrepreneur, no one turned a hair at the marriage of an East End barrow boy and the daughter of a professor. But the Walshes were married in their early twenties, when Terry still had his fortune to make. Which meant that either the girl with the cut-glass accent had already spotted his potential, or it really was love.

Deacon kept his expression wooden. 'We're fine. Just admiring the view.'

Caroline Walsh knew that Deacon's baby couldn't see the view and Deacon himself was not much given to aesthetic contemplation. She could have made an intelligent guess at why he was here. 'Terry's inside. Come in for a coffee.'

He was tempted. Terry Walsh's wife was an easy woman to like – confident, friendly, intelligent. Also, he'd known her for years. Jack Deacon didn't cry on anyone's shoulder; but if he'd needed to share his sorrows he could have done worse than share them with Caroline Walsh.

But common sense intervened. Accepting the invitation would have involved him in explaining to two different authorities. He could probably satisfy Division as to his motives for taking morning coffee with a target criminal's wife. He wasn't sure about Brodie. 'Better not,' he said, nodding at the baby. 'His mum'll be wondering where we've got to.'

'All right.' Caroline nodded her ash-blonde head, her hair curled so expensively it looked natural. She was wearing a cream blazer, a strand of pearls just visible at the neck. She walked round the car and coolly got in at the passenger door. 'Then I'll keep you company for a minute.'

He didn't think he was being propositioned. He didn't think either his professional or personal virtue was in any danger. He'd had a wealth of experiences in the last thirty years, but not many of them involved classy women trying to get him into bed. 'Did Terry—?'

She didn't wait for him to finish. 'No. I was on my way back from the shops and saw your car. Jack…you do know we're both thinking of you?'

Deacon always found kindness harder to deal with than violence. 'Yes,' he mumbled gruffly. 'Thanks.'

Caroline looked at the baby, jaunty in the baseball cap that kept the sun off his empty eyes, and reached a finger to stroke his cheek. There were tears in her smile. 'Such a charmer…' She cleared her throat, directed her gaze to the emotional safety zone of the Channel. 'I know you have to be careful – you can't take help from just anyone. But Terry's a businessman. He could find a way to do it that wouldn't compromise you. You don't have to choose between your job and your son.'

Deacon felt as if she'd reached inside him to knead his guts. He was at once startled and immensely touched. 'I appreciate that, Caroline. For what it's worth, if I thought it would make a difference I'd take you up on it. But it wouldn't. It's not a question of money. Brodie's seen every expert the world has to offer, and none of them think they can treat him.'

Caroline Walsh nodded, still looking ahead. 'How is Mrs Farrell?'

'Bearing up.' It was all he could think to say. 'I think she's pretty well resigned now to what's going to happen. In a way it was harder when she thought there might be a cure and she only had to find it.' He gave a mirthless little chuckle. 'All we're left with now is prayers. At least you can do that without leaving home.'

The woman laid her hand on his wrist in a gesture of compassion. 'Keep praying. Miracles do happen, you know.'

'But not as often as they don't.'

'No.' She squeezed his wrist, and got out of the car and walked towards her house.

Deacon called her name. She looked round, one perfect eyebrow arched. 'You do know I'm going to get him one day, don't you?'

Caroline smiled broadly. 'As I said, miracles happen.' She walked on up the drive, the pearls shimmering around her throat.

Chapter Twenty-Four

Jane Moss phoned looking for Daniel. Brodie explained that he wasn't available but she was familiar with the case and would be able to help.

But Jane knew what she wanted and it wasn't Brodie. 'Do you have his mobile number?'

'Yes.' Brodie heard herself and winced. She sounded like a jealous mother fending off her son's girlfriends. 'It's here somewhere.' She read it out. 'But I doubt he'll be able to help you any further.'

'I bet he does,' said Jane calmly.

After she'd rung off, Brodie sat peering at the phone for a long time, her thoughts unsettling. Daniel was finally doing what she'd wanted him to for most of four years. Why didn't she feel happier about it?

This was the first time Brodie had spoken to Jane Moss. Everything she knew about her had come from Daniel. The cool, self-possessed voice at the other end had been unexpected, but she of all people could appreciate strength of character. She didn't know what had made her hackles rise.

She wasn't sure what Daniel would do when he got

Jane's call. Given how she'd spoken to him last night, and the way they'd parted, only one person in a hundred would have felt any obligation to keep her informed. But Daniel was that person. Ten minutes later her phone rang again.

'Jane has an idea for settling things with Margaret Carson. Whether or not it leads anywhere, we can't bill Mrs Carson for any more work – she ended the commission days ago. You can take the cost of what I've done since then out of my wages. Anything else I do for them will be personal.'

It hurt her to hear him speak to her as an employer when they'd been so close. Closer than family; closer than lovers. Now they were reduced to talking in a manner carefully calculated to avoid misunderstandings.

'Fine,' she said. She should have left it at that, but the devil on her shoulder prompted her. 'I'll issue an invoice for our services to date, you can bill her yourself from here on out.'

There was a brief silence. Then Daniel said quietly, 'I've never put a price on friendship before and I don't intend to charge for it now.'

'As you like,' shrugged Brodie. 'You're a free agent.'

Another, longer pause. When he spoke again there was a yearning in his voice. 'Brodie, what's happened? To us – to you? Why are you treating me like this?'

She pretended not to know what he meant. 'What happened to me is that my child got sick and I haven't as much time as I once had to feather-bed your feelings. And maybe I haven't the patience I once had, either.'

'You never had *that* much patience,' Daniel remembered wistfully, and Brodie had to concede that he was right.

'But we were good friends. Now you talk to me as if I'm your enemy.'

'Oh, get over yourself, Daniel,' she said tartly. 'Everything isn't about you. I'm just a bit too tired and too fraught to tiptoe round you at the moment. If you need someone to hold your hand, try Jane. What idea, anyway?'

'What?' He was off balance, struggling to deal with her new coldness.

'You said she had an idea about Margaret Carson. What idea?'

Daniel didn't want to discuss it. He remained deeply uncomfortable with the idea, even if he could see some merit in it. Now Jane wanted to show him something and wouldn't tell him what. 'It's all a bit off the wall. I'm hoping she'll have second thoughts.'

'Yes? Well, good luck with that.' She went to ring off.

He made one last attempt to get through to her, his voice in her ear plaintive. 'Brodie...can't we at least *talk*?'

'Daniel, we've *been* talking. But I'm busy. There are things I have to get on with. My assistant walked out on me last night.'

'I didn't...' He stopped and took a deep, unsteady breath. This wasn't about who'd said what to who, or who started it. It was much more fundamental than that. They could argue about the symptoms, they could blame the malaise on one another, or they could try to cure it. 'Don't throw away what we had. If you've no use for it at the moment, pack it away carefully so you can find it if you need it later. We're strong enough to survive this. We've survived a lot worse. Don't push me away. I care about you.'

'Yes? That's nice,' she said; and she kept her voice calm and rather patronising, and this time she managed to put the phone down.

But she went on looking at it for some minutes, appalled at what she'd done, half hoping it would ring again. If it did, she knew she wouldn't be able to go on with this. She knew she'd tell him everything. But it didn't. She sniffed, and took the diary out of the drawer.

When she opened it the first thing she saw was Daniel's small, precise, rather schoolgirly handwriting. And she burst into tears.

Jane picked him up at the netting shed. She had an adapted hatchback with sliding doors and hand controls, and her wheelchair was folded in the back. Daniel got in beside her. 'All right, I'm here. What did you want to show me?'

'Patience,' she said mysteriously. 'You'll see in a minute.'

She drove up Fisher Hill – Daniel staring rigidly ahead to avoid gazing forlornly into Shack Lane – and near the top turned off into the jumble of little alleys at the back. In Hunter's Lane she stopped the car and opened the door.

Daniel looked around. There were a few dusty shop windows – a locksmith, a barber, a charity shop – among the small stone houses. They'd been built for fishermen when Dimmock had a small fleet. But it never had a harbour, and launching the boats from the stony shore was the kind of hard physical labour that people stopped doing when the alternative was the dole rather than the workhouse. Daniel's home was a relic of the same period. Now there were no fishermen and the little stone houses were mostly occupied by widows and old men who rarely ventured further than Fisher Hill because, whichever way they turned, it was too steep for old knees.

While he was looking Jane had unloaded her chair and hefted herself into it, leaving Daniel feeling guilty. 'Er... can I help?'

'No need,' she said airily. There was no dip in the kerb. She hauled herself up backwards by the sheer strength of her wrists, then spun neatly. 'This is it.'

She was indicating one of the front windows. Like Brodie's office, it was hard to be sure if it was a shop or someone's front room. A curtain had been drawn across and there was a small brass plate beside the door. Daniel read it. Even then he didn't understand. 'He sells cars?'

'No,' said Jane with a heavy patience, 'Mr Daimler makes jewellery.'

Daniel gave a little jolt. 'I didn't know there was a jeweller here. When I took Margaret Carson's commission I reckoned I'd contacted every jeweller within a ten-mile radius. I never even heard the name Henry Daimler.'

'That's because he's discreet. He doesn't need to advertise. His name is well enough known in the kind of circles where they commission good jewellery. This is where Imogen and Tom's father came thirty years ago.'

Daniel's eyes widened. 'This is where the necklace was made?'

'It wasn't this Henry who made it, it was his father,' said Jane. 'But the workshop's the same and he still has his father's pattern books. If he can't copy Imogen's necklace, no one can.'

Daniel hung back. He really didn't want to do this. Jane gave him no choice. She herded him in with the wheelchair like herding a stubborn sheep with a quad.

With the result that when Henry Daimler junior looked up and saw the uncertain young man with the thick glasses and the determined young woman in the wheelchair, he thought they were shopping for a ring to mark an engagement only one of them wanted. Rather than produce the pattern books and talk through their preferences and their budget, he thought perhaps he would show them some that he'd made earlier. The reluctant groom might buy something from the cheaper end of the range rather than make a scene, but Mr Daimler was pretty sure that if he left a commission he'd phone up later to cancel it.

Only when the girl spoke did he realise he'd made a mistake. 'We were talking on the phone earlier. You're the young lady who's interested in star sapphires.'

Jane nodded. 'Jane Moss. My friend, Daniel Hood.'

Daniel hadn't realised she thought of him as a friend. Or perhaps it was just shorthand, to avoid a lengthy explanation.

'I want a piece making up. I have a picture of the original. It was made by your father about 1980. I want as close a copy as you can manage.'

Mr Daimler nodded. He reached under his counter,

lifted out a tray. 'I put together some stones after you called. If you see something you like we can start immediately. If not, I'll ask around, try to find what you want.'

Pinned to a cream velvet board, carefully angled to the light, was a pocket constellation. The stones varied in colour from nearly black to nearly colourless. The blue ones came in every shade from polar sky to indigo, the black ones from dove grey to charcoal. There were yellow ones as well, and some the colour of fire, and some the colour of blood.

Daniel caught himself staring. 'They're all sapphires?'

The jeweller chuckled in his beard. 'Everyone thinks sapphires have to be blue. They can be any colour. We call the red ones rubies, but they're all sapphires.'

'And the stars?' asked Jane.

'They're commoner in some colours. There are star rubies. There are blue star sapphires, the best of them from Burma and India. Black sapphires produce the most stars, and the best of those are mined in Thailand.' He indicated a smooth oval stone the colour of Indian ink. 'The rays are gold.'

Jane was looking intently at the stones. 'That's what I want. Gold rays. But I want twelve of them.'

Mr Daimler blinked. 'Those are rarer. Dearer.'

'That's all right.' Jane looked directly at her companion. 'Isn't it, Daniel?'

Daniel gave an uncomfortable shrug. 'It has to be twelve,' he admitted.

'And cut like that,' said Jane. 'Round, like a pillow.'

'All star gems are cabochon cut,' the jeweller pointed

out politely. 'To show off the rays. What about size?'

She looked around the tray, then pointed. 'About like that.'

Mr Daimler's eyes widened perceptibly. 'That's thirty-eight carats. That's a big stone.'

'It has to be the same as the original.'

He nodded slowly. 'Well, you can find any stone, at a price. How deep a black?' Again she pointed. 'I'll make some enquiries. What about the mount? You said you had a picture.'

She reached into the pocket of her jeans, produced the insurance photograph. Mr Daimler looked at it. Then he looked closer. 'You want me to copy this?'

Jane nodded.

'Forgive me,' said the jeweller slowly, 'but…does the owner know? Only, people don't like seeing what's supposed to be a unique piece of jewellery worn by someone else.'

'I *am* the owner,' Jane said sharply. 'The legal owner. It was stolen from me.'

'Oh.' He was plainly taken aback. 'Then obviously I'm mistaken. I thought… I'm sorry. For a moment it looked familiar.'

This wasn't what they'd come here for. Even Jane, who'd known they were coming, hadn't expected this. Daniel felt as if someone had knocked him off a chair. 'It did?' he said weakly.

Jane raised herself on her arms and leant forward until her chin was almost resting on the glass counter. You could have cut diamonds with her resolve. 'Mr Daimler,' she purred, 'tell me where you saw my necklace.'

Chapter Twenty-Five

After Caroline Walsh disappeared into her house Deacon settled Jonathan back in his car seat. But instead of driving off he found himself indulging in some outside-the-box thinking.

If Terry Walsh had done what Deacon wanted him to have done, he must have had a damn good reason. It had been out of character: first, to have any dealings with a jumped-up mugger like Bobby Carson; secondly, to make the kind of mistakes that left him exposed to the risk of discovery; finally, to protect himself in a way that actually drew attention to what had gone before. In ten years' hard looking, Deacon hadn't seen Walsh make those kinds of bad business decisions.

So maybe Voss was right and it wasn't business. He knew it was nothing to do with the bulk paper trade; the paper was only a fancy wrapping for how Walsh made his money. Drugs, gambling, girls, and dry-land piracy. When Terry Walsh stole from someone, it wasn't their wallet and their fiancée's necklace, it was a juggernaut full of cigarettes or whisky that left the motorway one junction short of its destination and turned up twelve hours later and a hundred miles away, empty but for the driver locked in the back in his underwear. Terry Walsh was *good* at business. If he'd made the kind of errors that waymarked the Carson case, he'd never have stayed ahead of Deacon for ten years.

But no one's judgement is foolproof when his emotions are involved. A lot of the things Deacon knew about Walsh he couldn't prove, but there was ample evidence for the fact that he was a good husband and father. If his family were threatened, Walsh might do anything, however ill-advised, to protect them. Perhaps, for once, the man was thinking with his heart, not his head. It wasn't much of an edge, but it might be the best Deacon would get. If he couldn't use it, he might as well resign himself to having Walsh around.

He found his gaze straying up the Walshes' drive. Caroline was a woman who wore jewellery. Deacon thought he'd never seen her without at least a strand of pearls and a pair of earrings. And a good watch, and of course her rings, and…

Never in a hundred years had Caroline Walsh hired Bobby Carson to hit someone with a car because she fancied her necklace. No one acts *that* far out of character.

What about the daughter, Sophie? As the keeper of Terry Walsh's genes it was possible that she took a direct approach to taking what she wanted. But Deacon had met her, and she didn't strike him as vicious. Anyway, it made no sense. If either of the Walsh women wanted a new necklace, all she had to do was pout prettily and ask for Terry's credit card. If he was unable to refuse his daughter the horses that could kill her, he certainly wouldn't draw the line at jewellery.

Deacon was sure he was missing something. If Walsh was involved, somewhere there was a touchstone that transformed his actions from bizarre and illogical to wholly understandable. Petty crime may be as casual and shallow as an airport paperback, at once undisciplined and oddly predictable, but a serious career criminal produces work like a classic novel – well thought out and skilfully executed. Terry Walsh didn't do sloppy work. He didn't start things on a whim, get bored halfway through and leave them unfinished so that an unravelled edge might trip him later on. He took a pride in what he did. If this was him, something had happened to undermine his meticulous professionalism.

But though Deacon, sitting in his car outside the Walshes' house, explored all the byways of possibility – including those that were overgrown with nettles and ended in a rusty gate, padlocked with a chain and a sign saying *My bull can cross this field in eight seconds* – the image his mind's eye kept seeing was Caroline Walsh in her string of pearls.

'I must have been mistaken,' insisted Henry Daimler. 'It was only a picture in a newspaper. It was just, it looked like my father's workmanship.'

'And it was this necklace?' Jane pinned the insurance photograph to his counter with her finger insistently enough that Daniel feared for the glass.

'No,' said Mr Daimler firmly. 'It couldn't have been. I

mean, it was a charity luncheon or somesuch. Who wears stolen jewellery to a charity do, when they know the papers might be there? I mean, that's the point, isn't it? You rope in a few local celebrities in the hope that other people will show an interest too. Nobody goes to a charity do who doesn't want to be seen. Nobody goes wearing something they don't want to be seen wearing.'

'Did you keep the paper?' asked Daniel.

'Afraid not,' said the jeweller. He was a man of about fifty with thinning hair and the greyish complexion of those who spend too much time indoors. 'It wasn't important. I just saw a necklace in a photograph and thought, *That looks like one of Dad's*. That's all. I never gave it another thought until today. Even when we were talking about star sapphires on the phone.'

'Correct me if I'm wrong,' Jane said slowly, looking at the gems on their velvet pad, 'but even to me they all look different. How the star is positioned. The way the rays shoot out of it. The depth of colour. I think *I* could recognise my stone, and I'm no expert. If we could find the newspaper, I bet you could compare the two pictures and know if it was the same necklace.'

Daimler rocked a hand. His hands were precision tools, slim but strong. 'Not the stone, not from a newspaper cutting. I could probably identify the setting. Every one is a work of art,' he said with the quiet pride of a man who'd seen the best and made some of them. 'Once you've seen enough you start to recognise the hand of the man that made it. I thought the necklace in the newspaper was made by my father. And maybe I was right – he must have made hundreds in his career. But it can't have been the same one.'

He looked again at the photograph of the Sanger necklace, and though his words said one thing the doubt in his eyes said something else.

'Do you remember which paper it was?' asked Daniel. 'And when?'

'It was *The Sentinel*,' said Henry Daimler. 'But it was a long time ago. Could have been a year.'

'No, it couldn't,' said Jane Moss quietly.

'Getting on for, then.'

So they went to *The Sentinel*. Like many of Daniel's acquaintances, senior reporter Tom Sessions looked forward to seeing him with a Coliseum mix of pleasure, curiosity and trepidation. They'd known one another for four years, since the day Sessions found himself talking in the street to a man whose death he had already reported. Since then they'd moved in and out of one another's orbits, developing something bordering on friendship, so that Sessions would have been glad to see Daniel even without the professional interest in what kind of a drama he'd got involved in this time.

And the first thing he noticed was that it was fundamentally different to usual. It wasn't Brodie Farrell he was following around today, a small yellow-haired comet circling its glamorous sun, but a scarred girl in a wheelchair. The chair was, of course, a clue, but he'd have recognised her anyway. He interviewed Jane Moss for the first time while she was still in hospital, then again when she went home to River Drive. He even remembered what she was wearing that day – a T-shirt printed with the legend *People in wheelchairs do it.* His first thought was that unfortunately the punchline hadn't printed. When he realised that the whole thing was the punchline he'd grinned, and Jane saw what he was grinning at and grinned too.

'How are you keeping?' he said now.

'Not so bad,' she nodded. 'You?'

'Fine.' He hesitated. 'Is this about the Carson case?' He assumed the answer was yes. He couldn't think what else she'd want to see him about. He was just breaking the ice.

'Yes,' said Jane, 'and no. Not about the court case. It's dealt with – he's gone where I won't have to look at him for a while, and there's nothing I want to say about that. This is about the necklace. We may know where it is.'

The reporter's attention sharpened. 'Really? When neither the police nor the insurers could find it? How?'

'Daniel...' And then she stopped, glancing at him uncertainly, unsure how much to say.

Daniel realised with a flicker of appreciation that she was concerned for his integrity. Part of his job – when he'd had a job – was discretion. Jane wasn't going to tell a reporter who he'd been working for and it was hard to tell the story without. He stepped into the hiatus. 'A commission I was working on brought me into contact with Miss Moss,' he said carefully, 'and then a third party who believed he'd seen her necklace. He could have been mistaken, but there are good reasons to trust his judgement.' He gave a rueful little shrug. 'Sorry I can't be more specific.'

'That's OK,' said Sessions. He was a tall, somewhat gangly man of about forty who always wore the same tweed sports jacket. 'How do you think I can help?'

'The witness thought he saw the necklace in a photograph in *The Sentinel*. We wondered if you could help us find it.'

In common with newspapers everywhere, they called it The Morgue. Once it had been a storeroom full of boxes and files containing every item ever printed on the thousands of people in and around Dimmock who might one day do something else worthy of note. For many of them this second fifteen minutes of fame would be their obituary, hence the name. These days it's more efficient to keep a morgue digitally, so the room contained just a couple of computer terminals and some fireproof boxes for storage. Although the new technology made life infinitely easier for journalists, many of them still miss the good old days when hunting through The Morgue involved flicking through files of crinkly, yellowing paper.

Sessions remembered the IT revolution. He remembered how many man-hours had been wasted doing what a computer now did in a matter of seconds. He logged on at one of the monitors and turned to his visitors. 'Do we know what issue we're looking for?'

Daniel shook his head apologetically. 'Nine or ten months ago?'

'It couldn't have been before October the twenty-second,' Jane said quietly.

Sessions didn't need to ask why. 'All right, let's start with the issue of October twenty-seven.' A few deft keystrokes and he had a miniaturised front page. 'Do we know who it was a photograph of?'

'Possibly a charity do. That's not very specific, is it?'

'It'll do for now.' More keystrokes and the page disappeared, to be replaced by ranks of tiny photographs. 'We'll get rid of the sports, the weddings, the cutesy kids, the prize vegetables and the dog-and-pony show.' Suddenly there were a lot fewer photographs, and he increased the scale so it was possible to see what was in them.

'If your informant thought he recognised a necklace, we're looking for a woman or a group with a woman in it. She was in evening dress, or at least formal daywear, and she wasn't across the room from the photographer.' He got rid of half the photographs on his monitor.

Which left him with about a dozen pictures of people attending the kind of functions where good jewellery is worn. Many of them had charitable connections. One by one he blew them up bigger than they'd have appeared on the page, and Jane examined each of them minutely. But she couldn't find her necklace, or anything that looked vaguely like it.

She looked at Daniel with soul-wrenching disappointment. 'It isn't there.'

'Patience,' said Sessions, 'we've only just started. Let's try the next edition.' They repeated the procedure, with the same result. And again, and again.

Then Jane pushed herself back from the terminal and turned away. 'He must have been wrong. Either that, or it wasn't *The Sentinel* he was reading.'

'We're only up to the end of November,' Daniel pointed out.

'But Bobby Carson was in custody by the end of

October,' said Jane. Her voice was dull with regret. 'The police had circulated a list of everything he'd stolen round half of southern England. No one would have risked selling the necklace after that, no one with any sense would have bought it, and if someone had been stupid enough to wear it in public it would have been noticed.'

'Then what was it that he saw? Our' – Daniel glanced at Sessions – 'witness.'

Jane shrugged. 'Who knows? Maybe it was one of the nationals he was reading. Maybe he had an away day to Penzance and picked up the local free-sheet down there. And maybe, whatever he saw, wherever he saw it, he was wrong. He only thought it looked familiar. If it wasn't in *The Sentinel*, suddenly the odds on it being my necklace are a lot longer.'

But Sessions wasn't ready to give up. 'Local papers work differently to the nationals. On the nationals, if you miss a deadline, that's it – even yesterday's news isn't usually worth printing. With us it's local interest that counts. On a busy week, less urgent kinds of news get bumped to the next issue. But they don't get binned. Sooner or later we find a slot for them. A photograph of the great and good at a charity function is a good example. We'd certainly print a picture, but it wouldn't take precedence over a genuine news story. It could hang around for weeks before making it into print. Let's keep going. The Christmas and New Year editions are always crying out for fillers – anything that was waiting for a space would be a God-send then.'

So they kept looking.

The Sentinel didn't skip issues. *The Sentinel* had never

skipped an issue. During various strikes it had produced some late ones, in times of paper shortage it had produced some skimpy ones, and once during a protracted power cut it printed courtesy of a tractor on the other side of a hole in the wall. The barren week between Christmas and New Year, that many publications incorporate into a Bumper Holiday Edition before or after, got its own issue of *The Sentinel*, although it was thin and padded out with items that barely qualified as news even in Dimmock.

One of them was the presentation of a cheque for £400 raised by an estate agents' fun run on the Three Downs in aid of the Chinese earthquake relief fund. Normally, this worthy but small event would have warranted a paragraph on page two. But this was the holiday week, and the editor was desperate for anything that would stop the adverts bumping into one another. He hadn't sent a photographer to the presentation supper, but one of the estate agents had submitted a picture and, knowing his dead week was coming up, the editor had kept it. Blown up, it filled almost a quarter of the editorial space on page four, and if it wasn't exactly hot news, at least the five people in it would buy extra copies for their relatives.

Two of them were Timothy Li, senior croupier at The Dragon Luck casino on the Brighton Road, and his wife Pearl, coordinators of the local effort to send relief to the victims of the earthquake in Sichuan Province. Also pictured were Edwin Turnbull, senior partner at Turnbull, Fitch & Stewart, and his wife Doreen, and though neither of them were fun runners he was presenting the cheque in his role as chairman of the local association of estate agents. The fifth member of the group was one of the management team at The Dragon Luck where the presentation was made.

Jane leant closer to the monitor. She took the insurance photograph from her wallet again and laid it on the desk. The eyes of all three of them skipped from the screen to the photograph to the screen to the photograph to the screen.

Finally Jane said, 'That's it. Isn't it? That's what Daimler saw. He thought it was the same necklace, and so do I.'

Daniel didn't even wince at her indiscretion. All at once he had much more to worry about than maintaining Henry Daimler's privacy.

'Who's that wearing it?' asked Jane, reading the caption under the picture.

'She's one of the major shareholders at The Dragon Luck,' said Sessions. 'She's also the wife of one of Dimmock's more prominent businessmen. You know her, don't you, Daniel? That's Caroline Walsh.'

Chapter Twenty-Six

Daniel liked to do things by the book – except on those rare occasions when he threw the damn thing out the window and leapt after it yelling 'Minnehaha!' He thought they should go to Battle Alley and put their findings to the senior detective on duty.

But the book Jane worked by was *String Theory* by Brodie Farrell – the theory being, if you can reach a string, pull it. 'You know Detective Superintendent Deacon,' she said impatiently. 'Call him.'

Daniel would have resisted for longer if he hadn't thought that it was what Deacon too would want. He knew Deacon was officially on holiday. He also knew that Deacon's definition of a holiday was something you do if you can't find anyone to arrest. He'd want to hear, immediately, about any developments in the Carson case, particularly if it involved the Walshes.

'All right.' They were back on the pavement outside *The Sentinel* building. Daniel moved to the kerb. 'But I'll stand over here. Get him at a bad moment and his language can knock you off your…' He winced. 'Blow your wheels off?' he finished lamely.

'Daniel,' said Jane Moss firmly, 'if you're going to stick around you have to get used to the idea that my legs don't work. I don't *like* being in a wheelchair. It's a damned nuisance, it makes everything harder than it ought to be, and I resent like hell the fact that someone did this to me. But it doesn't embarrass me. It doesn't say anything about me except that I was unlucky. If you're going to be around me, you have to stop being so coy. I'm stuck in a wheelchair, and it's looking more and more likely that I always will be. I'm sorry if that freaks you out, but protecting your finer feelings is not my highest priority. Get over it.'

Daniel stood looking down at her for perhaps a minute while the commerce of Dimmock flowed unheeding around them. Then, not oblivious to the curious stares of passers-by but braving them, he unbuttoned his shirt.

Jane's first thought was that, always somewhat eccentric, he'd finally gone mad and she ought to back away as quickly as her wheels would carry her. But his face, though pale, was composed and his mild grey eyes were steady on hers. Puzzled but intrigued, she looked at what he was showing her.

Her eyes widened. She leant closer. 'What the hell is that? Smallpox?'

Daniel shook his head. 'Burns. I'm told there were about three hundred of them. I lost count. They've healed pretty well. Four years on, these scars are all that's left. The doctors thought the worst ones might need skin grafts, but they didn't.'

What he was saying made no sense. 'Those aren't burns,'

objected Jane. 'They're way too regular. They look like...'

'Daisy chains,' nodded Daniel. 'I know. The guy doing it got bored. For most of a weekend all he had to do was ask one question, and I didn't know the answer. In the end he was just going through the motions. Doodling.'

He'd managed to knock all the breath out of her. 'Daniel...'

'Yes,' he said calmly. 'I was tortured. I didn't deserve it – not that anyone ever does, but I wasn't even who they thought I was. So it doesn't say anything about me, either, except that I was unlucky. But I *am* embarrassed. I don't usually show this to people. I don't like having to explain it. I don't like seeing the expression on their faces. So I keep it covered up.'

'Then...why...?'

'Why show it to you? Because... I think, because hiding it isn't as good a way of dealing with it as having it out in the open where people can see it and know about it and accept it as part of who you are. The way you do. It's more honest and it's more dignified. I'm not embarrassed by you, Jane, I admire you. You're a stronger person than I am – maybe stronger than anyone I know. I want to be honest with you because it's starting to matter to me what you think of me.'

Jane breathed lightly, getting a grip on her emotions. Someone had done that to him. Three hundred times. It had taken most of a weekend. She cleared her throat. 'I can't keep my shirt buttoned up over my misfortune.'

He flicked her a fragile smile. 'I don't think you would if you could.'

She shrugged. 'We'll never know. One thing I am sure of: we're not getting into the competitive suffering business.'

He gave a gusty little laugh. 'No. That really would be crass. I just... I wish we'd known one another before you were injured. I don't want you to think I'm sorry for you. Well...I am, of course I am, I'm terribly sorry about what happened, to you and to Tom. That's not what I mean.' He heard himself succumbing to verbal diarrhoea, made himself slow down. 'What I mean is, what I see is someone in a wheelchair, not a wheelchair with someone in it. Am I making *any* sense?' he wondered, awkward as a schoolboy asking for a date.

'No.' Jane gave a thin chuckle. 'But I think it was a nice thing to say.'

'So...I'll call Jack Deacon, shall I?'

'I think you should.'

Policemen come to the front door, not the servants' entrance. These days it's less of an issue than it was in the nineteenth century, when the landed classes genuinely believed they should be above the law, but it was a tradition Deacon followed scrupulously. He'd left muddy footprints across some of the best Persian rugs on the south coast.

Usually, though, if he was calling on business, he didn't have a baby in his arms.

Caroline Walsh was putting away her shopping when she was surprised – not startled, it took a lot to startle her – by a rap at the door she'd come through five minutes before. When she opened it, Jack Deacon held out his baby as if she'd won it in a raffle. 'I need to see Terry.'

She'd been speaking to him only a few minutes ago. Something had happened in the brief space between then and now, and his attitude was different – harder, intense, brittle as a diamond. She was astonished to hear herself stammering. 'I-I'm not sure he's...'

'His car's in the garage,' said Deacon shortly. 'He's not in the garden so I'm guessing he's in the study. I know the way.' He left her, frozen like Lot's wife, holding her improbable winnings, and beat a heavy tattoo across the parquet flooring of the hall. In deference to their long acquaintance, he walked round the Persian rug.

Walsh must have heard him coming. Herds of buffalo don't signal their approach more clearly than Deacon on a mission. But he turned, still at his desk, with an expression of mild surprise as the door opened abruptly and then shut again, just one decibel short of a slam, leaving the detective superintendent looming over him. 'Jack? Everything all right?'

'Bobby Carson was working for you.'

'No,' said Walsh, 'he wasn't.'

'Bobby Carson was working for you when he mowed down two young people with a car outside The Cavalier on Chain Down. He brought Jane Moss's necklace to you, and you gave it to Caroline. Terry, what the hell were you thinking? Did you actually have to wash the blood off it first?' His voice was quaking with anger.

Walsh kept his own low and calm. 'You've got it wrong, Jack. Bobby Carson didn't work for me. He was a vicious little amateur, and I didn't, and wouldn't, have any dealings with him.'

'Careful, Terry,' snorted Deacon, 'that was almost an admission. That you only work with professionals. Men like Lionel Littlejohn.'

'Yes, Littlejohn worked for me, for a time,' said Walsh levelly. 'I believe he's retired now.'

'Only as far as the taxman's concerned. For you, Terry, he's always available. Even if it means driving the length of the country to lean on someone who's asking inconvenient questions. That's almost the most offensive part, do you know that?' Deacon's glare would have stripped paint. 'That you thought Daniel Hood might get to the truth when I'd failed to. That's the bit I really can't forgive. That, and making Caroline your accomplice. Haven't you made enough dirty money down the years that you could afford to buy her clean jewellery? Did you have to give her something that had been stolen by a murderer?'

Terry Walsh measured the words out one at a time and pegged them out on the space between them. 'Bobby Carson was nothing to do with me. I never hired him, I never used him, I never bought anything from him or accepted anything in payment or as a gift. He told the court he was working alone, and he was. He was a loose cannon, and it's more dangerous working alongside one of those than it is to be in the firing line. I'm sorry, very sorry, about what happened to those kids. But I wasn't responsible, not in any shape or form, and I have nothing to feel guilty about.'

Deacon's eyes were hot. 'Then explain to me how

Caroline was photographed wearing Jane Moss's necklace three days after it was stolen from her. While she was in ICU and Imogen Sanger was organising her son's funeral.'

Not a muscle moved in Walsh's face. That, more than anything, told Deacon he'd struck gold. It stopped being conjecture, or a promising theory, right then. Walsh wasn't shocked. He'd known the photograph existed. He'd hoped the necklace would never be recognised, but he'd known that one day it might be. And he'd known what his response would be. 'Prove it.'

'The picture was published in a newspaper! Forty thousand people saw it!'

'They *saw* my wife wearing a necklace. What kind of a necklace? Who's going to know from a picture in a newspaper? It may have been something like the one that was stolen. It may even have been very like it. But you'll need to prove it was the same one.'

'Oh, I can prove it all right,' snarled Deacon. 'I have the jeweller whose father made it. If we give the newspaper shot and the insurance photograph to a photo analysis lab, they'll be able to say with absolute confidence that they're one and the same thing. This wasn't mass-produced, remember – it's a signature stone mounted in a setting made in his own workshop by a craftsman. There won't be another one exactly like it anywhere.'

Behind Terry Walsh's eyes the cogs of his brain were whirring. Deacon wasn't bluffing. Now his back was against the wall. If you invite a policeman to prove something and he can, that's pretty much the end of the game.

But Walsh hadn't stayed ahead of that game – ahead

of Deacon – for all these years by being Second XI. He started with natural talent, and the more he played the better he got. He wasn't ready to pull the stumps up just yet.

'All right,' he said quietly. His gaze was steady. 'I'm going to have to tell you what happened. Maybe it won't make much difference, except to your opinion of me – and funnily enough, Jack, that actually matters to me. Have you got five minutes?'

'I've left Caroline holding the baby.'

'Literally?'

'Yes.'

'Good. That's him safe and her occupied. We shouldn't be interrupted.' He gestured Deacon to a club armchair. After a moment, grudgingly, Deacon took it.

'I haven't lied to you. Well...not about this.' Walsh's grin carried all the old charm but not quite the old confidence. 'I wasn't involved with Carson before he stole that necklace. I didn't mean to be involved with him afterwards. As it turned out, though – as I discovered too damn late – there *was* blood on that stone.

'It took you, what, about two days to realise it was Bobby Carson you were looking for, another three to find him. By then he'd fenced everything he'd stolen and dumped the car in a reservoir. There were no forensics to tie him to the crime. It was Jane Moss's evidence that nailed him. That's an impressive young woman. If you were on a jury you'd believe her. If I was, I would.

'So Carson had five days to turn his takings into cash. In fact it didn't take him twenty-four hours. Before you were even looking for him he'd laid the stuff off with someone – I'm not going to tell you who – who'd laid it off with someone else, who took it to a disco looking for a buyer. The usual story: he needed cash quickly, it belonged to his late mother, he'd have liked to keep it but… You know the routine.'

Deacon was looking at him with overt disbelief. 'You're not telling me you fell for that? You didn't honestly think that a man selling jewellery in a disco had any legal title to it?'

Walsh gave a wry shrug. 'I knew there was a possibility it wasn't entirely legit. But I'd no idea what the thing was. You hadn't publicised it as stolen at that point. I'd heard about the hit-and-run but I had no reason to connect that with this. I'm not a jeweller – I didn't recognise what I was being offered as genuinely valuable. I thought it was probably one of a hundred identical necklaces in a box that fell out of the back of a van. I thought it was costume jewellery – good costume jewellery, good enough for a birthday present for my wife, but still not the kind of thing there'd be a hue and cry over. I gave him eighty quid for it.'

'*Eighty quid?*' Deacon's voice soared. 'Tom Sanger died and Jane Moss will spend the rest of her life in a wheelchair for eighty quid?'

Walsh shuffled uncomfortably. 'I didn't know that. You can believe me or not, Jack, but it's the truth. If I'd known – if I'd even suspected – do you think I'd have given it to my wife? Do you think I'd have let her wear it in public?'

And, reluctantly, Deacon did believe him. A successful

middle-aged man, Walsh was still what he'd always been –
a wheeler-dealer, a man with an eye to the main chance, a
man who didn't need to buy iffy jewellery from someone
in a disco but probably couldn't resist the temptation.
Deacon could see him in a shadowy corner of the noisy
establishment, surrounded by people who had no idea
what he was up to, cheerfully hammering the price down
because both he and the vendor knew that stolen goods
are a buyer's market.

'Did Caroline know how you got it?'

'No.' He said it firmly enough but Deacon was
unconvinced. He liked Caroline Walsh but he had no
illusions about her. She couldn't *not* know how Terry had
made his fortune. She knew, and she enjoyed it with him,
and whether she'd ever held up a tobacconist at gunpoint or
not, she was in every way that mattered a gangster's moll.
If Walsh had told her about the man in the disco, she'd
probably have worn the necklace at the first opportunity,
out of devilment.

Right now, though, that wasn't the point. Right now –
here, in the man's study – Deacon was where he'd spent the
last ten years working to be: with a case against Terry Walsh
that would open up his affairs as a judicious stab opens a
clam. Because it wasn't just the necklace. Maybe all Walsh
did was buy questionable jewellery from someone he met in
a disco. He wasn't going down for murder, or as an accessory
to murder. But handling stolen goods is a serious offence,
and that was all the leverage Deacon needed to crack the
ripe nut that was Walsh's business empire. He knew what
he'd find. All he needed was a lawful excuse to look.

'Do you want to tell her, or shall I?'

There were things about Walsh which were almost admirable. There had to be, or the fact that they had grown up in the same London neighbourhood would never have tempted Deacon to tolerate a personal acquaintance that had the potential to damage him professionally. One of them was that he was an intelligent man. He didn't shrink from violence – Deacon knew he didn't, though he couldn't prove it – but he used it sparingly, as a last resort, and never as a substitute for thinking. He was thinking now, trying to see a way through this, not panicked but intensely focused.

'I will,' he said. 'If I have to.'

Deacon snorted a gruff little chuckle, half amused, half indignant. 'Oh come on, Terry! You're not going to appeal to my better nature, are you? You know I haven't got one.'

Walsh gave another microscopic shrug. 'We've known one another a lot of years. I've always thought of you as a friend.'

'Really?' Deacon looked at him closer. 'That's interesting. Because I've always thought of you as a pimp, a thief and a thug.'

Unoffended, Walsh laughed out loud. 'No, Jack, don't spare my feelings – tell me what you *really* think.'

That flicker in the cragginess of Deacon's expression might almost have been a tiny smile. 'I think that you and I have been chasing one another around this merry-go-round for too many years for you to think I'm a soft touch. You're not going to try to bribe me, not because it's illegal or immoral but because you know it wouldn't get you anywhere. So that's not what this is about. There's something else you need. Something you think I just might help you with.'

He tilted his head to one side. When Brodie did that she looked like a curious magpie that has seen something glitter in the grass. When Deacon did it he looked like a vulture wondering how long something would take to die. 'What is it you're not telling me, Terry? If what you've told me already was the truth, why are you still keeping secrets?'

Walsh spread his hands innocently. 'I'm not. I told you what happened. I feel bad about it – of course I do. It was just a bit of fun. I thought someone had pulled a fast one and Caroline was going to get a nice little trinket because of it. If I'd thought for one moment that people had got hurt, I wouldn't have touched it with a bargepole. If I'd known Bobby Carson was involved, I wouldn't have. You know me, Jack. You know that's the truth.'

Deacon went on regarding him speculatively. The trouble was, he *did* know Walsh. He didn't think he'd sent Carson to wipe out a couple of young lovers for the sake of their valuables, and he didn't think he'd have handled those valuables if he'd known how Carson acquired them. So maybe he hadn't. The hit-and-run, the death of the boy and the terrible injuries to the girl, had been widely reported, but details of the robbery weren't released until four days later. That had been Deacon's decision. He'd thought his best chance of finding Carson was if he tried to fence the goods, which he wouldn't if their description had been widely circulated.

As it turned out, Carson had passed the goods on while the blood was still wet in the road. They'd gone through maybe three different handlers before Walsh bought the necklace from a man in a disco.

A man in a disco? He knew they were rather different types of men. For instance, Walsh had a social life that went beyond the occasional meal with friends in a nice French restaurant. But they were the same age, and from Deacon's experience – gained mostly from arresting people with amusing substances in their back pockets – the average age of those frequenting discos was about nineteen. Wouldn't Terry Walsh have been a little conspicuous among the teeny-boppers?

'What disco?' he asked.

'Scarlett's, on the Brighton Road.'

Deacon knew the one. It was about half a mile from The Dragon Luck. 'Were you there alone?'

'Yes.'

'Anyone see you?'

'Lots of people. I don't know how many would remember seeing me. It is nine months ago.' He frowned then, perplexed. 'Wait a minute. I've just confessed to a crime, albeit an unwitting one. Now you want me to *prove* it?'

'Can you?'

'I don't *have* to! *You* don't have to. I confessed. If you don't believe me, great – pick up your baby on the way out and I'll see you down The Belted Galloway sometime. But you asked me how Caroline came to be wearing Jane Moss's necklace and I told you. I didn't fence the thing for

Bobby Carson. But I bought it in circumstances that made it unlikely to be kosher, and if you want to hit me with that, go ahead. You know my solicitor. By the time he's polished my defence, Adam Selkirk will make me seem like an innocent abroad and you like a bully for taking advantage of me.'

He took a long, slow breath. 'And I just wonder if there isn't another way of dealing with this. If Miss Moss gets her necklace back, and my company undertakes to support her financially for the rest of her life, wouldn't that do more good than you and Adam shredding my reputation between you as you try to convince a court that I'm some kind of criminal mastermind and he tells them I'm a simpleton who shouldn't be allowed out alone?'

As bribes go, it was better than most. At least Deacon didn't feel the urge to knock him down for offering it. Of course, he couldn't accept it. He didn't think Walsh thought he might. 'Miss Moss *will* get her necklace back. After it's done its job as evidence.'

Walsh regarded him coolly. 'Serious money isn't to be sneezed at, Jack. Not many people can afford your kind of scruples. I can make a big difference to that young woman's life.'

Deacon sniffed. 'You could anyway. As a kind of apology. From jail.'

Walsh laughed at him. 'I'm not going to jail for an injudicious purchase in the back row at Scarlett's!'

'That's *cinemas*, Terry,' Deacon growled, exasperated. 'If you're going to lie, get the details right. Discos don't have a back row, and anyone who'd been in one in the last twenty years would know that. Wherever you got that necklace, it wasn't in Scarlett's. So why would you say that? Why would you tell me something so wildly improbable, when the man with the capacious overcoat could just as easily have been selling his wares in The Dragon Luck where you'd every reason to be?'

Walsh looked away. He still appeared quite nonchalant, but Deacon's experienced eye detected a growing unease. 'I've told you what happened.'

Deacon didn't think at lightning speed, but what he lacked in rapidity he made up in perseverance. There was something else he'd always admired about Walsh. He was a good husband and father. Deacon had known that Terry Walsh would gladly lay down his life for his partner and his offspring long before he knew that, actually, he would too.

'Yes, I rather think you did,' he said slowly. 'Except that it wasn't you at Scarlett's, was it? And I don't think it was Caroline. Sorry to be so blunt, but you're both too old. It was Sophie, wasn't it?'

Chapter Twenty-Seven

'No,' said Terry Walsh.

He'd been lying for long enough, and not just over trivial things but in circumstances where getting it wrong could cost him his freedom or his life, to know he had to keep his tone light. He'd have hacked his own arm off with a penknife to keep Jack Deacon away from his daughter. But right now she didn't need his blood so much as his skill as an actor. He didn't wring his hands. He didn't beg Deacon to believe him, either with his words or his eyes. He just shook his head and said calmly, 'No.' And waited.

But Deacon had dealt with lots of different kinds of liars in his time. Urgent ones, sullen ones, and some whose eyes shone with bright honesty as they told him that black was white. Civilians, and young policemen, think there's a magic to it. That you can spot a liar by the way his eyes drift off to the left, or right; by the tremor, or perhaps the unnatural steadiness, in his voice; by the unnecessary complications in his account, or else by the lack of detail. But there is no magic trick. Experience had taught Deacon to focus on the facts. If he was being lied to, sooner or later the facts wouldn't add up. Honest people make mistakes too, but they're different kinds of mistakes.

By and large – remember this if you're asked to take part in one – that's what reconstructions are for. They're not, as you'll be told, meant to jog the memory of an onlooker. They're an opportunity for someone to settle the question of whether he's a witness or a suspect by doing something he simply couldn't or wouldn't have done. Taking a seat on the blind side of a station café, for instance, when his statement said he'd checked the time on the platform clock.

So Deacon was listening not to the timbre of Walsh's voice, not to the presence or absence of a tremor, but to what he was being told. He was being told that an intelligent, hugely successful career criminal had bought stolen jewellery from someone he didn't know in a discotheque frequented almost exclusively by Dimmock's teenagers. And that simply couldn't be true.

'What were you doing in Scarlett's?'

'The pubs were closed and I fancied a drink.'

'Not the quietest place for a quick tipple.'

'No, it wasn't. I won't be going back.'

'Were you driving yourself?'

'Certainly not.' Thus spoke the family man, indignant at the suggestion. 'Colin was driving. You know Colin.'

Deacon knew Colin would say he'd driven his boss up to the front door of Buckingham Palace if that's what he was told to say. 'Didn't we do him for speeding a couple of years ago?'

Walsh nodded. 'I believe you did. I had a severe word with him at the time.'

'It must have made an impression,' said Deacon, straight-faced. 'If he's now driving so slowly that you couldn't wait for him to cover the half-mile between Scarlett's and The Dragon Luck, where your wife is a major shareholder and I don't doubt the drinks are both better and free.'

Walsh shrugged. 'And where there's always someone with a problem they want my advice on or a tale of woe they want me to listen to. Sometimes it's nice *not* to be related to the boss.'

It was plausible. But Deacon wasn't buying it. 'So the necklace was for Caroline's birthday, was it?'

'That's right. It was the next day. She wore it that night at the function at the casino.'

'An eighty-quid necklace bought from a man in a disco? Isn't that a bit tight for a man of substance?'

'It wasn't the only thing I bought her. As a matter of fact I bought her a new car. It's out on the drive now, if you want a look.'

'Seen it.' Deacon was thinking. 'What did Sophie buy her?'

Walsh blinked. It was that Cuba moment, when the protagonists were eyeball to eyeball with the missiles ready to fly, and finally one of them blinked. 'Er…'

'Come on, Terry. You've only got two children – you must remember what they sent. Your son's in New York, isn't he? He probably got his secretary to send flowers. You bought Caroline a car and an iffy necklace. What did Sophie give her? If you can't remember we'll ask Caroline. Better still, let's ask Sophie.' He had his phone out. 'What's her number?'

There was a tiny whine in Walsh's voice. 'It's nine months ago, Jack!'

'But Caroline hasn't had another birthday since. I bet she and Sophie both remember. Come on, let's ask.'

Walsh said nothing. He made no move towards his phone.

Deacon's voice dropped softer. 'How old's your daughter now? Twenty, twenty-one? She works in a riding school, doesn't she?'

'An eventing yard,' murmured Walsh.

Deacon nodded. 'For what it's worth, I approve. It's good for the kids of wealthy families to go out and earn their own crust. Gives them a sense of values. Only thing is, working with horses never pays well, does it? Which maybe isn't the highest priority if you're doing something you enjoy and learning on the job, but it does leave you without much disposable income. I mean, *you* buy a present for a member of your family and it's a car or a holiday or maybe a horse. Sophie hasn't got that kind of spending power. You told me yourself, she likes living within her means, so I expect she'd rather not come to you for a sub.

'In that context, a pretty necklace bought from a man in a disco for eighty quid makes perfect sense. It was all she could afford. And Caroline was so proud she wore it at the first opportunity, to the charity bash at the casino. She thought it was just a trinket, but it was something her daughter had bought with money she'd sweated for instead of heading up to town with your credit card, and that made it precious to her.'

In a way Deacon was making this up as he went along. Except it was more like solving a crossword puzzle: every word he got right helped him find half a dozen more. He kept going, with mounting confidence. 'Then a few days later you heard where it had come from. How it had been stolen. You told Caroline, you disposed of the necklace, and you hoped Sophie wouldn't wonder why her mother wasn't wearing it any more. Then you hunkered down behind the firewall and waited to see if there'd be any repercussions.

'As the days and weeks passed, you felt increasingly secure. Caroline only wore the thing in public once, and if anyone had recognised it they'd have said so when the newspapers were full of the outrage at The Cavalier. The only potential danger was a picture taken by an estate agent at the casino that turned up in *The Sentinel* two months later. But it was just a snapshot; the chances of anybody noticing what Caroline had round her neck were pretty minimal. Bobby Carson was caught, charged and convicted, and still your name never came into it. It had been a close shave, but nine months later you were pretty sure you were safe.'

There was nothing cheery about Deacon's smile. 'Except then Daniel Hood started taking an interest. You'd no idea why, but he was asking questions in the very places where a connection could be made between Carson and Sophie – among the not-quite-honest, not-entirely-crooked local dealers who'd passed it among themselves, muddying its provenance each time, until one of them sold it to Sophie in Scarlett's. And you know a little about Daniel, but maybe not quite enough. You know that he's stubborn and smart, and if he was determined to find out what happened to Jane Moss's necklace he just might succeed. And you know that a private citizen can be scared off much more easily than a policeman. He doesn't have to fill in forms in bloody triplicate to explain why he isn't following up on a lead that looked promising right up to yesterday.'

He raised an interrogative eyebrow. Walsh made no response, by word or gesture. Deacon shrugged and carried on. 'So you called Lionel Littlejohn. You had a good relationship with him before he retired; he probably said if you ever needed him he'd come. You didn't want to use local muscle because of the risk of association. Also, you could trust Lionel not to get carried away and do the sort of damage that can't be hushed up. You didn't want Daniel hurt, just scared enough to find something safer to do with his time.

'That's what I mean,' Deacon said then, 'about knowing Daniel a bit but not enough. *I* wouldn't have put the frighteners on him. I'd have known that there was nothing better guaranteed to keep him looking. You knew he was stubborn – you had no idea *how* stubborn.

'Running him down with a car puzzled me,' he admitted. 'That almost put me off the scent. It seemed… out of character. What happened? Lionel exceed his authority? Or did someone else, who was sent to watch Daniel, get a sudden rush of blood to the brain and think he could earn a Christmas bonus by using his initiative?'

Still Walsh didn't react. Deacon thought that was probably all the answer he needed. If that wasn't exactly what had happened, it was pretty close.

'You almost got away with it,' he said. '*I* suspected you, but then I suspect you when someone trips over a paving stone or the weather takes a turn for the worse. I had no evidence. I thought I was going to see you get away with this too.

'But there was that photograph. I didn't know there was a photograph, but you did. When it turned up in *The Sentinel* you must have pored over it with a magnifying glass, trying to decide if it mattered – if the stone was recognisable. But it was just a few pixels in the local rag. If I'd seen the paper I wouldn't have recognised it, and I had a picture of the Sanger necklace on my desk. It needed a very particular eye, and a very particular interest, to spot that someone in a newspaper photograph was wearing a specific piece of jewellery.

'You were desperately unlucky.' Almost, Deacon sounded sympathetic. 'Among the people who saw that snap in *The Sentinel* was probably the only man in the country capable of identifying it. Even that mightn't have mattered, because he didn't know that the necklace his father made thirty years ago and the one Tom Sanger was killed for were the same. In the days following the murder we circulated pictures of it round Dimmock's jewellers, but we didn't know about this guy handcrafting individual pieces essentially on his kitchen table. He takes discretion to a whole new level. He doesn't advertise, he isn't in the Yellow Pages, and the slate by his front door doesn't mention jewellery. We missed him.

'Daniel found him. He wanted to get a copy of the

necklace made, so he went back to the workshop that made the original for Tom Sanger's parents. He produced a picture of what he wanted, and the rest' – he smiled lugubriously – 'is history.'

While he was talking Walsh had been planning his campaign. After all, he didn't have to listen too closely – he knew what Deacon was going to say. A lot of it was speculation, but once he was on the right track he would inevitably come to the right conclusion. Walsh needed to know how he was going to deal with it. Before Deacon had finished, he did.

Even so, he took his time. He'd get one chance at this – a maximum of one chance. If he got it wrong the consequences would be unthinkable. He leant back in his chair, weighing Deacon up. 'There's only the two of us here, Jack,' he said quietly. 'No witnesses. Not even Caroline; not even Jonathan. Nothing either of us says need go any further – and couldn't in any event be proved. Unless you're wearing a wire. You're not, are you?'

Deacon answered his slow smile with one of his own. 'You know I'm going to do my job, Terry. You *know* that.'

'Yes. Your job is catching criminals. Right now you have the chance to catch one you've been after for quite a while. I can make it easy for you, Jack. Not so easy that people will suspect, but easy enough that you'll get what you want. You want me in prison? You can have it.

'I can do time,' he said thoughtfully. 'I've always known I might have to at some point, and this is it. I've told you what happened. All you have to do is believe me. If you do, everyone else will too.'

'But that's the problem, isn't it?' said Deacon softly. 'I *don't* believe you. It wasn't you who bought that necklace for Caroline, it was your daughter. It was Sophie.'

'It was me,' insisted Walsh, and his face was like stone.

Deacon found himself in a terrible quandary. Walsh was right – this was what he wanted above everything else. Or nearly everything. They got Al Capone for tax evasion, and if he could get Terry Walsh for handling stolen goods it would do just as well. That was only the beginning. Everything else would follow.

But it wasn't right. He *knew* it wasn't right. He knew Walsh was never in Scarlett's, and since he believed that the story he'd been told was essentially the truth, that meant Walsh didn't buy the necklace. He'd undoubtedly handled stolen goods at regular intervals over the last forty years, but not this. Not the Sanger necklace. That was Sophie. Her father wanted to take the rap for her.

Which is a father's prerogative. You try to shield them from harm, even if it means taking the hit yourself. Deacon understood what he was doing. And he so wanted to let it happen. But it wasn't *right*. To charge Walsh with handling these particular stolen goods he was going to have to lie. And to his surprise he found he was no more willing to do that than Daniel would have been.

He said slowly, 'It's not that I don't appreciate the offer. But you know – you must know – that you being charged with handling stolen goods and Sophie being charged with handling stolen goods are entirely different things. You're a professional. You do this – don't bother to deny it – for a living, and you have done most of the time I've known you. We get you in court, you're going down for a very long time.

'Whereas Sophie's a decent, respectable, hard-working girl who made a silly mistake. She's not responsible for who her parents are – I don't hold that against her and neither will the judge. He'll see a twenty-year-old girl who had too much to drink in a disco and did something foolish. He'll accept that she didn't know what the necklace was. She should have guessed it was stolen, but not that it was evidence in a murder case. I'm guessing she'll get probation or community service. Jane will get her necklace back, and you and I can go on chasing one another's tails for a bit longer.

'I will have you behind bars, Terry. But I'd like to have it clean. I don't want to cheat, even if it is only you and me that know.'

'You can't have Sophie,' Walsh said softly.

'I don't *want* Sophie,' growled Deacon. 'But she's the one who did this so she's the one I'm going to charge. It's not a huge deal. She'll get a slap on the wrist and be told not to be such a silly cow in future.'

'It's a huge deal to me,' said Walsh fiercely. 'Because if she ends up with a criminal record, everything she's achieved is for nothing. She worked hard at school. She's working hard now. She's putting distance between my background and her future. Don't think she's ashamed of me, because she's not. She loves me. She knows…not everything but enough. And she knows she doesn't want to live like that. She doesn't want a life of privilege paid for, even in part, by my ill-gotten gains. That's why she's shovelling horseshit for a living. She loves me, but she doesn't want to be like me.

'You charge her with handling stolen goods, all that goes down the tubes. For the rest of her life, no one will ever believe that she wasn't a fully paid-up member of the Walsh family business. One silly mistake shouldn't cost her everything.'

He sat up straight in his chair. 'Well, I can do something about that. If she was anyone else's daughter caught buying a stolen necklace, like you say, it wouldn't be any big deal. She'd do her community service and stay out of trouble, and that would be the end of it. But Sophie is *my* daughter. I've put her in a situation where one stupid mistake could get her stuck with my reputation for the rest of her life. And I'm going to get her out of it. Turn a blind eye, Jack. It's good for her, good for you, good for me. Let it happen.'

Deacon actually found himself thinking about it. But he shook his head. 'I can't.'

They stared angrily at one another, two strong stubborn men, both doing what their consciences demanded. If the Cuban missile crisis had been down to them, the world would have burnt.

The study door opened. Caroline Walsh came in, still cradling Jonathan, carrying the post. 'A letter for you,' she said quietly, proffering it to her husband.

Deacon had been a policeman for thirty years, a detective for twenty-five of them. Also, he wasn't stupid. He saw that the envelope had been opened. Either Caroline Walsh had taken to checking her husband's mail or it hadn't just arrived. So she wanted Deacon to know what was in it.

Walsh looked quickly at her, took the envelope but put it on the desk, face down. 'Thanks.'

'I think you should read it,' said Caroline, her quiet voice with its cut-glass accent implacable.

Still Walsh hesitated. 'Now?'

Deacon breathed heavily. 'Go on, Terry, it's obviously part of the show. Let's by all means see what's in it.'

Walsh bit his lip. Then he took out the letter and pushed it, still face down, across the desk to Deacon. Deacon picked it up and read.

He felt his heart thumping, the blood darkening his face. He clenched his teeth to stop himself saying something precipitate. He read the letter again, to make sure it said what he thought it said. Finally he lowered it, regarding Walsh over the top. His voice was thick with gravel. 'This is pretty low, Terry, even for you.'

'I was afraid you'd think that. Which is why I wasn't going to show it you. Not right now.'

'Some things can't wait,' said Caroline Walsh, gently rocking the baby.

'When *were* you going to show me?' demanded Deacon. 'After you'd given up trying to bribe me any other way?'

'I suppose,' admitted Walsh reluctantly, 'in a way. It was never meant as a bribe. I never expected to be having this conversation with you – not now, hopefully not ever. When I started looking into this it was as a friend.'

'A *friend*?' exploded Deacon. He picked up the letter in order to slap it down again. 'You saw it as an act of friendship, to make me choose between my duty and my son?'

Walsh passed a troubled hand across his eyes. His wife looked uncertainly at him. 'The timing's unfortunate,' murmured Walsh. 'I never meant to link this offer to anything you might do for me, now or in the future. Believe that or not, as you like, but it's true.

'The problem is, events don't happen in isolation. Things affect one another whether we want them to or not. Whether I like it or not, right now your child's future is the only weapon I have to fight for my child's future. It's crap but we can't get round it. I won't let you hurt Sophie while I can do anything to protect her. And right now I don't care about the Geneva Convention.'

Softly, persuasively, Caroline said, 'Please consider it, Jack. For Jonathan's sake, and for Brodie's. Terry's telling the truth. When he contacted the clinic in Uppsala he was just trying to help. He's supported their research for twenty years – it would be a poor show if he couldn't get a friend's child onto a drugs trial. He thought it was a last chance Jonathan wouldn't get any other way. He didn't do it because he wanted your gratitude – he did it because he was in a position to help a sick baby and he wanted to.

'But as he says, events have a way of taking over. Now, something that it would have been our pleasure to offer you as a gift we have to put a price on. I'm sorry about that,' she said, her eyes low. 'It *is* pretty despicable. But then, the way you feel about your son, that's how we feel about Sophie. That we'd do anything to protect her. Even this.'

'All you have to do,' said Walsh, 'is leave her name out of it. You can have me. You can have your day in court without even worrying that my high-priced legal team might get me off. I'll plead guilty. You'll be doing the town a service, Jack, you know that. Getting me off the street is much more valuable than having Sophie work in a soup kitchen for a month. And for that, Jonathan gets treated with the only drug in preparation anywhere in the world that offers a significant chance of curing him.'

'You know that's true,' urged Caroline. 'Brodie's searched the world for this chance and no one could offer it. We can. We can't promise it'll save him, but this is a highly respected clinic at the cutting edge of cancer research, and they're willing to take him because Terry asked them to. A personal favour. That's what we want in return.'

'It's not like anyone will ever know,' pleaded Walsh. 'What evidence there is points to me. No one but you would have thought to look that little bit further. Neither Division nor even Detective Sergeant Voss will ever suspect it was anything other than a good collar.

'And no one will ever hear that I got Jonathan on the drug trial. I'll hide the trail so well even *you* wouldn't find it. Do this one thing in return. Settle for me. Leave Sophie out of it.'

Chapter Twenty-Eight

After he'd finished at the custody suite – the names they made him call the cells these days! – Deacon made his excuses and left. He was still officially on leave so he had every right to. Sergeant McKinney, who was doing a stint as custody officer and so universally referred to as The Prince of PACE, thought the Detective Superintendent was probably going somewhere to get drunk. And he was right. But there was something he had to do first.

The house was quiet. Paddy wasn't home from school yet. Marta, in the flat upstairs, had no pupil thumping out novice piano with two left hands. There was no sound even of a vacuum cleaner or washing machine. Only Brodie's car in the drive, and the fact that he'd had Detective Constable Jill Meadows take Jonathan home and she hadn't brought him back, suggested the Victorian villa was occupied at all.

Deacon parked his car beside Brodie's and let himself in with the key which she'd felt obliged to give him and he'd felt obliged never to use. But today time was important. He didn't want Brodie to hear a garbled version of what had happened before he got there. Actually, he didn't want her to hear an accurate one either.

He found her sitting quietly in the living room, the baby on her lap, her body curved protectively around him. She looked up, unsurprised, at the sound of the door. He saw from her face she was expecting him.

The reason he'd sent Meadows instead of, for instance, Detective Constable Huxley was not primarily that she was a woman. It was because she could be relied on not to gabble. Most people said more than they intended to, more than they wanted to, when Brodie fixed them with her loftiest stare and demanded to know what was going on.

But Brodie had almost as many contacts at Battle Alley Police Station as Deacon had, and probably more friends. Meadows may have managed to say nothing beyond *Hello* and *How are you?* and *Here's your baby*, but as soon as she left Brodie would have been on the phone looking for information. Though Deacon had got here as soon as he could, Brodie Farrell never needed much time to wring information out of people. She'd had two hours. Whatever gossip was currently racing round Battle Alley would certainly have reached Chiffney Road by now.

But it wouldn't be the truth, the whole truth and nothing but the truth. Only he and the Walshes knew that.

Brodie was on the sofa. Deacon took the chair, facing her squarely. All the way over here he'd been wondering how to start. In fact it hardly mattered how he told her, as long as he did it at once.

She looked up unhurriedly. 'I gather you had an interesting morning.'

He nodded. 'Yes.'

'Productive?'

'I think so.'

'Do you want to tell me about it?'

'I need to tell you about it. First, I need to know what you've heard already.'

She looked away, dropped a feather-light kiss onto her baby's head. 'I know you've arrested Sophie Walsh.'

Strictly speaking, Walsh should have destroyed the necklace. As soon as he realised what it was he should have taken it for a short sail aboard his yacht *Salamander* and dropped it into the English Channel. That would have been the professional thing to do, and Terry Walsh took a pride in his professionalism. In fifteen fathoms off Beachy Head he could be as sure as death and taxes that it would never come back to haunt him.

What kept him from doing the sensible thing was not the value of the stone. It was valuable to Margaret Carson, who'd have needed a loan to buy it. To Imogen Sanger, who was comfortably off, it had immense personal value. To Caroline Walsh it was not much more than a bauble, except that it was a gift from her daughter.

Terry Walsh was a family man, and to an extent that made him a sentimental man. This isn't always a weakness, though it probably isn't a survival trait in a criminal. Once he was aware of its history, of how it was given to Imogen Sanger, to her son and to her son's fiancée, and how it was taken away, he couldn't bring himself to drop it in the sea. The blood on it was precious blood. He wrapped it carefully, put it in a watertight box and buried it at the bottom of his garden. Then he planted a rose bush on top of it. You'd need to know it was there to find it, and if someone knew it was there he was already in trouble. It was as safe as it could be and still where he could recover it. He had it in his mind that, one day, he might find a risk-free way to return it to its owner.

And in a way he had. Now Deacon knew the story, regardless of what he did about it there was no longer any need to keep the necklace.

Caroline Walsh didn't go to Battle Alley with her husband and daughter. Deacon advised her that he'd want a statement from her later. But she hadn't bought the necklace from a man in a disco, or lied about doing it, and while he might get round to charging her with attempting to suborn him, right now he was too busy.

Once she'd delivered Jonathan to his mother, Deacon had DC Meadows collect Sophie Walsh from the stables where she worked. He himself drove Walsh into town. He wished he could enjoy the moment more. But the triumph was for ever ruined by the price he'd had to pay.

Caroline was not a sentimental woman. She was a strong woman. She'd always known this day might come; she wasn't going to collapse in the hall and cry about it now. There were practical things she had to do. One was to call the family's solicitor, Adam Selkirk. If anyone could get Pol Pot let off with an ASBO, it was Adam Selkirk. When she'd done that she went into the garden shed and selected a sturdy fork.

* * *

'And her father,' said Deacon.

'What for?'

'Her for handling stolen property. Him for attempting to pervert the course of justice.'

Brodie thought about that. 'I've heard he doesn't always recycle his drinks cans, too.'

Deacon gave a snort. 'I know, it's a bit like charging Hitler with behaviour likely to cause a breach of the peace. It's true, it just doesn't cover all the bases. But the important thing is it'll stick. I can use it to pin him to the dartboard. Then I'll throw all the other stuff at him and see how many trebles I can hit.'

'You got him then. You finally got him.'

'Yes. I don't think even Terry's wriggling out from under this one.'

'And the daughter?'

'Will get her wrist slapped, nothing more. What she did was more stupid than wicked. She was just very unlucky that the bargain necklace she bought from a man in a disco was the one Bobby Carson ripped from Jane Moss's neck two nights before. She didn't know that. There was no way she *could* know it. The magistrate will take that into account.'

'So you get what you wanted. Terry gets what he deserves. Jane gets her necklace back, Margaret Carson gets closure on her son's crime, and Daniel gets to feel smug because none of this would have come about if he hadn't taken Mrs Carson's commission and kept going even when she told him to stop.'

There was something terribly odd about the way

Brodie was speaking. Not so much the words as the tone. Deacon couldn't be sure if it was irony, or satisfaction, or disappointment, or something else entirely. She was too quiet, her body too still. She should have been demanding details from him, trying to make them show that she'd solved his case. Instead she just sat there, nursing her baby, a cocoon of stillness enfolding her.

He tried to stick with the facts. 'I don't think Jane will get her necklace back. The Walshes know where it is but they're not going to tell me. It was part of the payment for accepting their version of events. At least Mrs Carson will have the satisfaction of knowing she did all she could to find the necklace, and it's thanks to her that we know what happened to it – how Bobby got rid of it before we got to him, and why it never turned up again.'

Brodie didn't answer. She glanced at him speculatively for a moment before returning her gaze to Jonathan's sleeping head.

'There's something else,' mumbled Deacon.

'Oh?'

'That you need to know. That I have to tell you. You'll be angry. More than angry. You'll think I was wrong. Maybe I was. I'm not as sure about anything as I used to be.'

'Tell me.'

To his astonishment she listened in silence. It was like the quiet at the eye of a hurricane: ominous, stifling, pregnant with power. Once he'd started to tell her Deacon didn't dare stop because he knew that when he did the weight of the storm would fall on him. Driving over here he'd tried to prepare himself, to be ready for what she would say. But actually he couldn't imagine what she would say. He couldn't imagine how she would feel. After all she'd done, that had been for nothing, he'd been given one last chance. The cost really hadn't been that high. But he'd turned it down. They were never going to know if it would have saved their son's life. Probably not; but they were never going to know.

She'd throw him out. He'd never see her again. But before she did that she'd want to tell him…what? What possible words could express how she felt about what he'd done – the choice he'd made? People believe that strong enough emotions go beyond words, that words can't express the soul-deep turmoil of a heart. Deacon knew better. He knew Brodie would find words like chisels, and hammer them into him with a remorseless fury that even his blood wouldn't appease.

And he knew he had to let her. It was the only penance he could offer: the right to repay hurt with hurt.

It didn't take long to tell her what he'd decided. It just felt like half his life. When he was sure she understood he fell silent. Silence – such a silence – filled the room.

He knew that she'd understood. So she wasn't struggling to get her head round it. She was sharpening the chisels.

'Terry Walsh offered to get Jonathan onto a drugs trial? At a Swedish clinic where he makes a research grant?'

Deacon nodded. Then he saw from Brodie's face that that wouldn't do. 'Yes.'

'A reputable clinic? Not some backstreet quack trying to cure cancer with spit and seaweed?'

'No. A proper clinic. One of the leaders in the field. Terry's paper business has given them research funding for years.'

'And they knew about Jonathan? Terry told them about him – about his condition, and how sick he is. And they're testing a new drug that might cure him, and they were willing to put him on the trial.'

It was a triumph of the abridger's art: brief, accurate, to the point. Deacon grimaced. 'Yes. Terry had a letter confirming it.'

Brodie's look bored through his skull. 'And you said no.'

Deep in his gut was an unfamiliar sensation a lesser man might have recognised as fear. Soon it would be audible in his voice, soon after that visible in the shaking of his fingers. 'Yes.'

Brodie appeared to give this some thought. 'Did you think it was too late? That he's too ill to travel to Sweden? Maybe you thought, If only this had come along a month ago…'

Deacon shook his head. 'I didn't think that.'

'Then maybe you thought it was a cruel hoax. That Terry Walsh had nothing to offer. That it was all smoke and mirrors, and once you'd crossed the line there'd be nothing to justify it. You'd have compromised yourself and risked your career for nothing.'

Deacon drew an unsteady breath. 'No, I didn't think that either. I think what he was offering was genuine – if I'd done the deal he'd have got Jonathan on the trial. Which isn't the same as saying it would have worked, but

I think he was in a position to offer what he said he could offer.'

'A chance. A last chance.'

'Yes.'

'And you said no.'

'Yes.'

'Why?'

This was the question he'd known would come. All the way over here he'd been trying to find a satisfactory answer. Not just for Brodie – for himself. 'Because what he wanted in return wasn't mine to give.'

'He wanted to confess to a crime! You *know* he's a criminal – you've been trying to charge him for ten years. And he wanted to put his hands up to a crime. And you know, and I know, and Terry knew, that he was giving you the key to Pandora's box – that you were going to pull things out of it that were never going to go back in.'

'Of course he's a criminal,' agreed Deacon. Obstinacy was like gravel in his voice. 'But he didn't commit *that* crime. And I knew that, because I knew who had. I couldn't charge him with something I knew he hadn't done.'

'He was trying to protect his daughter! That's what you do when you're a parent. At least…' She let the sentence tail off in the most hurtful way imaginable. 'What happens next?'

'To Sophie, nothing very much. Nobody thinks she was part of the robbery. Terry will go to prison, probably for years. Now I have a lawful excuse to pick his business apart, the whole damned empire is coming down. No one will ever put it back together again.'

'And that'll be an end to the drug trade in Dimmock, will it? There'll be no more prostitutes – no more whisky shipments taking a wrong turn?'

He frowned, unsure where she was going with this. 'Someone will take up the slack. But it won't be Terry. He won't be as clever as Terry. It won't take me ten years to bring him down.'

'But that won't be the end of anything either, will it?' said Brodie. An ember was burning in the depths of her eyes. 'You're running up a down escalator – it takes everything you have just to stay level. You're not pulling the plug on anything, you're just stirring it round a bit.

'I thought, maybe that was what you had in mind. That you could save someone else's child – from drugs, from prostitution. That you threw away Jonathan's last chance so you could save other people's children. But you can't. You don't even think you can. All you can do is knock the cock off the top of the midden and wait for the next one to climb up. And for that you said no to something that might have saved our son's life.'

Try as he might, he couldn't avoid the killer words, the inescapable bottom line. 'I had to. I hadn't the right to do anything else. My pay cheque doesn't just buy my expertise, it buys my loyalty. It has to. It's the only way the system can work.'

Brodie had a bottom line too. It was this. 'You put your obligation to the job ahead of your duty to your own son.'

Deacon thought about that, but he couldn't really argue. 'Pretty much.'

They went on regarding one another, with a bizarre degree of calm as if the matter was way too serious for shouting. The moment Brodie told him to, Deacon would leave. But if there was more she wanted to say, more vitriol she wanted to throw, the least he owed her was to take it.

She still didn't start shouting. Without disturbing the sleeping baby she picked up a Manila envelope that was lying on the coffee table and passed it to Deacon. 'Open it.'

What was inside was heavier than a letter. When he lifted the flap and tilted the envelope, it slid out onto his palm.

He found himself looking into the eye of the universe. He had no idea what it meant, that it had been sealed in an envelope on Brodie's coffee table, but he knew immediately what it was. Not a copy, not a substitute, not a lookalike – it was Jane Moss's necklace. He didn't have to be a jeweller – he didn't even have to be much of a detective – to recognise that twelve-pointed golden star at the heart of a stone the colour of ink in champagne. Improbable as its presence here was, he knew the chances of it being anything else were even slimmer. 'How...?'

'Caroline Walsh was here. Now hiding it isn't going to achieve much, she wanted Jane to have it back.'

He couldn't stop the detective in him asking, 'How did she know where to find it?'

Brodie managed a thin smile. 'She said Terry whispered to her as he kissed her goodbye. You don't have to believe that, but you may find it hard to disprove.'

Deacon's eyes rolled to the ceiling. 'He did it again, didn't he? Daniel. Against all the odds, and not even the way he intended, he got Jane's necklace back for her. I can never decide, is it luck? Is he smarter than he looks? Or does he have one of those special angels that look after fools and...?' He heard what was coming and managed to get it stopped. But the horror showed in his eyes.

Brodie finished the saying for him. 'Fools and children. It's all right, Jack. Maybe there are such angels. Hester Dale believes there are. And today I think so too.'

She leant forward carefully. There was also a magazine on the coffee table: underneath it was another envelope. She didn't pass it to him. 'Do you want to know what's in this one?'

Deacon nodded mutely.

'A letter of authorisation for an executive jet to take us from North Menner airstrip direct to Uppsala, and a booking in my name for an apartment near the clinic. The taxi'll be here in half an hour. I will kill you if you try to stop me.' It wasn't a figure of speech. She meant it.

'Caroline?'

Brodie nodded. 'She apologised for trying to blackmail you. She said she was desperate. Once Sophie had been charged, she saw no point in withholding something that might help us and would be no use to anyone else.'

Struggling to make sense of it, Deacon muttered, 'I suppose it'll look good in court...'

'I suppose it will,' agreed Brodie, expressionless.

And actually, Deacon was too honest a man to leave it at that. 'But that's not really why she did it, is it?'

'I don't think so, no.'

'Terry said, if there was any way he could help he wanted to. He found a way. If I hadn't gone to see him, he'd have come to see me. Or you. This wasn't organised overnight, because he thought I was on his heels. He did it because he could, and he hoped it might do some good.'

'Yes,' said Brodie.

Deacon was still thinking. 'Cancel the taxi.'

'You're taking us to the airstrip?' She was making sure. He could still have tried to stop her.

'Yes,' he said. 'And then I'm coming to Sweden with you.'

'Won't that look bad?'

'Yes. But not nearly bad enough to stop me doing it,' said Deacon grimly.

Chapter Twenty-Nine

There followed a series of hurried phone calls, knocks on doors and surprised expressions.

Deacon called DS Voss from somewhere over the North Sea. Actually, Voss wasn't all that surprised, mainly because he knew his boss pretty well by now. As soon as he could get away he went round to the netting shed.

Daniel was not so much surprised as dumbfounded by the story he had to tell. Behind the thick glasses his eyes widened and widened; at one point Voss had to remind him to blink. It wasn't just that the necklace had turned up. It wasn't just *how* the necklace had turned up. It wasn't even that Brodie and Deacon were now en route for Sweden and a possible treatment for their son's illness thanks to a notorious criminal. It was that none of these things would have happened but for his own clumsy attempts to do a job he had no talent for and didn't really like. It was almost enough to make you believe in...

Oh God. He'd made a promise. If Jonathan lived he was going to have to find a way of keeping it. It would be worth it, but the mere thought made him feel sick with trepidation.

'And the chief wondered,' said Voss, 'if you'd like to tell Jane Moss and Margaret Carson that the necklace will be evidence for a while, but after that Jane will get it back.'

Daniel was white. He looked as if a draught from an open window would blow him over. 'You're sure it's the same one?'

'Of course it's the same one. How could it be anything else? You think Terry Walsh keeps a stock of fake jewels in biscuit boxes under his roses?'

'That's where it was?'

'Caroline dug it up. After it became obvious it wasn't going to buy her anything she wanted.'

'And they sent Jonathan…?'

'To Sweden,' nodded Voss. 'On the company plane. So no drive to Gatwick, no waiting at check-in, no waiting for baggage – a much easier journey for all of them.'

'I don't understand,' Daniel said weakly.

Voss made a grimace that was the facial equivalent of a shrug. 'That thing between Terry and the chief – it's a complicated relationship. I think, in spite of everything, they're more friends than they're anything else. It didn't affect how either of them did their job. But when Terry was able to help the chief's kid, he wanted to. Makes you wonder, doesn't it?'

For once, a sense of urgency made Daniel feel he couldn't walk fast enough. He phoned to check that she was in, then had Voss drive him to Margaret Carson's house. He wanted to tell Jane first. But Mrs Carson had paid good money for his services, and he owed her the news first.

She greeted him warily, unsure what had brought him

back when, to the best of her knowledge, the business between them had ended in recrimination.

'Can I come in?' asked Daniel.

She didn't move out of the doorway. 'If you think I'm going to change my mind and sit down with Miss Moss...'

'That's not what I want to talk about. There have been developments.'

Reluctantly, she took him through to the living room. He waited until she was sitting down, then told her what had happened to the star sapphire after it was stolen. How it passed from hand to hand so quickly that by the time it was being offered for sale under the multi-coloured lights of Scarlett's two nights later it had almost earned a kind of legitimacy. How a twenty-year-old girl bought it as a last-minute birthday present for her mother.

When Mrs Carson could find a voice she asked, 'What will happen to her?'

'She'll be prosecuted. She'd no idea how it was acquired, but she must have realised it was shady. That makes it handling stolen goods.'

Margaret Carson was still trying to take it in. 'And all this time...?'

'It's been in a biscuit tin under a rose bush in somebody's back garden,' said Daniel.

'And will it be returned?'

'Oh yes. Jane Moss is still the lawful owner. It was given to her by someone who had the right to give it, and taken by someone who hadn't. It's hers. Once the police have finished with it, they'll give it back.'

Margaret shook her head in wonder. Then a thought occurred to her. 'Do I owe you some money?'

'Not for this,' said Daniel quickly. 'Mrs Farrell will bill you for the time I was working for her on your commission. But all this happened after she sacked me – I don't see how you can be charged for that.'

The woman gave a gusty chuckle. 'So I got exactly what I wanted, all that I asked of you, and I never even had to buy the thing. I can't help feeling I've short-changed someone.'

'No, you haven't,' Daniel said firmly. 'I'm just glad it all worked out. I hope' – he glanced at her shyly – 'you'll be able to put this behind you now. What happened wasn't your fault. But the fact that it's been resolved is down to you. To your determination to make amends for what Bobby did. Jane will recognise that. It was the only thing anyone could do for her that would have made things a little better, and you did it.'

'*You* did it,' Margaret corrected him. 'If I hadn't come to you that necklace would never have turned up. I won't forget that, Daniel. Whatever peace of mind I can enjoy now, I owe it to you. It makes you wonder, doesn't it?'

Voss had said that too. Daniel hadn't known what he meant. 'What does?'

'If there isn't some kind of a hand at work.'

Daniel bit his lip. 'I think we just got lucky.'

'I know I did.'

Another phone call, then Daniel did what he never did – he called a taxi. He couldn't wait to share the news with Jane. His only regret was that he couldn't take her the necklace as well.

She was waiting for him in the open door of the house in River Drive. Her eyebrows climbed as the taxi drew up. 'Won the lottery?' she enquired tartly.

'In a way.' And he would say no more until they were inside.

He told her everything – more than he'd told Mrs Carson. He told her where Brodie and Deacon had gone, and why. He told her about Terry Walsh, and the long-standing game of cat and mouse he'd played with Deacon, and how it had finally ended. He told her how a moment of poor judgement by a tipsy girl in a disco was going to bring down a criminal empire. And how, in spite of that, the Walshes had wanted to do two things before the sky fell on them. One was to help Deacon's son. The other was to return Jane's necklace.

When she managed to find a voice Jane asked, 'Have you got it?'

Daniel shook his head. 'The police need to keep it for now. But Charlie Voss has seen it. It's fine. You'll get it back after the court case.'

'Good God.' She blew her cheeks out, stunned by the development. 'I never thought I'd see it again. I was resigned to it – you know that. I was going to have the copy made, and never wear it but take it out and look at it sometimes to remind myself how much Tom loved me. To get the real thing back – the actual stone that his father chose, that Imogen wore as long as he was alive and then kept for her son to give to someone *he* loved...' She ran out of words. Her eyes were bright with tears. She'd cried over Tom but never for her own predicament. She was crying now.

After a moment's hesitation Daniel leant forward and took her hand. He half expected her to shake him off, but instead she smiled through the tears. 'I owe this to you, don't I?'

He was awkward with embarrassment. 'Maybe a little bit. And to Margaret Carson. And to the Walshes. Anyone else who'd acquired it by the back door would have dumped it as soon as they realised what it was. But the Walshes are used to living dangerously. They didn't panic and throw it in a river – they put it where it would be safe until they went back for it. They always hoped some day to be able to return it.

'Not like this, obviously – more in an anonymous packet posted in Venezuela. But they didn't want to destroy something that Tom died for. Maybe that was sentimental. It certainly wasn't very professional – they'd have been safer with it gone. They must have thought the risk of keeping it was minimal, and if they were able to send it back one day it would make them feel better.'

'I can see all that,' nodded Jane slowly. 'I realise that when I get it back it'll be thanks to the goodwill of a number of people, including several you wouldn't expect it from. But none of it would have happened but for you. If you hadn't taken Margaret Carson's commission, she wouldn't have tried the next name on her list. There *is* no list. Round here at least, no one else does what you do – did,' she amended tactlessly. 'If you'd sent her away she'd have given up. She'd have had to. Maybe she'd have made a donation to charity instead, but I wouldn't have got my necklace back.

'And if you'd given up when the search looked like costing more than the thing was worth – the way the police did, the way I think Mrs Farrell would have done – I wouldn't have got it back. If you'd given up when Walsh wanted you to I'd have lost it. Also if you'd buggered off when I told you to, or when Margaret Carson told you to, or when even the least bit of common sense would have told you to.' An impish smile, only slightly twisted by her scars, robbed the words of any sting.

'A real pro wouldn't have got it back for me. A real amateur *couldn't* have got it back for me. The only reason I'm getting it back is that Margaret Carson went to someone naive enough to join her crusade, stubborn enough to pursue it, and stupid enough to ask questions of the kind of people who think it's a friendly answer if you can get yourself to the hospital afterwards.'

'Oh,' said Daniel uncertainly. It might have been a compliment. 'Er…thanks…'

Jane chuckled at his expression. 'You look like you're still half expecting me to throw you out.'

'You've done it before.'

'I didn't know you then.'

'No. Most people,' he admitted honestly, 'feel the urge to throw me out more keenly when they've known me a while.'

'Really?' Her eyes were innocent. 'I can't imagine why.'

Daniel shook his yellow head, amused and puzzled in

equal proportions. 'This isn't what I expected.'

'What isn't?'

'You. This…' He couldn't find a label for it. 'I thought you hated me. Now I feel like we've been friends for ages. Or am I fooling myself?'

'Daniel,' she said softly, and the tears had cleared from her eyes leaving something new, 'don't rush it.'

He was genuinely confused. 'Don't rush what?'

'I'm twenty-four years old,' she said, picking her words carefully. 'Wheelchair or no wheelchair, I'm not going to be a nun for the rest of my life. I loved Tom with all my soul. I was ready to marry him. But that's no longer an option. A time will come when I'll want to be in another relationship. It's not here yet. But – I don't know – maybe, if you've nothing better to do, you might want to hang around…?'

She'd succeeded in astonishing him. It was the last thing he'd expected her to say. It was not, however, the last thing he wanted her to say.

He almost blew it. He did what he always did: searched for the right words. He spent so long searching that she thought he was looking for a way out. A dark flush spread up her cheeks. 'Of course, if the wheelchair *is* a problem…'

His eyes flew wide, appalled that he'd let her think that. 'The wheelchair isn't a problem, Jane. An iron lung wouldn't be a problem. It's just… I thought I was entertaining a little fantasy. I was afraid that, once the business between us was finished, I'd never see you again. I didn't want that to happen but I didn't know what to do about it.'

She was on her way to forgiving him. There was still a bead of censure in her eye. 'Daniel...sometimes you just have to go for it. There's always a risk of rejection. But it's not as sad as wishing you'd had the courage to try.'

Daniel was nodding slowly. 'Courage was never my strong suit.' He thought it was true. 'I'm also a bit lacking in practice.'

'You and Mrs Farrell...?'

'We've been close friends for four years. I wanted more, she didn't.'

'But you stuck around. Ever hopeful?'

'Not really. That *was* a fantasy. I always knew it. I stuck around because my life was richer for having her in it. It wasn't enough, but it was a lot better than nothing. And then...' His brow furrowed. 'I don't know what went wrong. Of course, she's been worried sick about the baby. I didn't mind her taking that out on me. But all the time she seemed to be pushing me away. Maybe she just got tired of me.' He managed a wry little smile. 'I told you – people tend to when they've known me for a while.'

Jane shook her head in disbelief. 'Tell me, when did you first notice this change in her attitude?'

'Just this last week, mostly.'

'Since you and I met.'

'I suppose. I don't think there's any connection...'

'You weren't lying, were you?' she said ironically. 'You really haven't had much practice at this. Daniel, I think your friend Brodie is trying to teach you to fly. I think she wants something better for you than playing Buttons to her Cinderella.'

Daniel shook his head firmly. 'Oh no. You don't know her. She's...she wouldn't...' But now the idea had been seeded in his brain he couldn't get rid of it. 'Would she?'

'She cares for you,' Jane explained carefully. 'She wants the best for you. She knows what you want, and also what you need. Yes, Daniel, I think she just might.'

Chapter Thirty

A thousand miles away Brodie and Deacon were settling into the apartment, something else Terry Walsh had arranged before his ability to arrange anything was suddenly curtailed. They were likely to be here for some time, and it had occurred to him that sharing the close confines of a hotel room with either of them wasn't a fate he'd have wished on his worst enemy.

They'd gone to the clinic first. The doctor conducting the drug trial spent some time with them, examining Jonathan and going over his X-rays, explaining the science behind the drug he intended to use. He promised nothing. That was the purpose of a trial: to evaluate whether a new drug was any better than what went before. He didn't want to give them hope only to dash it.

But nor was he a cruel man. He didn't want them to feel they were wasting their time here. Jonathan's tumour was typical of the type the drug was designed to tackle. Preliminary results had been promising.

Hope is a hawk with sharp talons. Just sitting quietly on your wrist it can draw blood. But they wouldn't have had it otherwise. They were both realists – the last six months had left them no alternative. They knew the cancer could still win. But for the first time in weeks it no longer seemed inevitable.

Unpacking their bags at the apartment felt strange. They'd never lived together. They'd never before had to agree which side of a wardrobe was whose.

Finally Deacon said, 'What did you think? About the clinic.'

Brodie looked for a non-committal reply. As if sounding too enthusiastic could jinx the process. 'It seems very professional. I think we're in good hands. We've been incredibly lucky.'

It had been a long day. Deacon was too tired for clichés. 'Do you think it'll work?'

'I don't know, Jack,' said Brodie frankly. 'I'm scared to look that far ahead. It's enough that we're here, that Jonathan's being treated by someone who thinks he has a chance. That the choices, the decisions, are all made, and all we can do now is wait, and hope.'

She put the baby down to sleep in the bedroom. They moved into the sitting room next door. Deacon felt her watching him oddly. 'What?'

'What do you suppose happened?' Brodie's voice was edgy, spiked by troubling thoughts.

Deacon frowned, not understanding. 'You know what happened. Terry Walsh arranged it. We know how many pies he's got fingers in. His paper mill probably gets tax concessions for supporting medical research, something like that.'

'Yes. But... Doesn't it strike you as a hell of a coincidence?

That the one thing in the world that we need, someone you know is in a position to do for us. And not even someone who owes you a favour. You and Terry are *enemies*! You're sending him to prison.'

Deacon shrugged hefty shoulders. 'That's different. That's business. This was personal.'

'I know. But I keep wondering if it would have happened if…'

One of Deacon's thick eyebrows cranked higher than the other. 'Go on – spit it out.'

'If I'd never met Hester Dale.'

Deacon considered. 'You mean, we prayed for a miracle, and God sent us Terry Walsh?'

Brodie laughed out loud, then swallowed it as if someone might be listening. 'But if this works it will be a miracle. You weren't there – in all those consulting rooms. They put it different ways, but what all the best doctors in the business were saying was, "If your baby survives, Mrs Farrell, it'll be a miracle." Maybe this is how it works. Maybe it's never a flash of light and a guy with feathers and a trumpet. Maybe it's always a subtle shifting of realities, so that someone turns out to be less ill than he thought, or someone else comes along with a cure in the nick of time. And *everyone* says, "We've been incredibly lucky." Maybe it wasn't luck.'

'Terry Walsh as the agent of the Almighty?' Deacon shook his head bemusedly. 'Anyway, why us? Every sick kid's parents must pray for a miracle. Why should we get special treatment?'

She looked at him sideways. 'Maybe we earned it.'

'By the exemplary manner in which we've conducted our lives?' snorted Deacon. 'I don't think so.'

'Don't sell yourself short,' Brodie said softly. 'You've done a lot of good in this world, Jack, and you haven't always got the credit for it. Mostly that's your own fault – if you tell people you're a nasty bastard you can't complain when they believe you. *I* know you're a good man – not just a good policeman but a good man. And Charlie Voss knows it. I'm not sure anyone else does.

'But Dimmock, and a lot of people in Dimmock, owe you more than they realise. Some of them owe you their lives. Maybe this is how the balance gets redressed.'

But Deacon shook his head again, stubbornly. 'That's my job. What you're suggesting would be like getting a knighthood for something you've already been well paid for.'

In the adjacent kitchen the kettle boiled. Brodie returned with mugs of coffee, just different enough to what they got at home to taste foreign. 'And then,' she murmured, sitting down again, 'there's Daniel.'

Deacon cocked an eyebrow. 'You think Daniel's owed a miracle?'

'You don't?'

They both considered that. Deacon said, 'Daniel thinks you're his miracle. Brodie, why—?'

But she cut him off. 'We both know he's wrong about that. I've done him much more harm than good.'

'He never held that against you. You couldn't have known you were going to get him hurt.'

'I could have guessed. At least that it was a possibility.

But that's not what I mean.' She bit her lip. 'I've stood in his way for too long. He's thirty years old, and me and Paddy and Jonathan are the closest thing he has to a family. I shouldn't have let that happen. As soon as I realised he wanted more than I could give him, I should have made him look elsewhere. But I liked having him around. I used him. Maybe…' She didn't finish the sentence.

Deacon heard it just the same. His voice came out a shocked whisper. 'You think…what happened to Jonathan is because of how you treated Daniel?'

'No,' she said, unconvincingly. 'Maybe. Oh, I don't know. Only, if someone is keeping a tally, balancing the scales…'

But Deacon wouldn't have it, and not just because he didn't want her to blame herself for what he might have called an act of God but actually believed was nothing more than vicissitude. 'And right there is where you get into difficulties with the whole faith business,' he said gruffly. 'If there is a God, and He gives babies cancer because their mothers behave badly, we shouldn't be worshipping Him. We should be finding a way to bring Him down..'

Brodie's horrified look, as if even now his lack of reverence could cost them everything, wasn't enough to silence him. '*I* believe in balancing the scales. I believe in the marble lady holding them on top of the Old Bailey. Because what she measures out is as close to justice as honest people can make it. She looks at the facts – not rumour, not hearsay, not belief or opinion but fact – makes a small allowance for human nature and gives a fair and decent reckoning. She makes us pay for our shortcomings.

She doesn't put our children on the altar.'

Brodie swallowed. The problem was, she'd never been religious either. She didn't know how much you were allowed to question before the vats of judgement were upended on you. 'Jack, please be careful…'

In deference to her anxiety he managed not to sneer. 'In case Someone Up There changes His mind?'

She managed a watery smile. 'Am I being stupid?'

Deacon sighed. 'No. You're still just trying to do the best you can for Jonathan, same as you always have.'

There had been times when she'd wondered if he blamed her for Jonathan's illness. Not consciously, perhaps, but in the long lonely reaches of the night. His kindness brought a tear to her eye.

But Brodie didn't admit to crying. She cleared her throat. 'For a moment there you almost sounded like Daniel.'

'I don't need Daniel Hood to point out the flaws in someone's case,' sniffed Deacon. He saw that something was still troubling her. 'What is it?'

Travel doesn't just broaden the mind – it makes it easier to unburden it. Brodie would never have spoken to Deacon this freely in her living room, or his bed. The rented apartment was neutral territory. They could say things here that wouldn't be witnessed by the fabric of their ordinary lives and brought up later to reproach them.

Her voice was sombre. 'It mattered to him, you know. His lack of faith.' But the words were wrong. It wasn't a lack of anything: Daniel's atheism was as strong as any creed. She tried again. 'The fact that his own conscience was the highest authority he acknowledged. It really mattered to him. I spoilt that for him. I can't seem to stop hurting him.'

Deacon was sceptical. 'I doubt it's something we can much affect in someone else, one way or the other. Either you believe or you don't. The arguments for make more sense to you than those against, or vice versa. You can't make someone believe, and you can't stop them believing.'

'No. But I made him go against his beliefs. I made him put my needs above his ethics and choose between a lie and an apostasy – pretend to pray when he believed there was no one to listen, or abandon a conviction he'd lived his life by. It was a terrible thing to do to someone I care about.'

Deacon feigned a negligent shrug. This friendship between the mother of his child and another man made him as uneasy today as it always had. He'd got past feeling it was an immediate threat to his relationship with Brodie. But he was a conventional man, and the fact that he could never find a pigeonhole for it left him not knowing what to do with the thing. He knew it was real. He knew it had been of enormous importance to both of them. He was pretty sure that, Brodie's recent behaviour notwithstanding, it still was.

'It's not as bad as that,' he said, clumsily reassuring. 'Daniel had gone home by the time Hester Dale arrived. Maybe you were ready to sacrifice his beliefs for Jonathan, but it never came to that.'

Brodie was staring as if he'd said something extraordinary. 'Jack...*how* long have you known Daniel?'

'As long as you have. Four years.'

'And you think that, because there was no one there to watch, he broke his promise?'

Put like that... '*You* think he went home alone and prayed to a God whose very name offends him, because he told you he would?'

'That's exactly what I think.'

Deacon was nonplussed. 'But Brodie...by then you'd insulted him, mocked him and all but thrown him out! He left your house bleeding every way but visibly. You can't treat people like that and still have them want to please you. Even Daniel.'

She didn't look at him. She said in a small, quiet voice, 'I didn't say I expected it. I said it's what he did.'

'You *asked* him?!'

She shook her head, the cloud of dark hair tossing. 'I didn't need to. I know him, Jack. Nothing would have stopped him keeping his promise. He wouldn't even wonder if he needed to. He raised his objections when I asked him to do it. After he'd agreed, nothing would have stopped him.'

And Deacon knew she was right. 'Why?' he asked softly. 'Why did it matter so much to you to involve Daniel in something you knew was anathema to him? You must have known that, even though he'd do it, he'd never forgive you.'

'That was my sacrifice,' she whispered.

She'd lost him. 'What do you *mean*?'

She stumbled to put it into words. 'What we were asking – for Jonathan – it wasn't like a charm to cure a verruca. He was dying of the sort of illness that shows up on X-rays. Reordering reality enough to get round that wasn't going to be easy. A miracle that big I expected to have to pay for. I offered up my best friend to save my son. I offered up his conscience, his soul, his dignity. Every way but actually, I crucified him. Daniel's friendship was the only thing of real value to me that I could give up, and that was the only way I could think of doing it.

'And I nearly didn't, Jack. I nearly decided it was too much. Even for my baby. I nearly decided the sacrifice was too great.' The tears were running down her face openly now, spilling either side of her mouth.

Deacon felt he'd been sideswiped by a wrecking ball. Finally he understood. The things she'd done, the things she'd said, that had made no sense to him at the time – finally they did. She'd given up almost the biggest thing in her life for the one thing that mattered more. For the tiny chance that someone was listening who might appreciate the gift enough to save her son. His voice was weak, hollow. 'When I asked why you were treating Daniel like that, you said he deserved it.'

Brodie managed a broken smile. 'It's true, Jack. He deserves much better than me. And I think now he has a chance of something better. But I didn't think he'd take it unless I pushed him away.'

'Jane,' realised Deacon, the surprise in his eyes like a sunrise. 'You think… Daniel and Jane…? *Daniel?* And Jane?'

She shrugged helplessly. 'Who knows? But it's a chance. The way he talks about her – the things he's done for her

– there's something there. I don't know if he knows it yet. I don't know if she feels the same way. But sometimes you just have to see half a chance of happiness and jump at it. And you can't do that if someone's holding you back.'

Deacon said softly, 'It wasn't your fault. That friendship – even the kind of friendship you and Daniel had – wasn't enough for him.'

'I could have tried harder,' she said sadly.

'You mean, you could have lied. You know better than that, Brodie. You know that would have broken his heart faster and surer than anything else you could have done.'

Knowing he was right didn't help much. The last few years had been the most extraordinary time of her life. She'd got a business, a lover and a child out of them, and though she couldn't be sure what the future held for any of them, at heart she felt a certain cautious optimism.

And then there was Daniel. Knowing him had been key to her growth from an embittered, embattled ex-wife to the woman she was today. It was a journey she couldn't have made without him. Her only regret was the nagging worry that he'd been a much more positive influence on her life than she had been on his.

'The worst of it is,' she admitted, 'I do love him. Still. I always will. Just, not in a way that's any good for him.'

If she'd been telling him something he didn't know, Deacon might have objected. 'You did what you had to do. What you honestly felt was best for all concerned. I think you were probably right. I'll tell you something else. When the dust's settled and Daniel thinks about what's happened, he'll know exactly what you did and why you did it. He'll forgive you.'

'Even lying to him? I told him I didn't care if I hurt him!'

Deacon shrugged. 'Love makes liars of us all. You had to do the best you could for Jonathan. You wanted the best for Daniel. You found a way of reconciling what should have been impossible opposites. I'm pretty sure Daniel's going to understand that.'

Her eyes were mournful. 'I doubt if I'll ever know. I don't think I'll see him again. I think that was part of the payment. Like giving up chocolate for Lent.'

One of Deacon's eyebrows rocketed. 'You think Daniel's gone for good? That the angry words of a desperate woman were enough to make him want to put the last four years behind him?' He passed a weary hand in front of his eyes. 'Brodie, sometimes I think that – in spite of everything – you hardly know him at all. Maybe he and Jane will get something together. I hope they do. But if they do, or if they look like they're going to, the first one he's going to want to tell is you. If they don't, the shoulder he'll want to cry on is yours. Even if they faff around for the next six months wondering if they will or not, he's going to want to know how Jonathan's doing. You're not rid of Daniel yet. I promise you.'

He went into the bedroom to check on the baby.

Brodie so wanted to believe him. It just seemed too much like having your cake and eating it – winning this precious chance for Jonathan, and getting a refund on the only thing she'd possessed that was valuable enough to pay for it.

After a minute it struck her that Deacon hadn't come back. Her stomach knotted hard, her weary legs launching her towards the bedroom. 'Jack...?'

Jonathan was asleep, cradled against his father's chest. Deacon was looking at the twin beds. 'I suppose what I'm wondering,' he said without much preamble, 'is, do we push them together or leave them where they are?'

For a moment Brodie had thought something terrible had happened. That you can't have your cake and eat it, and you shouldn't even try. But she'd been wrong. She slumped on the nearest bed as all the strength went out of her. 'Oh Jack...'

Predictably, he misunderstood. If she'd been watching she'd have seen a faint flush creep up his stubbly cheek, but he feigned unconcern. 'Fair enough. You're probably right. Too much water under the bridge.'

She'd managed to hurt him again. Inadvertently, but that didn't make the hurt any less. She reached out a long-fingered hand, resting it on his arm where Jonathan's head lay sleeping. 'Sorry. I thought...'

She nodded at the baby, and Deacon's eyes flared with understanding. She was jumping at shadows, but that wasn't her fault. Not with all she'd been through, all that lay ahead. He was going to have to be gentle with her. He could do that. It was what he wanted, what he'd always wanted. He still didn't know if it was what she wanted.

'Or,' he said carefully, essaying a compromise, 'we could leave them where they are for the moment.'

She looked at him, holding their baby, and it was like seeing him for the first time. There was a lot that was wrong with him as a partner. But then, there was a lot wrong with her too. She'd let him down, not the other way round. She'd never expected him to forgive her that, but she knew now that he had. She didn't know what the future held for any of them. But perhaps you didn't need to know. You had to jump. To make a leap of faith.

'Water under the bridge?' she said impatiently. 'That's what bridges are *for*! Jack, I don't know how far we can go with this. We've made mistakes, God knows we've made mistakes, but we've survived them. We're neither of us lovesick teenagers – we've been around the block a few times, each on our own and both together. We know not to expect too much – of one another, of other people, of life. And knowing that gives us a better chance of surviving the new mistakes we'll make.

'I don't know if we can grow old together, Jack, or if we'll break one another's hearts and bones trying. But I do know everything worth having is worth fighting for. Give me the baby.' She put him back in his cot. 'You take the headboard, I'll take the footboard. Now...*shove...!*'